Flaming Tree

Books by Phyllis A. Whitney

FLAMING TREE
DREAM OF ORCHIDS
RAINSONG
EMERALD
VERMILION
POINCIANA
DOMINO
THE GLASS FLAME
THE STONE BULL
THE GOLDEN UNICORN
SPINDRIFT
THE TURQUOISE MASK
SNOWFIRE
LISTEN FOR THE WHISPERER
LOST ISLAND
THE WINTER PEOPLE
HUNTER'S GREEN
SILVERHILL
COLUMBELLA
SEA JADE
BLACK AMBER
SEVEN TEARS FOR APOLLO
WINDOW ON THE SQUARE
BLUE FIRE
THUNDER HEIGHTS
THE MOONFLOWER
SKYE CAMERON
THE TREMBLING HILLS
THE QUICKSILVER POOL
THE RED CARNELIAN

Flaming Tree

PHYLLIS A. WHITNEY

DOUBLEDAY & COMPANY, INC.
GARDEN CITY, NEW YORK
1986

Grateful acknowledgment is made to Random House
for permission to quote lines from "Night," by Robinson Jeffers. Copyright © 1925, renewed 1953, by
Robinson Jeffers.

Library of Congress Cataloging in Publication Data

Whitney, Phyllis A., 1903–
Flaming tree.

I. Title.
PS3545.F55   1986   813'.54
ISBN 0-385-23095-8
Library of Congress Catalog Card Number 85-1601

ACKNOWLEDGMENTS

I will long remember the beauties of the Monterey Peninsula, with its rocky seacoast, white sand beaches, and windshaped cypress and pine. I enjoyed the little town of Carmel, not only because it is unique, but because of its creative and friendly residents, who were generous in offering help and hospitality.

Margaret Pelikan of the Carmel Public Library and Dorothy Steven of the Monterey Public Library helped invaluably with introductions and research materials.

I appreciated the hospitality offered by Michael Stanton of the Normandy Inn, where I stayed, and which appears in this story in another guise.

Linda Rockwell became my "foreign correspondent," sending me pictures of Nepenthe and other spots I had visited and wanted to write about, as well as answering endless questions. She also introduced me to Linda Stephenson, whose beautiful home in Carmel Highlands I adapted for my book.

Ann Yost's enthusiasm and involvement with Robinson and Una Jeffers brought them excitingly to life for me at Tor House.

Here at home, Chuck Anderson, teacher, writer and filmmaker, loaned me books and counseled me on the creating of documentary movies.

While my settings are real, none of the characters in *Flaming Tree* exist outside of my imagination.

For Edith Forsyth
Friend and counselor—a doctor
who has never needed "lessons"
in compassion.

Flaming Tree

I

THE YOUNG BOY ran along the top of the cliff, teasing his mother, half in anger, half in fun. Behind him, where water cut a gash inland through granite, the Pacific roared, sucked in its breath, and roared again, sending rainbow spray high in the air.

"No, Jody—no!" The mother reached for her son, and he slipped away, laughing exultantly, the rim of the chasm much too close to his flying feet. When she reached him he tried to push her away—pushed with both hands, so that she stumbled backward, clasping him desperately at the same time. For an instant they clung together on the very edge, seeking for balance, and then disappeared, the boy still laughing as his mother screamed. The ocean's voice covered all other sounds, and the warm California sun burned brightly down on the Point of the Sea Wolves.

A short distance away, behind a gnarled oak, a solitary figure, kneeling on the dry grass of this high sea meadow, watched the two vanish from sight, and after a stunned moment, rushed to the edge of the ragged gash above the ocean.

Phyllis A. Whitney

The two hadn't fallen into the water but lay far below on a ledge of rock where spray washed over them. Unmoving, mother and son were still clasped in each other's arms.

When water retreated and left a moment's quiet, the watcher (who until now had done nothing) called down to them: "Ruth! Jody!"

The two lay still as broken dolls. No one could survive a fall so terrible. It was better to let it end there. Better not to see, but to go quickly away, and be forever safe.

II

KELSEY walked along the white crescent of beach, carrying her sandals in one hand, a fine powder of sand slipping under her feet. She could taste the salt air, and its cool touch on her face seemed to calm her, stilling her unrest.

The early October sun had gone down in a flash of orange beneath lowering clouds that dulled the ocean. At this moment she needed only the beauty and peace of the scene around her, with no suffering—not her own nor that of others. Perhaps the loveliness of this Carmel beach would help to heal her, help the nightmares to stop.

She was a tall young woman in her early thirties, with straight brown hair cut feather-close to her head, shaping it nicely, even when it was blown by a breeze from the Pacific. Only a few years ago Kelsey Stewart had met the world with a wide, open look. Now, though her brown eyes still held the same direct and searching quality, there was a hint of wariness as well, and a loss of laughter that had once bubbled so readily.

Back home in Connecticut, she had often felt the joy of achievement, and sometimes the despair of failure. The children she'd worked with as a therapist had all suffered injury of some sort—at birth, or by accident, or even by suicide attempts. When nothing could be done, she grieved—too much. They'd warned her in school—those teachers who were skilled in working with the brain-injured—that she must not become too deeply involved with any one child, lest failure destroy her own ability to cope. She'd never managed to remove herself sufficiently, but had gone right on caring. She had even imagined that she'd plumbed all depths of feeling and could take anything that might happen.

Not until that moment at the wheel of a car driving along a snowy highway from Connecticut to New York did she know what suffering could really be like. She'd been on the way to pick up her husband at Kennedy Airport. Carl Stewart was a sports announcer (failed athlete, in his case) and he was always off with some team, snatching time at home between games. There'd been no one to leave their son Mark with that day, so she'd brought him with her. At three he was a remarkably cheerful, energetic little boy, and she'd enjoyed having him beside her, strapped into his special seat.

At the crossroad, the patch of ice had been impossible for the other car to miss, and it had plowed straight into Mark's side. When Kelsey woke up in the hospital later, she didn't remember the crash. Carl was there, angry and condemning. They hadn't had much of a marriage for a long time, and only Mark had held them together. Mark, who was to grow up and become the successful sports star his father could never be. But Mark, with his clear blue eyes and shining smile, had died that night on a Connecticut highway. And for Kelsey, everything else had died with him. The fact that it was an accident meant nothing to Carl. He saw only that he had lost what was to be a vicarious second chance at the life he'd wanted.

Kelsey scuffed sand and went down to where an unhurried wave lapped coolly over her toes. If only she could stop weaving the threads of memory over and over. If only she hadn't taken Mark in the car that day. . . . It had happened two years ago, and some sort of healing should have begun. Perhaps if Carl had been a different man—a loving, supporting husband—she'd have begun to recover by now. Her own physical injuries were slight, and she'd mended quickly. But together with her terrible grief, Carl's bitterness over the loss of his son had been impossible to bear. Two months ago there'd been a divorce. She was free now to do what she wished and go where she liked. Wherever that was. . . .

Not to her parents in Florida. They'd wanted her to come, but she'd known that her mother would be a quivering jelly mass of sympathy and heartbreak, while her father would have held back his feelings stoically, though she'd have been aware that all the while he was blaming her for the loss of his only grandson no less than Carl had blamed her. Then, a week or so ago, her mother's sister, Elaine Carey, had written a rather peremptory letter inviting her to come to Carmel and stay at the inn she owned. Kelsey had accepted in desperation. Aunt Elaine was as salty and bracing as a sea breeze, and her healthy, no-nonsense approach to life might help right now.

She had meant to visit Elaine's Manzanita Inn long before this, but somehow it was always her aunt who made the trip east and stayed briefly because she was eager to return to the town she had adopted. She'd made a real success of the inn she had opened ten years ago, and she could never stay away from it for long.

Kelsey had no private patients at the time, and she'd dropped everything to board a plane for California. She had been here for three days. Days of rest, of isolation, of seeing no one but her aunt, and sometimes Denis Langford, who assisted Elaine in managing the inn.

Carmel inns were distinctive and individual. The Manzanita presented its peaked roofs and half-timbered façade to Ocean Avenue, and wandered back in a series of rustic galleries, courtyards, and balconies that was endlessly fascinating and bewildering. There was always a waiting list of guests, so the rooms were full, but since Elaine's apartment was in a small cottage that was part of the complex, and had its own guest room, Kelsey could avoid the inn's comings and goings, and keep to herself. This she had managed to do until Elaine had chased her out this afternoon.

"Go down to the beach and blow the cobwebs away, Kelsey. It's time you took yourself in hand. As soon as you come to life I've got a job for you."

"Right now, I don't want a job," Kelsey said.

"I can see that. What you want is to wallow in your grief, enjoy your pain. But you're needed and sooner or later you'll revive. You're not really the wallowing type."

Elaine could be formidable when she chose, but Kelsey had resisted. She still felt too sore and lost to start living again. There was nothing to pull her back into life, and in a way it was better to feel numb and uncaring. This state was more comfortable than hurting all the time.

She turned back up the beach and waded through pools left by the tide, approaching the higher level of sand at the foot of Ocean Avenue. A cypress tree, its lower limbs bone-white in the graying evening, grew near the edge of pockmarked sand. The Monterey cypress and pine were wonderful trees, native to the peninsula. The cypresses, small and twisted, were bent by sea winds into strange shapes, while the pines stood tall and straight, their green heads held high for seventy years or so.

"Hello, Kelsey."

Startled, she looked around to see the man who sat in a low crotch of cypress branches, observing her, oddly unsmiling. Odd because whenever she'd seen Denis Langford at the inn, he'd been a cheerful man with a ready smile and easy laughter. He had a way with guests that seemed to please them, Elaine said, and she had encouraged Kelsey to talk to him. So far, not a successful effort.

Now he looked grave, and not very happy, so that her attention was caught. Lately she had begun to run from happy people.

"Wait a minute before you go back to the inn, Kelsey," he said. "Sit down and let's talk a bit." He gestured expansively toward the sand, still not smiling, his gray eyes searching her face in a curiously intent way. For the first time she glimpsed an underlying sadness behind what had always seemed his ready smile. She dropped down on the sand and began to put on her sandals.

"Did my aunt send you to soothe my troubled spirit?" she asked.

"I volunteered. Look, Kelsey, I know something of what's happened to you, and I know what you must be feeling."

She rejected that quickly. "Nobody knows, and I don't want to talk about it."

Denis Langford was a few years older than Kelsey—perhaps thirty-eight, though he'd seemed younger to her, much more like a youthful twenty-eight. Perhaps his fair hair gave him a younger look than might have been expected. He ran a hand through it now, smoothing back strands the wind had dropped into his eyes.

"Don't worry—I'm not going to talk about what's happened in the past. Either to you or to me. It's the present that scares the wits out of me. If you'll just stop being so damned aloof and standoffish for a moment—"

His words upset her. Until her aunt, and now Denis, no one had ever accused her of being standoffish, or uninvolved, and suddenly she didn't like what must be happening to her. She drew her knees up to her chin and watched him with the steady gaze that was sometimes disconcerting to others.

He managed a fleeting grin. "That's better. Now you're looking at *me*. The reason I said I knew what you must be feeling is because I've nearly been there myself—in a different way. In fact, I'm still there, just as you are, and the going is pretty rough."

He was reminding her that other people had troubles, tragedies, and she knew she'd been too immersed in her own to care. For the past two years she had been able to throw herself only into her work with children—those whose need was desperate. She could still care about those who were young and lost and frightened. It was the problems of other adults she had wanted to push away. She sighed, waiting for Denis to go on.

"Your aunt wants you to meet someone—a woman who is coming to the inn in a little while. Coming to see you."

This sounded alarming. She knew that Elaine Carey liked to manipulate and arrange, and right now Kelsey didn't want anything to be arranged for her. Again she waited.

"I think perhaps you should say no to what your aunt wants of you."

That surprised her. He was taking a lot on himself for such short acquaintance. "Tell me why."

He left the tree and stood looking out along the crescent of Carmel beach toward a point of land that made a black protrusion into the sea. With the ocean calm, the sound of the waves was hushed, and there was a scent of woodsmoke on the air. An orange streak still stained the sky but the gray of evening was coming down.

Denis spoke over his shoulder, almost absently, as though he puzzled aloud. "Do you believe in good and evil? I mean as separate entities inside ourselves?"

"The demon and angel within?" she asked, finding his words disturbing. In her profession no one talked much about good and evil as such, and she felt a little self-conscious. "I don't think I've thought much about it."

"Neither have I until lately." He came to lower himself to the sand beside her, and let a handful of white grains dribble through his fingers. "It's the thing we do these days—we excuse those who behave badly. We let them off because of a miserable childhood, an unloving mother, a brutal father—whatever. Sometimes I wonder if the old religions didn't have a clearer idea—that evil really exists. That some men, some women, *are* wicked clear through—and very dangerous."

His words made her even more uneasy. "I'm not sure what you're talking about. I don't think this is an abstract conversation. Do you really know someone you think is evil?"

He flung away a handful of sand. "Maybe you shouldn't get involved in whatever Mrs. Carey asks of you."

Kelsey crossed her feet and rose lightly. It felt good to have her muscles under control, even though she'd neglected them lately.

"In that case," she said, "I'd better get back to the inn and find out what this is all about. Unless you'd like to tell me?"

He rose as easily, and she sensed in him an agitation that he made an effort to conceal. "You'll have to make up your own mind. But I'll warn you that it's a nasty situation. Anyway, I don't suppose it matters, really, because nothing can be done about the boy."

"What boy?"

"His name is Jody Hammond. He's my nephew, and he was nine a few months ago. But I'd better let your aunt tell you the rest."

As they followed the incline of Ocean Avenue, he fell into step beside her, and he seemed to draw his more usual, cheerful manner around him, submerging the intensity he'd shown on the beach.

"I wish I'd been here in Carmel's early days," he said. "The life would have suited me. It wasn't all that long ago—early in the century. These trees were planted down the center of this street because it used to rush with water and sweep everything away."

He had slipped easily back into the lighthearted host who enjoyed informing a guest. Kelsey listened with half her attention as he went on.

"Of course Carmel's trees are either glorious or notorious, depending on your viewpoint. If you're a visitor who's just tripped over an uneven sidewalk because trees have the right of way, you may not be enthusiastic about preserving their roots. But Carmel protects its trees lovingly, and sidewalks, streets, houses, all accommodate their presence, and go around where necessary. There's even a city ordinance that you can't sue for an injury if you were wearing high heels."

She wondered if he might be chatting on in this vein because he wanted to counteract his lapse into something he hadn't intended to discuss.

They turned down a side street that ran between the inn proper and the three cottages across the way. The architecture was fairytale whimsical—gingerbread houses with more peaked roofs, after the Carmel style.

"I'll leave you here and get back to the office," Denis said. "Just don't rush into anything, Kelsey."

"Thanks—I'll watch it."

She went up the short walk to her aunt's cottage and through an open door. The small sitting room had a California flavor, with touches of Spanish influence in the dark, carved furniture, and Indian motifs in bright, handwoven rugs and hangings. A small woodburning fireplace offered warmth against chill evenings, with a stack of driftwood near the hearth. On a long, low bookcase stood a fanciful, armored knight, lance in hand—an imaginative Don Quixote wrought in tin.

Her aunt came into the room while Kelsey was staring at the knight. "A sculptor friend made him for me," Elaine said. "He's modeled after a huge old rusty statue that somebody once put up on a hilltop overlooking Big Sur."

"Denis Langford came for me," Kelsey said. "You wanted to see me?"

"Yes. I had a call. Ginnie will be here any minute, and I'd better tell you what the score is."

Her aunt dropped onto the long sofa, and began to pluck absently at the blue lightning pattern. For once, she seemed not entirely at ease.

"Whatever it is," Kelsey said, "I don't want to get involved. Not yet. Please, Aunt Elaine, I need more time just to be let alone."

"Of course, dear. I wouldn't think of pushing you."

But that was exactly what she intended, and Kelsey regarded her with loving exasperation. At fifty-six, Elaine was still a handsome, well-built woman, her silvery hair done in the upswept style of another decade, which nevertheless suited her well. She had authority, dignity, but not always a sense of humor. Kelsey watched her, still wary and on guard.

"About two months ago a terrible accident happened out at Point Lobos," Elaine went on. "Ruth Hammond, the daughter of a dear friend of mine, had taken her nine-year-old son out there on a hike. Jody was always a mischief, and he was teasing his mother by running along a rocky cliff that dropped into the sea. She tried to stop him, and somehow they fell together. They were caught on a ledge just above the water, and they must have lain there for a long time before someone heard Ruth's calls. They were taken to the hospital in Monterey, and Tyler Hammond, Ruth's husband, came at once. Ruth and Jody were still alive, but that was about all, God help them. Ruth is Denis Langford's sister."

Kelsey listened, remembering Denis's words, knowing that

she must not let any of this reach that core of herself she now held remote, inviolable. Not because Denis had talked mysteriously about "evil," but because she had no strength left for anyone else's grief, however terrible.

When Kelsey asked no questions, Elaine continued. "Ruth can speak and move her arms, and her mind is clear. The rest of her is helpless. The specialists who were called in say that Jody's brain damage is so severe he will never be anything but a vegetable. 'Chronic vegetative state' is the term they actually use. He's still in a coma, though after a month, Tyler brought his wife and son home from the hospital. Ruth's mother came up from Palm Springs to take care of her. Dora Langford has been my friend from way back, and she's had nursing experience. However, the boy needs full-time nurses around the clock. That's where Ginnie comes in.

"Ruth went to college with Ginnie Soong, and she asked her to come and take care of Jody. Ginnie's a good nurse, and she's been looking after him during the day for the last month. There seems to be no hope for his improvement, and it's a dreadful time for all of them. I went up to Carmel Highlands last week to see Dora and Ruth. Dora is terribly worried because Ruth has given up completely. If only Jody could be helped, perhaps she'd want to live again."

Kelsey still kept silent, trying to resist what she was hearing.

"Doesn't any of this reach you?" Elaine asked.

"I don't want it to reach me! I don't like the way I am now, but I can't bear any more, and there's nothing I can do." She heard the anguish in her own voice, and knew it was entirely for herself. She had nothing left of compassion for others. The last two years of trying had drained her.

Elaine went on in spite of Kelsey's resistance. "Tyler means to put his son in a nursing home up near San Francisco, where he can live out his years—whatever they are. Ginnie doesn't want this to happen, and she's talked to me about it. So I thought of you."

"But if the doctors are right, this may be the best solution, hard as it is."

Elaine went calmly on. "Ginnie will be here any minute, and she wants to talk with you. I told her I'd arrange it. So you must at least see her. She's an interesting person—Ginnie Soong. Her father owns a Chinese import company in San Francisco, and her mother helps in the shop and writes exquisite poetry on the side. As I said, Ginnie went to college near L.A. with Ruth Langford. She was her roommate, and even after Ruth married Tyler they kept in touch as good friends. Just before the accident, Ginnie had come to visit Ruth, and was in the Hammond home as a guest when it happened. I want you to listen to what she has to say. You can do that much, Kelsey."

She couldn't very well get up and walk out. "All right—I'll listen, but that's all. What about Mr. Hammond? How is he taking this?"

Elaine's hesitation indicated uncertainty. "Badly. He's a strange, gifted man—a brilliant man who never wears his feelings openly. I've never liked him very much, though I admire his work. He's written, directed, and produced some very fine documentary films, two of which have won awards. He's not working now, and I'm not sure he ever will again. Ginnie says he's withdrawn into himself, and he's holding everything back. Anger, grief, despair—he's closed himself off. He's lost both his wife and his son, and it would take someone pretty strong not to be destroyed. He *is* strong, but for now I think he's given up as much as Ruth has."

Kelsey knew very well that Elaine wasn't thinking only of Tyler Hammond's double tragedy. She was thinking of Kelsey's own loss as well. It was easy to see the wheels turning and to guess what her aunt's first purpose was going to be.

"There's nothing you can do about Mark or Carl," Elaine said. "That's all over and past. But Ruth and Jody Hammond are *now*. Perhaps something can be salvaged if the boy can be helped."

"Have you told these people anything about me?" Kelsey asked.

"Ginnie knows only that you've worked as a physical therapist." Elaine broke off and stood up. "Here she is now."

The young Chinese-American woman still wore her uniform, though without the cap of her nursing school. She came in briskly, and her dark eyes went at once to Kelsey, questioning, perhaps even challenging. Her black hair had been fluffed gently to frame a rounded face. Though she was small, she looked sturdy, and the hand she gave Kelsey offered a firm clasp. The effect she conveyed was one of pleasant, straightforward efficiency, so that it might be hard to refuse whatever this woman asked. Kelsey braced herself.

"How is everything up at the house?" Elaine asked.

Ginnie shook her head. "Not good. Tyler's made his arrangements to send Jody away, and Ruth has agreed. I think he believes it will be better for her when the boy is out of the house. She's seen him only a few times, when Tyler has carried her down to Jody's room, and each time she's been terribly ill afterward. She might feel better if only her mother or Tyler could get her to open up about what happened. She won't talk to me either."

"Ruth can't accept her own condition," Elaine said, "much less what the doctors say about Jody."

"Why haven't *you* accepted the doctors' opinions?" Kelsey asked Ginnie directly.

The nurse didn't hesitate. "Because I'm not sure they're right. They aren't God, you know. Coma isn't something with exact boundaries—it's a sort of catchall word when there's nothing else to use. Jody's eyes are open, but they don't track or follow anything. We simply can't tell for sure if he sees us, or if he understands anything. Just the same, I've had a feeling now and then that I had some sort of eye contact with him—that it wasn't just an empty look, but as though he saw me. I've tried all sorts of signals, of course, but there's no response. He can't blink as I've asked him to, or press my fingers, yet I still have a feeling that there's something there—that maybe his mind isn't a complete blank. If you could just come to see him, Mrs. Stewart—"

"What could I do that you can't?"

"You've had more experience with such cases. Tyler Hammond won't listen to me, but he might listen to you if you thought there was any hope at all. Mrs. Carey tells me you have healing hands—and that's something I believe in because I've seen it happen."

This was surprising, but Elaine nodded at her.

"Have you forgotten the time I did the rounds with you, Kelsey, in that nursing home where you were working with brain-damaged children? One of the nurses there used that phrase about you. She said the children responded to your touch and your voice."

"That's not very scientific," Kelsey said.

"Science!" Ginnie exploded passionately. "This is a small boy who needs help! There can be more to healing than some doctors realize. The rotten part is that Tyler's not going to give us a chance to find out."

"Why not?" Kelsey asked.

"He blames Jody for what happened. He wants him out of his sight."

A sudden stillness possessed Kelsey. A listening stillness.

Elaine said, "It's true, and it's dreadfully unfair. When Ruth was able to talk and give an account of what had happened out at Point Lobos, Tyler knew that Jody was to blame, and he made absolutely no allowances for a child's silliness and lack of judgment."

"Sometimes," Ginnie added more softly, "I almost think Jody senses how his father feels. Though the doctors say his brain is too badly damaged for him to understand anything."

"If he can understand anything at all, such treatment is terribly cruel!" Kelsey cried.

"Of course it's cruel," Elaine said. "That's why the boy needs help. I know Tyler's suffering, but Jody needs someone who can step in and *do* something before it's too late."

"There've been EEG tests and brain scans, of course?" Kelsey asked.

"Yes," Ginnie said. "And the waves, or lack of some of them, tell a pretty grim story."

"Just the same," Kelsey spoke half to herself, "even the experts admit that no one knows for sure about the brain." The stillness inside her was being replaced by something else. She knew what injustice and blame were like, and she was already disliking Tyler Hammond intensely. "There have been patients who came out of deep comas with their brains functioning enough so they could relearn some of what was lost. Sometimes they even repeated conversations they'd heard around their beds when they were supposedly unconscious."

Ginnie sensed the change in Kelsey, and her eyes held a challenge. Yet Kelsey still hesitated, knowing that she was being manipulated, pressured—by both her aunt and Ginnie Soong. There was something here that she distrusted, that she couldn't yet evaluate.

"When do you want Kelsey to come?" Elaine asked, settling the matter.

Ginnie's smile had a triumphant edge to it. "How about tomorrow morning around eleven? By that time I'll have Jody ready for the day."

"Has his father authorized this?" Kelsey asked.

"I've taken care of that," Elaine said quickly. "I talked to Tyler on the phone the day after you came, Kelsey, and I guess I made it pretty strong. I'm Dora's friend as well as Ruth's and he had to listen. So he will give you this one chance to see Jody before he sends him away."

"You'd no right to do that!" Kelsey protested. "I don't think I can change Mr. Hammond's mind, and I'm not sure I ought to try."

"Maybe you underestimate yourself," Elaine said.

Ginnie spoke quickly, as though staying any longer might lose whatever ground she'd gained. "I've got to get back now. Dora Langford, Ruth's mother, has been looking in on Jody, and I mustn't leave him for too long. You will come, won't you, Kelsey?"

It was easier to give in and do as they asked. Tomorrow would have to take care of itself.

"All right," she said, "I'll come. Just this one time."

"Tyler won't let you come for more," Elaine said, but she had relaxed a little.

Ginnie left quickly, and again Kelsey sensed a curious triumph, however repressed, that seemed out of proportion to anything that a stranger, an outsider, might be expected to accomplish. A conflict was clearly building in the Hammond household that perhaps did not entirely concern Jody.

"I expect you'll want to change your clothes," Elaine suggested, cutting short any further discussion. "We're going out to dinner tonight, and Denis is coming with us. He can fill you in a bit about his sister and this whole miserable situation."

Kelsey gave up and went off to her room. The cottage was on two levels, and her upstairs windows looked out upon a fantastically gnarled oak tree that was nothing like the tall oaks back home. Its roots had pushed up the cement of the sidewalk, and its limbs looped upon themselves in strange contortions, like something out of Edgar Allan Poe. Hinged shutters had shaded the room from afternoon sun, and when she had folded them open to the breeze, she could glimpse the ocean only a few blocks away, though barely visible now, its color matching gray skies where only a hint of sunset remained.

She took a light cotton suit from the closet and put it on. Her dark hair complemented the wheat color, and with a quick brushing its feathers fell into shape. She used a mere touch of lipstick, and put on lapis earrings, delicate and dangly, that added a further hint of color. Somehow she looked less pale this evening than she had earlier. A touch of sun? Or a touch of interest in life?

Whether she had invited it or not, something of a mission had been forced upon her. She knew that she wanted to see Jody Hammond, who was being so unfairly blamed by his father, and perhaps by his mother, for the harm that had been done. She could probably make no difference in his condition, but she had to see for herself. A somewhat combative eagerness that was rather pleasant had begun to stir in Kelsey. She almost looked forward to meeting Tyler Hammond. Someone ought to take Jody's side, and her hands weren't tied as Ginnie's must be.

She went downstairs with more of a lift to her step than she had felt for a long time.

III

THE ONLY MEAL the Manzanita Inn served to its guests was a continental breakfast, so Elaine, who liked to cook, often made her own meals in her kitchen at the cottage. She took guests of her own out to one of the many restaurants in the "village." Since parking was difficult in Carmel, cars were a nuisance, and Carmelites usually walked. So Elaine, Kelsey, and Denis went on foot to the La Playa Hotel a few blocks away.

The great pink building made a right angle around lawns that sloped down the hillside and were trimmed with flowerbeds in bright splashes of color. Inside, the lobby's soft lighting and subdued Spanish touches were soothing to Kelsey's senses. Tiles rimmed the steps of a curving staircase at one side, carriage lamps glowed here and there on the walls, and a wide stone fireplace with sofas grouped before it invited one to linger.

Elaine led the way through to a white dining room with a tiled floor where windows ranged around two sides, framed in white fretwork. The many well-spaced tables were set with lemon-yellow cloths and napkins. Beside a window, their table looked out on lighted lawns and walks, and a beautiful, lacy gazebo in which several people were having cocktails graced the lawn. Carmel, Kelsey was beginning to find, was full of such romantic touches. Again she felt a soothing sense of peace. Perhaps she could simply mark time until tomorrow and stay quiet.

Denis wore a light jacket over a beige pullover sweater, the top of his jacquard tie showing. Elaine, when she wasn't wearing pants, liked the flowery prints of California, and her dress matched the flowerbed below their window. Since Carmel's weather was often on the cool side, she wore a white cardigan. Earlier, Kelsey had seen mists on the Santa Lucia Mountains that made a backdrop for the town, and it was those mists and fog from the sea that kept the climate comfortable.

Her sense of peace, however, didn't last long. When they'd ordered seafood dishes, Elaine went straight to the matter that most absorbed her.

"Kelsey has agreed to go to Tyler's tomorrow and see Jody," she told Denis. "Ginnie was able to persuade her, as I thought she might."

Denis cocked one blond eyebrow at Kelsey. "With your aunt's help, I'll bet. Do you really want to put yourself through this, Kelsey?"

His tone was light, but she remembered his strange words earlier when they were on the beach. "Perhaps this is something I must do," she responded, "whether I want to or not. Besides, it's easier to go than to fight with Aunt Elaine."

"Very wise," Elaine said complacently. "Denis, tell Kelsey a little about your sister. She needs to be armed with a bit of background before she goes tomorrow."

"Armed" seemed a militant word, and Kelsey waited for Denis's response.

He buttered a piece of roll and sat staring at it absently as he spoke. "Kelsey's not likely to see Ruth at all."

"Probably not," Elaine agreed. "Just the same, she needs to know something about the situation. You can tell her better than I can, Denis."

He set down the bite of roll uneaten. "Ruth is younger than I am by a couple of years, and ten years younger than Tyler. Maybe around your age, Kelsey. She was always a sweet kid. There was so much gaiety about her—she loved everyone, trusted everyone. We could laugh at the same jokes, but she was never unkind. Tyler came along and swept her off her feet. I don't know why beautiful, happy women are so often attracted to moody men who hold in their emotions—except when they explode."

"While I don't like Tyler very much," Elaine said, "he can be pretty compelling, and there's no denying his amazing talent. I suppose most men with a touch of genius are hard to live with."

"I don't know how she managed as well as she did," Denis went on gloomily. "Sometimes she even coaxed him into laughing at her little jokes."

"He obviously adored her—still does," Elaine said. "That's what's so tragic when she's changed so much."

"Being paralyzed would change anyone," Kelsey said mildly. "It takes time to get one's courage back and accept a different sort of life."

Elaine sighed. "I'm not sure Ruth can ever manage that. I hope you will meet her, Kelsey. I want to know what you think."

"Look," Kelsey said quickly, "I'm a physical therapist, not an analyst."

"You're a lot more than you realize, dear. Denis, do you think something could be arranged? I mean for Kelsey to see Ruth."

Denis shook his head. "Tyler wouldn't allow it—not as things are now. Ruth doesn't want anyone to see her the way she is, and Tyler's stiff with pride over what he regards as his private affairs. It's hard even for *me* to get to see her—and I'm her brother."

"Tell me how she has changed," Kelsey said.

"There never used to be any hatred in her." The pain Denis felt was evident in his voice. "I hardly know her now. She's even cross with Mother, who takes care of her with such devotion."

"It's probably temporary," Kelsey said. "Most people fold up in despair at first when they're hit by something so awful. It takes time to see everything in a new way." She sounded so reasonable, she thought wryly. But her own sounder perspective had vanished in the last two years.

"I don't know," Denis said. "This is more like a violent change of character that's out of all proportion, no matter what's happening. Ruth always had so much courage. She was the leader when we were kids, even though I was older. Now Tyler has only to stand by her bed and stare at her and she falls apart. She knows how she must look to him, how useless she is as a wife." His voice broke.

Elaine put a hand on his arm. "Let it go, Denis. I'm sorry I've opened all this up. I thought it might help if you could give Kelsey more of the picture since she'll be seeing Jody. Let's skip the people and talk about that fantastic house. Tell her about La Casa de la Sombra."

Their young waiter—in Carmel, waiters were likely to be out-of-work actors, or part-time musicians—brought their appetizers and made sure all was well.

"The house, Denis," Elaine prompted. "Tell Kelsey about the House of Shadow."

This was something he could warm to. "It was built back in the early days, up in Carmel Highlands. There are lots of

Carmels. That's why the town is called Carmel-by-the-Sea—at least in print. Nobody says all that. In the beginning, when the Spanish moved in and called the river the Rio del Carmelo, to honor the Carmelite order, Carmel was just an unimportant country neighbor to the old capital of Monterey. But nothing in California matches Carmel for beauty, so artists and writers have always come here, along with the very, very rich."

"It's still a creative community," Elaine interrupted.

Denis went on. "La Casa de la Sombra was built by a writer lucky enough to have money. In style, it's Mediterranean, and it drops down a steep hillside on several levels. The big vaulted living room used to be a gathering place for the literary crowd long ago—Jack London, and George Sterling, who really put his stamp on Carmel, along with Mary Austin. Carmel was perfect in those days for a 'bohemian' existence. Go back a little further, and Robert Louis Stevenson left his own mark, working here for a while."

"I hope you get to see more of the house than Jody's sickroom," Elaine added. "I remember when Francesca Fallon did a radio interview with Tyler in the handsome library up there. That was a wild broadcast. Tyler absolutely lost control for a moment, and Francesca got pretty mad. She was a really terrible woman."

There was silence while the waiter served them, and when Denis spoke again, his tone of voice put an end to Elaine's chatter.

"Francesca's dead." The words had a stark, almost challenging ring, though Denis looked at neither of them.

"Who was Francesca Fallon?" Kelsey asked.

"I shouldn't have brought her up," Elaine said quickly. "What happened can give Carmel Valley a bad name that it doesn't deserve. Anyway, she has nothing to do with the present problems at the house."

Denis still looked troubled.

Elaine went on. "Legends were always built up around Francesca. Empty legends, I think. She liked to encourage them since she hadn't all that much substance. When she was young she used to act bit parts in B pictures. Then she disappeared for a while, thanks to alcohol and probably drugs, as rumor has it. When she got herself straightened out, she started writing a gossip column for a Los Angeles paper, and did pretty well, since that was her thing. Until she dropped it and bought a small ranch in Carmel Valley, though not, of course, to do any ranching. That was when she started her local radio program out of Monterey. She always thought she belonged on big-time television, but she couldn't make it there."

"Tyler should never have done that interview," Denis said gloomily.

"Oh, I don't know." Elaine dismissed his words, and Kelsey wondered if this was something her aunt wanted to gloss over. "After all, he and Ruth and Francesca were old friends back in the Los Angeles days."

Denis disagreed. "I wouldn't say *friends*. Anyway, why do we keep talking about her?"

But by this time Kelsey was curious. "What happened to this Francesca?"

Elaine said, "She was murdered about six months ago, right there on her own little ranch. The police never found out who did it. Now let's get off that subject. You know, for a time, when Tyler and Ruth first moved into the House of Shadow, things were pretty lively again. Ruth tried to revive the custom of holding a salon for writers and artists. Though 'salon' is too formal a word for Carmel. It was fun for a while."

"It didn't last?" Kelsey asked.

Elaine sighed. "Tyler hated it. He's a recluse at heart, I suppose, and he disliked all the traipsing in and out, and all the chatter that he thought was superficial. Some of those people preferred talk to production. So he put a damper on Ruth."

"Even if he was right, he doesn't sound like much fun," Kelsey said.

Denis snorted. "Fun isn't the word you'd use around Tyler. Fun was Ruth's thing, but of course he squelched it out of her. Now he's becoming more of a hermit than ever, shutting everyone out, sealing himself in. How can Ruth recover at all in an atmosphere like that?"

There seemed to be no safe topic, Kelsey thought, and her own depression returned. She had lost her brief eagerness to see Jody and face Tyler Hammond. He sounded more and more formidable and she didn't want to fight anyone. She would be glad when tomorrow was over and she could forget the troubles of strangers, and begin to pull her own life together.

They finished the meal with coffee, skipped dessert, and walked silently back to the inn. Elaine wanted to stop at the office, where messages were waiting, and while she leafed through them, Denis drew Kelsey aside.

"I'm sorry all this has been thrown at you. I never wanted Elaine to involve you in the first place. Kelsey, would you care to go down to the beach for a while? When I walk beside the ocean at night it always calms me down. And we might talk a little."

Elaine heard him, and she held up a piece of paper. "Come back to the cottage first. There's a message here for either you or me, Denis, to call your mother at Tyler's."

Denis looked alarmed. "Something's happened!"

"We'll find out," Elaine said calmly.

They hurried down a flight of rustic steps outside and through a passage at the rear. Lights had been left on in the cottage, and under the peaked roof its windows looked warm and welcoming. In the sitting room Elaine picked up the phone, dialed, and then set it on the amplifier so the others could hear.

Dora Langford, Ruth and Denis's mother, answered at once. "Thank you for calling back. I wanted to let Denis know that everything's all right now—more or less." She paused, and Denis spoke quickly.

"I'm here, Mother. What is it?"

With an effort, Dora Langford went on. "Ruth tried to kill herself tonight. I went to make a call away from her room, and while I was gone, she picked up a fruit knife and was trying to cut her wrists. I stopped her before she'd lost much blood." Again Mrs. Langford paused, as if to get her breath.

"Are you all right, Mother?" Denis asked.

"Don't worry about me. It's Ruth's mental state that frightens me. Tyler's with her now, and I hope she's sleeping."

Denis said, "I'll come at once."

Her voice broke. "No—Tyler said not to. I'll call you tomorrow and let you know how she is."

"I'd like to see for myself." Denis was insistent. "I want to talk to her."

"Not now, please. She's been given a sedative. But don't worry. Either Tyler or I will be with her every minute."

"That's what I'm afraid of," Denis said. "You know Tyler hardly helps her state of mind, Mother."

Elaine thanked Mrs. Langford and hung up the phone.

Denis had dropped into a chair and he sat for a moment staring blankly at nothing. "Ruth has given up. Just given up altogether. She thinks she has nothing to live for—and God help her, maybe she's right."

"That's another reason why I want Kelsey to see Jody tomorrow," Elaine told him. "You mustn't let this get you so far down that you're ineffective, Denis. Your sister's hardly responsible for her actions right now. And she needs you desperately."

Kelsey was beginning to feel even more sympathetic toward Ruth, the more she learned about Tyler. She knew exactly what it felt like to be powerless against circumstances one couldn't control.

"What about that walk on the beach?" she reminded Denis. "I'd still like to go." Perhaps by this time he needed it even more than she did.

He looked at her gratefully. "I'd forgotten. I'm ready whenever you want to leave."

Kelsey ran upstairs for a sweater and in a few moments they were walking down Ocean Avenue together. Denis moved fast now, as though he needed to release pent-up energy, and Kelsey matched his stride with her own long legs. Since Carmel had no streetlamps, he'd brought a flashlight, and the beam played ahead as they reached the foot of Ocean Avenue. They climbed down a sandy bluff and went around tide pools to the lower level of the beach.

Everything seemed totally different at night. Moonlight brushed the ocean with rippling silver foil, and the cypresses, never growing far from the water, twisted in black silhouette against the sky. The lights of Carmel shimmered among its many trees, and more lights rimmed the crescent of Carmel Bay, following Scenic Drive, and rising among the pines to Carmel Highlands.

Denis gestured toward the dark point of land that cut into the water across the bay. "That's Point Lobos out there— *Punta de los Lobos Marinos*. The Spaniards called our sea lions sea wolves. It's out there that it happened, Kelsey."

"Tell me," she said, knowing that he needed to talk.

"The area's a park, a state reserve now, with trails running through the pine groves. Rangers look after it. The entire shoreline's rough and rocky, with sharp gashes where the sea rushes in. That's where they fell—because Jody was teasing his mother."

The thrust of the point was only a black shape rising above silvery water, and Kelsey felt the tightening inside her. She could so easily become involved with the little boy who lay in a coma up there in his father's house on the highlands. And that could mean even more pain ahead.

"Point Lobos was Jody's favorite place for a hike," Denis continued. "Ruth used to call him a sea boy because the ocean excited him and drew him. She said he was trying to go back to it. The beach is down the hill from Tyler's house, and it's always been hard to keep Jody from running down there alone. He can swim like any fish, but he has no caution, and the currents along here are treacherous."

Denis broke off, recognizing that he'd spoken in the present, and that everything concerning Jody now lay in the past. Kelsey's private pain stabbed with sharp reminder. Mark, her own small son, had been filled with just such bursting energy. He'd always needed to be restrained. She said nothing, resisting the pain.

When Denis paused, she stopped beside him, looking into his face as he studied her in the shadowy moonlight.

"I'm sorry," he said. "I don't know why we should inflict our troubles on you."

"It's all right. I'm further along than you are, though I haven't even begun to reach a quiet shore yet—no calm waters. But I've had more time than you have. Once I even wanted what Ruth tried to choose tonight—to make the hurting stop. But I know it's better to—just wait."

"You have a lot to live for, Kelsey."

She knew he was thinking of how little Ruth had left. Kelsey had been lucky, if you wanted to call it that.

"Tell me more about Jody," she said. "Were you close to him?"

Denis hesitated, then took another course. "Jody idolized his father, but sometimes he was afraid of him, too. Tyler loved his son, but he wasn't always good with a small boy."

"I was thinking more in terms of how *you* might help Jody. Perhaps even more than his father can. Sometimes stricken fathers become almost useless in their grief. They can move in mistaken directions because their pain is so terrible. That's why I wondered if you were close to your nephew."

He turned away to hide his own feelings and started walking again. "I can't even talk about that. My sister's son!"

In the past, Kelsey had found that the powerful emotions which could swirl around a helpless child were often the hardest problem of all to deal with. Now that she knew how it felt from inside, it became even more difficult to deal with the pain of others. Her sense of sympathy had heightened, but she also knew better now how hard grief could be to deal with.

They walked on again, and after a little while Denis began to talk. It was as though the moonlit night, the rhythmic sound of the sea rushing in, the wind touching their faces, calmed him, and gave him a new freedom to speak.

"Where some kids are scared of heights, or scared of the water, Jody was never afraid of anything physical. He was a brave, bright little boy. I loved him a lot, even when he teased us all."

In another place, another time, Denis might never have said these words, and Kelsey liked him for speaking out of his own intense feeling. She'd learned something of the need for that in her work with injured and brain-damaged children.

They moved to drier sand away from the water's edge, and the walking grew harder. For a time they were silent, and Kelsey savored these quiet moments. The sand under their feet added its own whispering sound to the pulsing of the waves. Other walkers were out on the beach tonight, and two or three couples, as well as several lone joggers, passed them going the other way.

"The beach is really Carmel's community center," Denis said. "It stretches from Pebble Beach to the Frank Lloyd Wright house down on the promontory. On the Fourth of July, bonfires are lighted, and all year round picnic suppers on the beach are a big thing. In the old days there were abalone roasts, before all the abalone went elsewhere. That's when George Sterling started that great old abalone song that goes on for endless irreverent verses. Tonight's unusual because there's no fog. It often rolls in at sundown and people can lose children and dogs on the beach, as well as their sense of direction."

He was talking to free himself of tension, and when his stride lengthened she kept up with him. Not until they were out of breath from the brisk walk did they slow down and turn back.

"You don't say much," Denis remarked. "Not that I've given you much chance. I think you really listen."

"I like to listen. Tell me about you. You haven't always been an innkeeper, have you?"

"No—I fell into that, I suppose. Elaine's an old friend of my mother's and she roped me in. I seem to be doing all right."

"What would you like best to do?"

"I wish I knew. I suppose I'm moderately good at a few things, so I haven't run long enough on any one track. I envy Tyler his passionate involvement in film work. Or at least he used to be passionately involved. There's one thing I like especially about Carmel—the General was never here. So I needn't feel him breathing down my neck."

"The General?"

"General Schuyler Bridges Langford—my father." Denis spoke the name wryly.

"Tell me about him."

Denis drew a deep breath of sharp, salty air. "He died in Vietnam. Though not in battle—which I'm sure he'd have

preferred. Hepatitis got him. He's buried at Arlington. I didn't
go to the funeral, but Ruth and Mother went, and came home
with the flag."

"You didn't get along with your father?"

"That's putting it mildly. I hated him a lot of the time, and I
suppose I loved and admired him too. I don't think he had any
feeling for me one way or the other, except maybe anger
because I never wanted to go his way. Ruth got off easier than I
did. He couldn't expect to turn her into a soldier. And daugh-
ters often wrap their fathers around their little fingers. I owe
Ruth a lot for standing by me. She could face up to the General, who would take it from her, and no one else."

"What about your mother?"

"I suppose Dora was the perfect wife for an army officer. She
knew how to take orders and adapt to whatever he wanted.
Ruth and I were the usual army brats."

There was too much pent-up bitterness in Denis Langford,
and perhaps he'd denied it too much of the time, suppressed
what ought to be let out and aired. The quiet of the beach,
empty at this far end, and the pale moonlight that hid sharp
reality had perhaps allowed him to lower his guard. With a
stab of regret, Kelsey wished she could lower her own.

"What did you want to do that your father opposed?" she
asked.

"I tried a lot of things—he didn't like any of them. I still
paint a little, write a little. When we lived in the desert near
Palm Springs I tried movie scripts for a while, and Tyler said
some weren't too bad. I even acted in a couple of movies, but
that wasn't for me. For a while I switched to selling real estate,
and did all right. The list goes on and on, and it's pretty boring.
I suppose I was mostly trying to grow up, as well as aiming to
find something that would make the General accept me without my being a soldier. That wasn't possible. Enough about
me. What's your spell, Kelsey? I don't usually go on like this

with anyone. At least I was doing pretty well here in Carmel until this—this terrible accident happened to Ruth and Jody." The words seemed torn out of him. "Now things have fallen apart for all of us. Maybe that's why I can talk to you—because you know about falling apart."

She liked his almost matter-of-fact dismissal of self-pity. "Yes, I do know about that," she said.

"So now it's your turn. This physical therapy you do—I should think that would be awfully painful at times. I mean working with other people's children."

"It can be. That's why I wanted to take some weeks off. But it's satisfying too when there's any improvement. Sometimes the wiggling of a finger is practically a miracle. And the children are wonderful. Brave against the most shattering odds. They're ready to laugh at silly jokes, and so often loving and needing love. And of course they're cranky and difficult sometimes. It breaks my heart in the cases where there's so little that can be done. Maybe that's one reason I don't really want to see Jody Hammond tomorrow. But there's no standing against Aunt Elaine once she's determined about something."

He started to laugh at the thought of opposing Elaine, and then sobered. "I wish you didn't have to see him either. It won't matter for Jody—he's out of it. But what happens may make everything seem that much more hopeless for Ruth. And Tyler will probably be as rude and insensitive as only he knows how to be."

That small knot of indignation had begun to tighten in her against Jody's father. More and more, he seemed an impossible man.

"What about Ginnie Soong?" she asked.

"I'm not exactly sure. I've known her on and off for years because of the time when she roomed with Ruth in college. She's bright, and she's a good nurse. But sometimes—well, you'll need to make up your own mind eventually."

"I don't know if there'll be an 'eventually.' I'll go up to Mr. Hammond's house because Aunt Elaine wants me to. But I need to get my own life back in order."

"You will," he said gently. "Thanks for listening. I can be a good listener too, if you ever want to try me."

Now, as they followed the beach, they had most of the long stretch of sand to themselves. Sometimes, Kelsey thought, it was easier, perhaps even more comforting, to talk to strangers than to close friends. With a stranger there were no preconceived attitudes, and much less unwanted advice likely to be given. She wished she could speak about her husband. Carl had not been an especially gentle or sensitive man, and there were still angers against him that she'd never expressed. But she couldn't talk about this to anyone yet.

"Do you paint anymore?" she asked instead.

"Everybody paints in Carmel, or sculpts, or writes. It's catching. I've even exhibited a few pictures once or twice. There's a whole street of good art galleries, and they aren't just for visitors. Carmel may look like a quaint tourist attraction, but even though tourists are our main business these days, the town is for the people who live here and wouldn't want to live anywhere else."

"Do you stay at the inn?"

"I have rooms there for now. For a while I lived at Tyler's but that didn't work out. What he'd like best is a cave with no one else around—except maybe his wife and child. Or at least that's the way it used to be. Let's not talk about Tyler. What was your husband like?"

The question caught her off guard. "I'm afraid I wound up not liking him very much. Any more than he liked me. It was a mistake, except for Mark. That part would have been fine. Afterward, Carl couldn't stand the sight of me. He blamed me because Mark was in the car I was driving. We didn't quarrel—

we just walked in opposite directions. I'm sure he'll land on his feet."

"You will too."

"Of course," she agreed. But the earth still had a tendency to tilt, and sometimes it was all she could do to keep her precarious balance.

"How do you plan to get to Tyler's tomorrow?" Denis asked. "I can drive you up there in the morning, if you like."

"That would be fine. Thank you."

They reached the town end of the beach, climbed the sandy bluff to the street, and started up the steep slope of Ocean Avenue. Denis took her to the door of the cottage and went off to his own rooms, in a wing of the inn.

Elaine, dressed in a tailored robe, lay stretched in a lounge chair, reading a Mary Higgins Clark mystery. She looked up at Kelsey's blown feathers of hair and pinkened cheeks.

"You look a lot better than when you arrived. You haven't been doing so well since you came, have you?"

Kelsey shook her head. "It's my own fault. I mean to get out more now."

"Look, dear, the atmosphere at Tyler's may be worse than ever after what Ruth has attempted. So if you'd like to postpone seeing Jody for a few days, I can arrange it. Tyler's mood will be blacker than ever, and I don't want you to take on a rough situation too soon."

"It doesn't matter. I'm ready now, and I'd better go through with it. Denis has offered to drive me to the house tomorrow. I think I'll go to bed now since I'm not quite over Connecticut time."

"Fine. Have a good sleep, dear."

Elaine Carey wasn't a demonstrative woman, and she never invited embraces, but Kelsey bent to kiss her cheek. "Thank you for helping." Her aunt patted her hand, and Kelsey was touched to see tears in her eyes.

She went up to her room, got ready for bed quickly, and then lay awake in the dark, sorting out the day. Denis, at least, seemed to be a plus. In a strange way, she felt more comfortable with people who had also suffered disaster. The untouched were too carefree for her to be around. Tomorrow she would need to be strong, because otherwise this small boy, Jody Hammond, could tear her apart and open wounds that had still not healed. His father didn't want her there, and perhaps he was right. Both her aunt and Ginnie Soong seemed to be looking for a miracle.

Right now, Kelsey was fresh out of miracles.

IV

MISTS smudged the high ridges of the Santa Lucia Mountains as they ran parallel along the coast. Carmel's Scenic Drive wound its way south above the beach and through a residential area of small, distinctive houses.

This morning Denis seemed more subdued than he had last night, and Kelsey suspected that by daylight he might be regretting the frankness with which he'd spoken during their walk on the beach. Perhaps he felt as she did, that they were on a hopeless mission that must be performed quickly so they could escape from its awfulness as soon as possible.

The highway ran past a narrow side road that led uphill. A sign indicated Carmel Highlands, and she glimpsed an impressive inn built on the hillside above. Up there were large homes as well, set apart from one another in great stands of Monterey pine. Denis kept to the main road until he came to a driveway that led downhill on the right-hand side, ending in a paved space before the garage of La Casa de la Sombra.

They left the car to follow steps dropping to a still lower courtyard. Kelsey paused beside a huge aloe vera bush to look down upon sloping, red tile roofs and steel-blue walls of the house below. A front wing met the main house at a right angle, framing two sides of the court, and bougainvillea reached purple tendrils across blue stucco. At the corner angle where walls met, a flight of narrow stone steps with a curving iron rail mounted to an upper entrance on the second floor. Denis went to the lower door and raised the knocker beside carved fretwork panels.

A Japanese-American maid greeted them and invited them into a square anteroom with a dark tiled floor and pine-paneled walls. An iron lamp hung from the high ceiling, and a hall opened into the huge living room that Denis had mentioned. Kelsey could see straight through to a far balcony, with pine tops dropping away, and the blue sea visible beyond.

A moment later Ginnie Soong came briskly into the room, professional and efficient this morning in her white uniform, a cap pinned to her black hair. She looked even more concerned than she had yesterday, and greeted them gravely.

"Please call Mr. Hammond, Hana," she said to the maid.

"I couldn't get through by phone this morning," Denis told Ginnie. "Nobody would talk to me. I wasn't sure whether Kelsey should come or not, after what happened. How is my sister?"

"She's sleeping, I think. That's best for now."

"And Tyler?"

Ginnie shook her head doubtfully. "I've hardly seen him. And he's not permitting anyone except your mother to see Ruth. Even as an old friend, I don't count right now. Come with me, Kelsey, so you can see Jody alone for a moment."

A side door opened down a hallway and led into what had probably been a guest suite, since it had its own bath, sitting room, and small kitchen. Now it was furnished with an electric hospital bed, white utility tables, and a metal cupboard. The tiled floor could be easily cared for, and the setup seemed ideal for its purpose. Beyond the bed, two casement windows opened on green pine tops and made the room bright, in spite of dark paneling on the walls. On a table near the bed a television set talked to itself.

Kelsey paused in the doorway, taking in the room at a glance, trying to hold her feelings in check. Somehow she must be cool, objective, and not allow her own emotion to stand in the way of anything she could offer this child. He lay on his back, his slight body barely discernible under a light blanket—a handsome boy with an empty face and large gray eyes that stared at nothing. Kelsey felt the touch of Denis's hand on her arm, urging her forward, and she walked in and stood looking down at Jody Hammond's thin face. Denis came with her and stood near the end of the bed.

A plastic tube inserted in one nostril was connected to a suspended bag filled with liquid food to sustain life. Jody's dark hair had been trimmed short, except for the bangs over his forehead, and a small patch of bandage showed where hair had begun to grow back in the shaved area of damage. The usual urine bag had been clipped to the bed, and the tube that led to a catheter disappeared under the blanket.

Jody's sickly pallor, his soft child's mouth and rounded chin caught at her heart. She had a quick vision of the way he must have been, his eyes alive with fun, his legs strong and swift. In the same instant a memory of her own Mark stabbed through her, and the longing to hold a child in her arms was intense. She glanced at Denis, wanting to escape, fearful lest she wasn't strong enough to go through with this.

He stood watching her steadily, and his nod was just perceptible. With the quick turning of a knob, Ginnie stilled the television set that Kelsey knew was there for the purpose of offering possible stimulation to the boy in the bed.

"You never know what they can hear," Ginnie said, and the quiet words were steadying.

Kelsey bent over the bed. "Hello, Jody." She watched intently for the slightest flutter of lashes, for any change in his breathing. There was nothing. His arms, reaching from a short-sleeved hospital gown, lay inert on the covers. Gently, Kelsey picked up one limp hand and found it pliant in her own, but without any sign of life in the slender fingers. There was no return of the firm pressure she gave him; no response of any sort, and she had expected none.

Ginnie said softly, "We try. We try everything. At least I do."

"I know." Kelsey stroked the slim hand that lay in her own and began to speak to him slowly, clearly. "I've just come here from Connecticut, where I live, Jody. Back home I work in hospitals, helping children who've been hurt. Sometimes I have helped them to get well. Some of them are walking and talking again now. It takes time, Jody. We know how frightened you are inside. It's very scary not to be able to move and talk, but you can come out of that. We all want to help you."

She bent so that she could look directly into his unfocused eyes, and it seemed for an instant that he was looking at *her*. But one of the most frustrating things in such cases was that you could never be sure, and one's own strong wish might make the impossible seem real.

"Can you try a little, Jody?" she said. "Can you just press my fingers?"

There was still no response, and her throat felt full of tears. No matter how many times she saw a child in this condition, it always broke her heart.

A sudden change in the atmosphere of the room pierced her like a chill. There had been no sound, but her own acute senses were aware that both Ginnie Soong and Denis had stiffened. She turned and saw Tyler Hammond in the doorway. In spite of all she'd heard, she was unprepared for the force of the man —a dark, furious, pent-up power—as though he might explode at any moment; that without reason he was already angry with her for being here at all.

"Good morning, Mr. Hammond," she said. "I'm Kelsey Stewart."

He threw Denis a quick, dismissing look—though Denis didn't move—and walked to the opposite side of the bed, where he faced Kelsey.

"I suppose you know what happened to my wife last night—what she tried to do?"

"Yes, I know," Kelsey said. "I'm very sorry." She glanced at the unhearing, unseeing boy. "But we shouldn't talk here."

He didn't answer or move. His eyes held the force, she thought grimly. His look was nearly as unblinking as his son's—an almost destructive stare, as though it pleased him to disconcert and confuse. Kelsey stared back, examining him as he examined her. He was tall—more than six feet—and inclined to stoop a little, as though ordinary doorways might defeat him. His thick hair was as black as his son's, and his eyes much darker. Unlike his son's, his skin was tanned, his thin, long-fingered hands brown and strong. An angry arrogance seemed to stamp his manner, as though he had been so long accustomed to command that he hardly considered the feelings of those around him. Kelsey reminded herself that this was a man who had endured—was enduring—an almost unbearable pain, and his anger could be a protective shield. But she had no desire, no strength to stay and try to fight him. It could very well be that the father was as much the problem as the boy in the bed, and she had no strength left for dealing with impossible fathers.

"You're right," she said, answering his unspoken words. "I'm afraid there's nothing I can do that's not already being done." She glanced at Ginnie with a forced smile. "Your son is in very good hands with Ginnie Soong."

He brushed her words away with a flick of his fingers. "I've let you come this morning only because I respect Elaine Carey. Now I've done what she wished, but I have made other arrangements for Jody. He'll be driven by ambulance to a place in San Francisco next week where every possible care can be given him."

"Custodial care?" Kelsey asked. "Someone who will watch and protect him, and be too busy to help him?"

"That's all that's needed now. I've had the best specialists in to see him, both at the hospital and here at home. The doctors all agree that when a coma lasts more than forty-eight hours, it's less likely that the patient will come out. The chances for even a slight recovery are—"

"But I've *seen* them come out!" Kelsey interrupted. "I've seen them come out after months. You're giving up too easily. Too soon."

"Thank you for stopping in, Mrs. Stewart. There's no point in your staying."

He started for the door without a word for either Denis or Ginnie, and Kelsey went right after him. "Just a moment, Mr. Hammond."

He turned, staring her down. "Yes?"

"There's no such thing as knowing for sure how hopeless a case may be. Not for a long time—if ever. You haven't allowed Jody enough of a chance."

His mouth was as grim as his eyes. "Don't try to tell *me!* I'm thinking now of my wife's sanity—maybe of my own. We lost our son two months ago. Don't you people ever consider the families who may be destroyed by having"—he broke off and gestured toward the bed—"a shell like that in their midst? We can't pick up whatever lives we have left while he's here to remind us every moment of what he did—what he caused!"

For an instant of inner rage Kelsey hated him furiously. Yet she knew the unhappy truth in his words. In such cases there was always this desperate problem to be faced, and sometimes no other choice than to send the brain-damaged patient away. However, this was a big house, and Tyler Hammond could afford all that was needed to give Jody whatever chance might still be left. Even in the best of institutions, there were too many other hopeless cases, and too few nurses and aides for real nurture. Aides came and went, and some were good, and some weren't.

He didn't wait for her answer, but walked out of the room and down the hall. Kelsey closed her eyes and felt the weakness of total defeat flowing through her.

Denis touched her arm. "You can see that it's no use. Let me take you back to the inn."

Ginnie spoke softly. "Wait. Look at him!"

Kelsey stared at the boy in the bed. His eyes were still open, but now a big tear was falling from one gray eye, rolling slowly down his cheek. Tears could be a reflex to pain, but this was more. This seemed an indication of understanding. She watched for only a moment, and then ran out of the room after Tyler Hammond. He was about to disappear around a jog in the corridor, and she called to him.

"Wait a minute, Mr. Hammond! Please come back!"

He kept going without a pause, and anger with him trembled in her voice.

"Are you afraid to see what you've done?" she cried.

He turned slowly. Thick black brows met above his nose, drawn down in an anger that equaled her own.

"What did you say?"

"I asked if you were afraid to see what your words have done to your son."

He strode back down the hall past her, and she ran to keep up with him. In Jody's room he stood beside the boy's bed. Ginnie Soong looked as though she too might cry, as now more tears coursed down Jody's thin cheeks.

"What does this mean?" his father demanded.

Kelsey answered, trying to keep her voice steady. "I believe it means that some part of Jody's brain is listening and understanding, and can be hurt. It has the power to make him cry." She picked up one of the boy's small, limp hands again. "We know you can hear us, Jody. We know you can understand. Even though you can't move yet or speak to us, you do understand. Your father is sorry for what he said. He thought you had gone away, Jody."

For an instant she expected the man beside her to deny her words and make some further explosive utterance—out of his own pain. Instead, he touched the boy's forehead, smoothing back his hair before turning toward the door, speaking to her as he moved.

"Come with me, Mrs. Stewart. We need to talk."

Denis made a small gesture, almost as if he wanted to stop her, and Ginnie said, "It's all right. Let her go."

The hallway jogged around the interruption of Jody's suite, and continued to a corner room on the ocean side of the house. Tyler Hammond went ahead, not bothering with formality, and sat down behind a big desk set diagonally across a corner, between two windows. He gestured her to a green leather chair nearby.

Kelsey sat down, trying to still the turbulence inside her. The room was filled with deep browns, set off by a thick, soft rug in the green shade of meadow grass in spring. Except for the steel desk and green leather chair, the furniture was dark and beautifully made, hand-carved. There were no draperies at the wide glass of the windows, and she could look over pine groves that cascaded down the hillside and ended where sand began and the ocean took over. Paintings on the walls seemed to be of local scenes, and one in particular caught her eye—a tower built of irregular stones, rising against a misty sky. Her angry inner trembling had lessened and now she could give all her attention to the man who sat watching her behind his desk.

"What do you think you can do for him?" he demanded. "Can you bring back my son?"

"The way he was before? Probably not. But those tears may really mean that he can understand—something. Nobody can tell how much, or what he thinks about. But I don't believe he was crying because of physical pain. He cried because you hurt him with your words. So I do believe he understood something."

The man behind the desk didn't flinch. "If you came here to work with him, what could you do? I understand you're a physical therapist. But he can't move a finger, so I don't see that he has any need for you."

"I don't limit myself," Kelsey said. "I like to use anything that might help toward healing. In a way, there would be more freedom for me to work with Jody here than in a hospital or institution. There are always boards of directors who must protect the hospital. These days there are too many lawsuits, and sometimes patients die before a board convenes and makes up its mind. The unknown can often seem threatening and dangerous."

He watched her without belief. "You're setting yourself up against medical authority?"

"Not really. I just feel that the only way to accomplish anything is not to give up. Not to accept passively anyone who says something can't be done. Not even a doctor who makes that claim. All he can mean is that *he* doesn't know anything else to do. But there's always one more step—somewhere. So we hunt for it. Maybe there's a chance here to find it."

She heard the passion and conviction in her own voice, but Tyler Hammond remained unmoved.

"I'm not going to change my plans," he said. "A week from tomorrow, the ambulance will come to take Jody away. If you want to visit him once more, and make what suggestions you can, perhaps I can pass along what you say. My son is not going to be anyone's guinea pig."

Kelsey suppressed quick anger at his words and made up her mind. "No! I want to come every day while he's still here. I want to stay for two or three hours each day and work with him."

"That's impossible."

"I won't hurt your son. I only want to stir what may be there to awaken in him. I can't make any useful change in him in a week's time, but I can begin to find out something about Jody Hammond."

"It's not entirely up to me," he told her stiffly. "Jody's mother must give her consent too, and she's in no condition for that at the moment."

Kelsey nodded, waiting.

"My wife agreed with me days ago that it would be better to have Jody out of the house. Better to make a clean break. She has a long road ahead herself to any sort of emotional recovery. She may never walk again, and she knows that we've already lost our son. Right now she doesn't want to live, and she must be watched constantly. I can't see that Jody's tears necessarily mean anything except a reflex or some faint glimmer of understanding. He can't move or talk, and to have him here in this house puts an additional strain on my wife."

She longed to point out that this very attitude meant sure defeat, but in spite of herself she'd become partisan as far as the boy was concerned, and she didn't want to anger Tyler any more than she already had.

"Let me come every day for this remaining week," Kelsey said. "I don't want to be paid, and you needn't feel obligated in any way. Aside from doing this for Jody, I'm doing it for Aunt Elaine, who is Mrs. Langford's friend. Besides, my aunt thought it would be good for *me.*" She put a challenge into her emphasis, and caught his attention.

"What do you mean?"

Perhaps this was using an unfair weapon, but she met his eyes directly, boldly, refusing to be cowed. "If I come into this house on any basis, you need to know something about me. Though not because I want sympathy. That's not for you to give. Two years ago my three-year-old son died in a car accident. I was driving. My husband never forgave me for taking our boy on that trip, and we've been divorced since. You see why I might feel especially drawn to Jody. I know what it's like to be blamed unjustly."

He turned in his swivel chair and stared out the window. She looked past him to the tremendous view of Carmel Bay, its shining surface enclosed in arms of land that pointed into the ocean on either hand—blue and clear and far-reaching. Way out on the water a white sailboat was skimming past, as though it flew in some special element between sea and sky.

But it was the man she watched, the man who held her first attention. She knew a little about color therapy—it was sometimes one of her tools. Color had to do with individuals, and she saw the stark hues that seemed to envelop him, with dark shades predominant—melancholy grays, the black of despair, all laced through by a startling streak of scarlet. She knew these colors existed only in her own mind, but she had a feeling that red was always there underneath—the true red of anger. He could be a dangerous man. Perhaps to himself most of all. Perhaps to his wife and son as well. Never an easy man to work with.

Nothing about him had softened or gentled in the least when he turned back to her. "Come tomorrow morning, and then we'll see. If she's able to talk to you, I want you to meet my wife."

When Kelsey reached the study door and glanced back, he

was staring out the window again, his eyes as empty as his son's.

She went quickly down the hall, to find Ginnie alone with Jody. The nurse sat beside his bed, reading to him from a child's picture book—too young for Jody's nine years as he had once been.

"I'm coming back tomorrow," Kelsey told her.

Ginnie nodded. "Maybe you *can* help. I've never seen him cry before, except when there's the reflex of pain. Denis has gone out to the car to wait for you. I'm glad you came, Kelsey. I *think* I'm glad you came."

That seemed a curious way to put it, and neither woman smiled, though for an instant their eyes held. Then Kelsey said good-bye and found her way out to the front door. She climbed the stone steps to the garage area on the hillside above. Denis sat at the wheel of his car, and he made no move to start it as she got in. He looked sick and shaken by grief.

"That was pretty bad," he said. "Jody crying. I almost cried myself. Tyler can be a brute. When I think of him married to my sister—and the way she is now—" He closed his eyes.

"We've got to help Jody," Kelsey said. "We've got to at least try."

"How? When Tyler won't listen to anyone."

"If your sister agrees, I'll come back every day for a week. I can't promise anything. But I can try."

Denis looked at her in wonder. "You managed that?"

"He said it would depend on Mrs. Hammond. If she's able, he wants me to meet her when I come tomorrow."

"I don't know how you did it, but I'm glad you got through. Just don't begin to hope for too much. I wish you didn't need to see Ruth at all. She may be discouraging because of her own despair."

Ruth Hammond was another facet of a complex problem, but she would postpone dealing with her until the time came.

"I've worked with children like this before," she told Denis, "and all I know is that I have to try. I can be tough and stand up to parents when it's necessary."

Though not as tough as she might need to be in this case, she thought wearily. She had to put up a front to convince others, and that in itself could be enervating.

Denis reached out to touch her hand lightly, and spoke the same words Ginnie had—"I'm glad you're here, Kelsey. Maybe you are the miracle we need."

"Don't ask for miracles—please."

"All right. I'll tell you what—this is my day off, so let's not waste it. Sooner or later you have to do the Seventeen-Mile Drive around part of the Monterey Peninsula. Let me take you this morning. We can go slowly, and stop for lunch along the way."

She was already shaking her head. "I don't feel like sightseeing."

"It will be more than that. You needn't look at the views, if you don't feel like it. There's someone I want you to meet. Someone who knows Tyler Hammond very well, and who may be able to give you some leads in dealing with him."

Kelsey gave up and tried to relax.

V

FROM CARMEL GATE, the Seventeen-Mile Drive curved through the Del Monte forest, turning, after some miles, toward the sea. Denis seemed quiet, and Kelsey didn't feel like talking. The events at Tyler Hammond's house were too recent in her mind, and too disturbing. She found herself increasingly concerned—dreading what might lie ahead when she returned.

Not that she would change her course—not after those tears on Jody's cheeks. The one faintly encouraging instant had been when Tyler had touched his son's forehead—an involuntary gesture that perhaps betrayed something beneath his grim exterior. At least, at the end of their talk, he'd seemed less certain about doctors' verdicts than he'd been at first. Ruth, of course, was still the big question mark.

As the road dropped toward the ocean, the peninsula's surf-fringed shore came into view and Denis slowed the car.

"Before we reach the House of Light," he said, "I'd like to tell you a little about Marisa Marsh."

"House of Light?"

"The opposite of Tyler's House of Shadow. Don't worry—it's not as pretentious as it sounds. Marisa has never called it that. It's the nickname visitors and friends have given it—you'll see why. She built the house for herself fifteen years ago, after her husband died. I suppose in another day people would have called Marisa a Wise Woman. Or maybe a witch! Of course she'd laugh at that. She's very down to earth, at the same time that she soars. By now she must be in her seventies, though you'd never guess it."

"Why are we going to see her?"

Denis smiled a bit ruefully. "I suppose because she has a gift for quieting rough waters, and quiet is what we both need right now. There are other reasons you'll understand when you meet her."

He turned the car off the highway and followed a narrow, climbing road away from the water. A few low-built houses overlooked the sea, and Marisa's house was at a high point, where the road ended.

"Do we just drop in?" Kelsey asked.

"It doesn't matter. Her door is always open. Here we are."

The house was built of adobe and redwood, with arched windows all around, and a small front garden of flowers blooming riotously to suit themselves. Stepping-stones led to a redwood entry porch. Before they reached it, Marisa Marsh appeared in the doorway, her smile welcoming—almost as though she'd expected them and looked forward to their coming.

She was a small woman, slightly built, though somehow giving an impression of height because of her manner. She held herself "tall." Her eyes were a sparkling blue, clear and direct in their gaze. She was not, Kelsey thought, a woman whom anyone would fool for long. Everything about her seemed distinctive. Thick, springy gray hair hung in a plait over one shoulder, and was fastened at the end with a turquoise thunderbird clip. Obviously, she liked the color of turquoise, since she wore a flowing skirt of that color, trimmed with a wide band of garnet red at waist and hem. Somehow the shades seemed to blend. A white blouse of thin cotton set off her slim, tanned throat, and dangling earrings were again a thunderbird design. She wore no other jewelry on brown hands and arms.

As they came up the steps she held out both hands to Denis, and then turned to include Kelsey in her welcome.

"This is Kelsey Stewart, Marisa—Elaine Carey's niece," Denis said. "I'm showing her the Seventeen-Mile Drive, and I wanted her to meet you."

"Come in, both of you." Marisa took Kelsey's hand and drew her into the house, continuing to hold it. When they were inside, she turned it over palm up, and studied its structure. Kelsey felt uncomfortable, but Marisa Marsh was without self-consciousness.

"A good hand," she assured Kelsey. "Strong—useful. A hand for helping. But you haven't quite found yourself yet, have you?"

This was a woman who would like to challenge and surprise, and Kelsey found herself uncertain. As far as she was concerned, she'd been tested a great deal in these past two years. She wondered what Denis's real purpose was in bringing her here to meet Marisa Marsh.

"You're right, as usual," Denis said. "I mean about Kelsey being useful. She's a special kind of physical therapist—with trimmings—and perhaps she's going to work with Jody Hammond."

Marisa looked intently into Kelsey's eyes, and again there seemed a challenge Kelsey couldn't read. "Sit down, please, both of you. I've something in the kitchen that needs stirring. Back in a moment."

Her movements were quick, and Kelsey sensed the vitality

and strength with which this woman would meet whatever happened in her life.

Her home was indeed a "house of light"—built, not in the Spanish adobe style that sought to protect from the heat of the sun, but to let in light and air on all sides. A main, central room with high arched windows ran the width of the house. Beyond, a terrace looked out toward the ocean, so that a gold and blue radiance poured in and bathed the entire room. The furniture was simply constructed of light woods. The chairs had turquoise seats, and turquoise cushions were tossed across a wheat-colored sofa.

Kelsey sat in a handcrafted chair with wide wooden arms, and rocked gently, beginning to feel more relaxed. This bathing of light and color soothed more than it invigorated.

"You feel it, don't you, Kelsey?" Denis asked. "Marisa claims that the color turquoise fights depression. Even when there's fog, light comes in, and the sea color is strong. On clear evenings, the blue darkens inside and out, and it's all the more a quiet room."

Kelsey could sympathize with the feeling for color, and there seemed almost a poetry in Denis's words. Yet she still wondered why she was here. No matter. For the moment she could be still inside, and watch Marisa, who was definitely the star in her own staging. Whether it was an artificial staging or simply natural, she couldn't tell yet.

When Marisa rejoined them, Denis told her what had happened with Jody that morning, and how Tyler had agreed to let Kelsey return every day for a week until the boy was sent away. Providing, of course, that Ruth consented. Then he added somberly, "Last night my sister tried to slash her wrists."

"I know," Marisa said gently. "Tyler called me late in the evening. Ruth seems to be all right. Perhaps it was more a cry for help than anything else." She turned to Kelsey. "Has Denis told you—I practically raised Tyler. His parents were my husband's and my friends a long time ago in Illinois. After they died, we arranged to take him. Adopt him. He was only ten when he came to us. Their death was a tragedy he never really got over. I'm afraid it still darkens his life."

Marisa's tone of voice had changed to a different cadence—a musical minor key. She could, Kelsey recognized, play emotions in her voice, as though it were an instrument, and again, whether this was natural or calculated, she couldn't tell.

Denis had grown uneasy with this talk of Tyler, and he changed the subject. "Will you show Kelsey your photographs, Marisa? They might help her to understand a little better what she's getting into up at the Hammonds'."

"You're a photographer?" Kelsey asked.

"I suppose I'm a lot of unimportant things. That's what happens to a person who can't decide about one talent. So I'm a dabbler. I do things for my own satisfaction, and I enjoy photography. Paintings interpret and require a very great skill. But a photograph catches one moment of life as I see it—when I'm lucky, that is."

"It's more than luck in the portraits you've done," Denis said. "I think you hypnotize people when they sit for you. They let down their guard and give themselves away."

She laughed—a light sound like wind chimes—and led them into a studio wing where terra cotta tiles paved the floor and there was very little furniture. Dozens of black and white photographs lined the walls, while at the rear a door opened into a small darkroom.

Here the ceiling was lower and had been painted pale blue. Across it, suspended invisibly, flew three lovely geese—perhaps a fourth of life size—as though seen far away against the sky. They had been fashioned from driftwood, partly natural, partly created by the artist who had seen the form in the wood.

"Beautiful!" For a moment Kelsey could look only at the three soaring birds, and her spirits lifted at the sight.

"Tyler carved those for me a long time ago," Marisa said, and now the timbre of her voice was melancholy again.

It was difficult to imagine that dour, unfeeling man creating beauty like this. Another facet of Tyler Hammond had been revealed that gave her a little more hope. Somewhere in him there was a sensitivity she hadn't suspected.

The richness of Marisa's black and white prints was due to the gradations that lay between deep black and pure white. Velvet gradations, so that one didn't miss color.

Some of the photographs were of the Monterey Peninsula and of the Big Sur coastline—not pretty postcard pictures but a revelation of wild elements in nature. For a woman who liked the calming influence of turquoise, Marisa had a surprising instinct for the violent. She had caught a vivid moment of storm where the sea churned with white water and flung its spray high against wet black granite. Marvelous contrasts there.

"Point Lobos," Denis said softly.

Marisa spoke quickly, as though to draw Denis away from thinking of the terrible thing that had happened in that particular place.

"I studied photography for a while with Ansel Adams," she said. "He lived here for years until his recent death, you know. I don't think anyone has ever equaled what he could do with a landscape."

The next picture, again devastating, showed Cannery Row in Monterey after a fire had destroyed most of the original buildings. Still another revealed the devastation on Highway One, where a tremendous landslide had wiped out the shore connection between Big Sur and San Simeon.

"They're tremendous pictures," Kelsey said. "And a bit frightening."

Marisa nodded, pleased. "I suppose disaster always fasci-
nates me. Natural disaster—the dark side of reality. The thing
mere humans can do so little about."

"Wrath of the gods," Denis said, and his shiver wasn't altogether pretense. "I guess I prefer a little insulation. Reality?—
there's too much reality around. What can we do but close our
eyes and pray? Let's look at the portraits—they're not so
threatening."

As they crossed the studio to an opposite wall, Kelsey
watched Marisa with growing interest. So much of her own
work dealt with the psychological as well as the physiological
that she was always curious about what drove and motivated
people. Marisa seemed a woman of many aspects. Perhaps not
all as healing as Denis seemed to think.

"Show Kelsey your portrait of Tyler," Denis said. "Now
that's reality."

Marisa gestured, and Kelsey stopped before a photograph of
Tyler Hammond that held a central place on one wall, with no
competition from other pictures. Its impact was shocking. The
lighting of the head against a neutral background was as dramatic as that in the scenic pictures, showing the stark, brooding intensity of the man. His eyes seemed shadowed with pain,
the brows heavily thick and dark—angry brows. His mouth,
set grimly, hinted at even darker thoughts, and black hair
swept away from a forehead that was surely formed of the
same implacable granite as those coastal rocks. It seemed a
tormented face, and Kelsey asked a question.

"When was this taken, Mrs. Marsh?"

"About three years ago—I think," Marisa said.

So the torment was not because of recent tragedy alone. It
must have grown from something he'd lived with for a long
time. In any case, if this was the essence of the man who was
Jody's father, she would stand little chance of persuading him
to anything he resisted. Hurling herself against him would be

like hurling herself upon the rocks of Point Lobos—as his wife and son had been hurled upon them two months ago. Kelsey looked up at the flying geese, so beautiful in themselves and seeming to reveal an imagination that could soar.

"He can be like that too," Marisa said gently.

"He's more like the photograph," Denis insisted. "You had to be warned—armed. This tells the truth about Tyler."

Marisa spoke quickly. "No—it's only one truth. This is what he gave me in a single instant of time. There are other moments. Look at this one over here."

In the background of the next picture rose a rough stone tower—the same tower Kelsey had seen in a painting in Tyler's study—and at its base stood a man and a boy. The man, Tyler Hammond, was obviously talking to his son about the tower, one hand gesturing, and he seemed a different man from the portrait. The boy's face was bright with interest as he listened. This was Jody as he had been—such a little while ago. This was the image she needed to hold in her mind as the goal she must reach toward. One certainty that no one had taught her in any classroom, but which she had learned painfully through trial and error, was that unless one could *believe* in a return to the normal, the impossible could never be accomplished. Sometimes grim determination not to give in counted for more than anything else.

She looked again at the high stone structure rising above the two figures in the photograph.

"What is that strange-looking tower?" she asked.

"That's the Hawk Tower at Tor House," Marisa said. "Robinson Jeffers carried all those stones up from the beach and built it himself. Tyler was doing a documentary film about Robinson Jeffers."

In college Kelsey had been drawn to the poet's unusual rhythms, foreboding beliefs, and stunning word pictures of this California coast.

"I should think Jeffers would make an exciting film," she said.

Marisa sighed. "Tyler hasn't touched it since the accident to Ruth and Jody. I don't know if he'll ever go back to it."

It was the boy, however, who interested Kelsey more than the father. "Have you any other studies of Jody?"

"There's one over here I rather like." Marisa's movements were always quick, and somehow a surprise, like the movements of a bird who might take off in unexpected flight at any moment.

Kelsey stopped before a picture in which Jody was completely lost in his own world of creation. He seemed to be modeling a clay head of a woman—a head that was half life size, and three quarters turned to the camera.

Again the boy's face was brightly intent, his fingers busy with the clay—a likeness clearly emerging as he worked.

"That's a really remarkable head of Ruth that Jody made," Denis said. "I expect Marisa had some hand in helping him to find her likeness."

Marisa dismissed that. "Not really. I taught him a little technique, but Jody showed a real talent for portraiture."

The boy's spirit shone in his face, in the very set of his mouth in eager concentration. This was what Kelsey wanted to carry with her when she returned to that boy with the blank eyes whom she'd seen this morning. These pictures would give her a goal, a standard toward which she could build.

Denis, however, was shaking his head. He turned away from the photograph as though it was more than he could bear to look at.

"The next one is Ruth," Marisa said. "You haven't met her yet?"

"Not yet." Kelsey stood before the delicate, clear-eyed, and somehow innocent face that looked out from the next frame. A happy face, the eyes thick-lashed, the lips soft, almost tremulous, the chin as rounded as a child's and all too vulnerable. This was no face to stand up to granite.

Denis spoke softly. "She's not like that anymore. That Ruth is gone. But I'm glad you caught her the way she used to be, Marisa. You have a really great instinct for portraits. I like these better than those wild scenes."

"Thank you, Denis. I value your opinion, since you really do know."

Denis seemed to shy away from whatever she implied. "You never cared much yourself for this picture of Ruth, did you, Marisa?"

"No—I wasn't able to catch her as I wanted to. Your sister's far more complex, more interesting, than this shows. Have you seen her since last night, Denis?"

He answered gloomily. "I haven't been allowed to see her. I barely managed to talk to my own mother since Tyler has Dora firmly under his thumb too. Sometimes he can be brutal."

"I know," Marisa said. "I know only too well."

Denis seemed to study her for a moment, and then asked an odd question. "Marisa, have you had any more—promptings?"

"No! And I don't want any!"

"But if you hadn't—"

"Skip it," she said curtly, and for the first time she seemed uncomfortable, dismissing the subject—whatever it was.

Denis touched Kelsey's arm. "We've taken enough of Marisa's time. We'd better run along."

Kelsey, however, had stopped before the next, head-and-shoulders photograph. The woman wore a pale blouse with a boat neck, and in contrast, a long string of black beads. Her large, rather myopic eyes gazed beyond the camera, and her mouth was fixed in a deliberate smile. Her nicely shaped nose was tilted slightly, the nostrils flared, as though the woman had caught an unpleasant odor. It was so perfect a nose that Kelsey wondered if it had had a little help. California interest in plastic surgery made you question perfection. Her hair—probably a wig—was smartly coiffed and fluffed around her face, as though to soften outlines that seemed hard. Her chin was too sharply pointed for beauty, yet the whole was an arresting and rather exotic face.

"Who is that?" Kelsey asked.

Marisa considered the photograph for a moment. "Never mind who—what does that portrait tell you?"

"I don't think I'd like her," Kelsey said.

Denis snorted. "You wouldn't have. Practically no one around here liked Francesca Fallon."

There had been talk about this woman at her aunt's—about her murder. But before she could ask anything more, Marisa spoke quickly.

"Look, you two—you needn't rush off. Do stay for lunch. My chili and beans are ready, and I can pop rolls into the oven. If you want to set the table on the terrace, Denis, I'll toss a quick salad."

"We'll accept gracefully," Denis said. "We were going to stop in Pebble Beach for lunch, but this will be much nicer. Thanks, Marisa."

Before she left the studio, Kelsey's eye was caught by one more dramatic photograph set apart at the far end. Unlike the others, this picture was in dramatic color. She walked over to it, her attention completely arrested. Again there was disaster. Against a night sky a tree stood burning—a twisted oak, its branches alive with fire. Orange and crimson flames leapt into the sky, and every leaf blazed in this instant of time. One could almost hear the crackle of conflagration, the windy roar. The whole thing must have raged for only a few moments before the spectacle was over.

Marisa had come to stand beside her, and she spoke softly, an almost relishing note in her voice. "I was lucky with that one. Friends were building a house out in Carmel Valley. They were planning to do some ranching—horses. I'd spent the day with them and we were camping near the site. A thunderstorm came up, and lightning struck that tree. That was years ago, before I turned entirely to black and white film. I took several shots, and this was the best one. Of course when they finished the house, my friends called their place Flaming Tree Ranch. Unfortunately, they failed . . . the house is empty now."

Denis spoke with a slight edge to his voice, as though the photograph of the flaming tree made him uneasy. "Let's help you with lunch, Marisa," he said, breaking the spell.

Marisa moved swiftly and capably, and Kelsey helped Denis carry dishes of creamy glaze and brown linen place mats out to the terrace. A table, its top inset with tiles from Greece in a fish pattern, was quickly arranged with salads of fresh greens, a big bowl of chili, and hot rolls and butter. When Marisa had brought glasses of iced tea, they sat down to eat. Their hostess looked like a young girl, curled up in a big wicker chair, with her turquoise skirt swirled about her. But she wasn't a young girl, and sometimes a knowledge that was almost ancient looked out of her eyes.

"Were you ever a dancer?" Kelsey asked.

Her laughter chimed again, and Denis said, "She still is."

"One of my many lives. You should have seen me in my Isadora Duncan phase! About a thousand years ago."

The terrace, with its widespread view of pines sloping toward the ocean, the rocky coastline, and strips of sand, seemed utterly peaceful, the air clear and cool and sunny. A pine tree cast its shadow over the table, and small, bright fish seemed to dart in the tiles around their place mats.

"It's heavenly," Kelsey murmured, once more feeling tension wash away—grateful for any respite from Tyler Hammond's problems, and her own.

"It's calm today," Marisa said. "We can be buffeted up here. Do you see that spot way out there near the rocks where white water is churning? They call that the Restless Sea because so many currents come in at that particular point. More than almost anyplace in the world."

For a little while longer it seemed good to postpone all the urgencies that lay ahead. Good for a little while not to fight for anything. The chili tasted hot and delicious, the creamy butter melted on Kelsey's roll, yet something still nagged insistently for her attention. That last portrait she'd seen in Marisa's studio had disturbed her for some reason.

"Tell me about Francesca Fallon," she said.

There was a moment's silence while Denis buttered a bit of roll and Marisa looked off toward the ocean. Clearly, neither wanted to talk about her, but Kelsey was thinking again of Elaine's words.

"She's the woman who was killed a few months ago?"

Marisa nodded. "Francesca was murdered in her home in Carmel Valley. No one knows by whom."

"Was she shot?"

"She died from a blow to the head," Marisa said grimly. "Though they never found the weapon. Whoever it was must have been scared off because nothing was taken. The houseworker who came every few days found her. The police think it was a random incident—someone who broke in looking for money or jewelry. Though knowing Francesca, I wonder."

"Unfortunately, she invited trouble," Denis said. "I imagine she had a few enemies, and maybe she got what she deserved."

"That's possible," Marisa agreed. "She did a radio program out of Monterey for a while, you know—a gossipy sort of hour, sometimes with interviews. She could dredge up trouble, cause a lot of nastiness to surface."

Again, Kelsey remembered. "Someone mentioned that she interviewed Tyler Hammond."

"She certainly did," Marisa said. "If you could call it an interview. Since he was hard to get, Francesca went to his house to do the broadcast. I was there, and I made a recording at the time because Tyler was on. It's still around somewhere."

"That broadcast didn't do either of them much good," Denis said.

Marisa went on. "Tyler, of course, has a splendid voice. It came across well on the air, and I still hope he'll do the commentary for the film he was working on about Robinson Jeffers."

"You ought to erase that tape you made," Denis said.

"Oh, I don't know—I think Tyler gave as good as he got. It was pretty lively to listen to, since nobody messes with Tyler. If the program hadn't been live and done right on the air, I don't think the station would have run it."

"We all knew Francesca Fallon when she was young," Denis said, "and I never liked her."

Marisa mused aloud, almost to herself. "I wonder if there's a wickedness scale for human beings. None of us makes a '10' when it comes to goodness—whatever that is—and some fall into the minus category. Perhaps I'd rate Francesca as around '2.'"

Here was the subject of good and evil again, Kelsey thought —the same topic Denis had brought up last night on the beach. Perhaps Marisa, whom he'd termed a "wise woman," was the source of his thinking about the subject.

Now, however, the luncheon was nearly over and they must follow the coastline, circling on back to Carmel, returning to all the troubles that waited to engulf them.

Kelsey asked an abrupt question before they left the table. "Where would you rate Tyler on your scale, Mrs. Marsh?"

She twisted her thick gray braid, toying with the thunderbird clip in fingers that were brown from the sun and wiry thin. The movement seemed nervous, and for a moment Kelsey thought she wouldn't attempt an answer. Her involvement with Tyler, her partisanship as his adopted mother was clear.

"Tyler came to a crossroad in his life a while back. He could have gone in several directions. I'm not sure he's ever really chosen."

"I think he has," Denis said gloomily. "If what you call evil means damaging others, then he's chosen."

"That's a bit strong," Marisa said, and rose from the table, uncurling herself.

Kelsey's mood had changed to a restlessness as great as those churning currents out beyond the rocky shore.

Marisa seemed to sense her need to be on her way. "Leave everything," she said. "I always think best when I'm being domestic. I'm struggling with an article right now. Something I've thought about for a long time, and that I've wanted to set down on paper—if only for my own satisfaction."

"What's the subject?" Kelsey asked as they left the terrace.

"Good and evil—what else? Just a modest little topic. I don't even know where *I* stand on the scale. I suppose we never know ourselves."

"I'd like to read it when it's done," Denis said. "You'd better think hard about Tyler."

"I always think hard about Tyler," Marisa countered.

She came to the door with them and held out her hand to Kelsey, not so much as a handshake as to take Kelsey's fingers in her own, as she'd done before, seeming to test their tensile strength, sensing at once a certain resistance Kelsey put into her hand.

"Stubborn," Marisa said, sounding pleased. "I don't think you give up on anything. But still unfinished—unsure. There's a hard fight ahead of you. No, don't worry, I'm not a fortune-teller. Anyone could read this, considering the situation at Tyler's. But Jody is my grandson—or I think of him that way—and I really hope you can help him, Kelsey. When I talk to Tyler again, I'll tell him he should listen to you."

"Thank you," Kelsey said. She took her hand back self-consciously, not used to being analyzed so openly. "I've loved coming here."

"You're to come again—and I mean that," Marisa said.

When they were in the car, heading toward the main road, Kelsey thought of something. "There wasn't a picture of you in Marisa's gallery, Denis. Why not?"

He grinned. "Oh, she's tried. But she never liked the result. She thinks I'm unfinished too—like you."

"Are you?"

He sobered. "I've always had trouble finding my direction."

"Doesn't Marisa Marsh have the same problem? All those things she does!"

"It's not the same. She has so many gifts, and she uses them well. She doesn't discard anything. All her skills add up, even though she doesn't have a drive toward one spectacular success. With me, every time I think I've found my way, something changes."

"Maybe that only means you have more depths than most people and you're still searching."

His smile was wry. "How long does that go on? Anyway, that's enough for confession time."

"I don't suppose anyone ever stops being unfinished," Kelsey said. "Isn't that what it's all about—growing? Anyway, I like Marisa a lot."

"So do I," Denis agreed.

They followed the road along the ocean, stopping now and then so Kelsey could enjoy the sight of sea lions and listen to their barking. Cormorants perched on rocks out in the water, and the sea rolled in endlessly. In one place, when they parked

for the view, small, greedy squirrels, tourist-fed, tried to jump
into the car.

They drove on again, mostly silent now. Kelsey liked Denis
Langford increasingly. His lack of pretense made a pleasant
contrast to what she'd seen of Tyler Hammond's arrogant per-
formance. Tyler's more secretive nature might be frightening
to probe. Even though he held back a bit, Denis was more
open.

"Let's stop here," he said, turning off to another parking
space. "This is one of our postcard vistas—the Lone Cypress.
We'll get out and stretch our legs."

On the bank below, a mass of twisted cypresses seemed to
entangle their way downhill toward the water. Some were
dead—gray-white skeletons that had long ago been deformed
by ocean winds. On the left, a tongue of land reached into the
water, ending in a spectacular rock with a high, jagged point
that cut into the sky. In the background across the bay the long
stretch of the Santa Lucia Mountains loomed on the horizon.
Lacy white fingers of surf broke at the rock's face, and swirled
inland through gashes in the granite. Near the top of the
rugged point, crowning it dramatically, stood the small lone
cypress tree—not twisted like the others, but a straight, fragile
silhouette against ocean and mountains, defying winds and
water boldly.

"Both Monterey pine and cypress seem to feed on the fog
and salt winds," Denis said. "They don't grow inland. We can
go down closer, if you like."

He held her hand as they descended the path, protected on
either side by wooden fencing. The way ended at a stone
support wall that guarded the tree. One could come to its foot,
and no farther.

Kelsey looked into green branches rising above her. "The
trunk is charred! What happened?"

"Vandals." Denis spoke with disgust. "Probably kids. Someone set the tree on fire. Luckily, it wasn't destroyed. I don't understand that sort of vicious destructiveness."

Neither did she. It seemed appalling that anyone could be willing to destroy something beautiful that was also a symbol for the region and had stood for so many years. The sight reminded her of that terrible burning tree in Marisa's photograph. But that tree had been destroyed by an act of nature, and nature had no conscience.

"I wonder if men without conscience—or women—are the truly evil that Marisa was talking about?" she said. "Whoever tried to burn this tree must have had no glimmering of conscience."

Denis thought about that. "I suppose when there were tribes, or strong families, even neighborhoods, and people cared more about religion, children were taught a few values. I don't think the very young have consciences at all—it's something that has to be learned. Maybe we all have a dark side we have to fight against."

"Is Tyler losing the battle?"

"Let's go back," Denis said abruptly.

Kelsey stood for a moment, staring, not at the tree, but toward the faraway headland of Point Lobos, from here only a series of rocky dots floating on the ocean.

When they reached the car, Denis sat with his hands on the wheel and made no move to start the engine, his dejection clear.

"What are you thinking about?" she asked.

"Mainly about Ruth, I suppose, and about Jody. They're never out of my thoughts for long these days, Kelsey. I can't help remembering the last time we came here together. Jody wanted to climb right up into that tree—he was always a great climber. I had to hold him back." He paused and then went on. "Maybe there's something else you ought to know about Marisa."

"I'm sure there's plenty to know," Kelsey said.

"This is special. You've seen that she's a remarkable woman, and sometimes she has an extra sensitivity. ESP—whatever you want to call it. She claims it's something we all have and mostly never develop. Marisa was the one who found Ruth and Jody after they fell. She was working in her darkroom when she had a sudden urge to drop everything and get into her car. She said it was overpowering—as though she were being directed in some way. She drove to the state reserve at Point Lobos and walked out on foot. That's a big place, but she let her own compass take over—and she found them! Then she rushed back to the office for a park ranger, and Ruth and Jody were brought up from that ledge above the sea. If it hadn't been for Marisa, they might have died there. Yet she doesn't want to accept this gift she has, or believe in it. When this sort of thing happens, it upsets her—makes her almost ill."

"It's happened before?"

"Several times—ever since she was a child. She's tried to ignore it—and then suffered guilt when someone might have been helped if she'd acted. I don't think it's a pleasant gift to have."

He started the car abruptly, and for a little while Kelsey no longer looked out at the view. Too many ramifications were coming at her much too quickly, bringing a sense of alarm and confusion. It was as though she walked on a surface that seemed secure, only to find it giving way unexpectedly beneath her feet. Marisa Marsh was closely connected with the Hammonds on several levels, and Kelsey knew that she must see her again. If she were to help Jody, she must know much more than she did now, and Marisa could be a source of needed information. Especially if she really had some gift of sensitivity. This might even be used to help Jody.

There was never just one road to healing, though sometimes the medical profession could be locked into its own narrow premises. Kelsey had learned that it was best not to discount anything, and to use every instrument that came to hand to treat the whole person. Yet there were always doubts, and she was torn by fear of the consequences if she failed. Could she really help that child who was locked so terribly into his own damaged brain? She only knew that she must try every possible course—if Tyler Hammond would give her a chance.

As the road curved on along the shoreline toward Carmel, Pebble Beach came into view, with its famous golf course, its lodge and fine shops. Denis drove past, and a few miles later, as they turned inland, the loop of the drive was completed at Carmel Gate.

When they stopped at the office of the inn, Elaine was behind the desk.

"I'm glad you're back," she told them. "Tyler's called several times. It seems that Ruth has decided that she wants to see you right away, Kelsey. She doesn't want to wait until tomorrow."

"That's wonderful!" Denis said. "She must be feeling better. Maybe I can see her now too. I'll drive you up there, Kelsey, and . . ."

"I'm sorry," Elaine was shaking her head. "Tyler told me that Ruth doesn't want to see you right now, Denis. The last time you visited her she got much too upset."

Denis drew a deep breath and let it out slowly. "That's because Tyler was there glowering when I saw her. *He* made her think I was upsetting her. God knows I only want to help my sister."

"Then perhaps it's best to stay away from her right now. Humor Tyler a bit until things calm down. Kelsey, you can take my car. I don't drive much around here. Do you think you can find the way?"

"I'm sure I can," Kelsey said. "I'll go right now."

She stopped to thank Denis for the morning. He looked

thoroughly depressed, wounded by the word from his sister. She wished she could offer comforting words, but there seemed nothing more to say. Helping Jody was her one real goal.

She followed her aunt out behind the cottage, where Elaine kept her car.

VI

SINCE the road along Scenic Drive was also the road to Carmel Highlands, Kelsey had no problem finding the way. Elaine's Mercedes was a delight to handle, and it was good to be at the wheel of a car she'd never driven before. She needed to escape the physical memory of her own car on an icy road in Connecticut.

As she drove, she thought again of the visit to Marisa Marsh, and the photographs she'd seen. Especially the one of Ruth—happy and guileless, with no inkling of what was to happen to her and her son. The instant of "truth" that Marisa's camera had caught was indeed only an instant and, as Denis said, might already be lost in the past.

She wondered why Denis had wanted her to see that darkly ominous portrait of Tyler Hammond. He'd said she needed to be warned. Of what? She had already glimpsed something of Tyler's unyielding character, so what more had Denis wanted to emphasize? No matter—Tyler was no photograph—no still portrait, however brilliant. It was the man himself she must deal with in all his complexity. A picture could never change, but a man might.

On the higher road the turnoff came up quickly, and she followed the short drive down to the Hammond garage and got out of the car. Someone must have heard her arrival, for when she followed the flight of stone steps to the lower courtyard, Tyler himself stood in the doorway, waiting.

He greeted her coolly and led her into the big, high-ceilinged living room. Heavy, dark beams arched above, and a great limestone fireplace tapered halfway up the wall, occupying most of one end of the room. The furniture was old—all good Spanish pieces, mostly dark like the beams. Lamps and paintings and ornaments showed the tastes of another day, perhaps of a former owner. Opposite the fireplace, a small minstrels' gallery of dark wood jutted out, high on the wall, with a narrow arched door behind. This was a room where parties had once been held, and spirited talk must have echoed against white walls. Now it was a silent, empty room.

Outside light filtered from a sunny white balcony, where a door stood open.

Tyler gestured her toward one of the two sofas slipcovered in brown-striped cotton, that faced each other before the fireplace. For Kelsey, the main effect of the room seemed heavy and oppressive. The party times were long gone, and had left no trace.

Tyler's stoop had become more pronounced, as though the recent tragedies weighed heavily on his shoulders. For a little while he sat absently silent, not looking at her, his thick brows —the brows of Marisa's portrait—drawn together in a frown. Although the silence grew uncomfortably strange, Kelsey made no attempt to break it. What happened now was up to this man who clearly had no welcome for her, even though he'd summoned her here.

When he finally spoke, it was to ask a question that surprised her. "Did you stop at Marisa Marsh's on your drive today?"

"Yes. Denis wanted me to meet her."

"What did she think of you?" Again, a strange question.

"She would have to answer that. I liked her very much."

"You would know how she felt," Tyler said shortly. "Marisa doesn't hold back her reactions."

"She invited us to stay for lunch. And she asked me to come to see her again. She also showed me some of her photographs."

For the first time he looked at her directly. "So?"

Kelsey shrugged. "I saw the happy one of your wife, and a not very happy one of you—but as Mrs. Marsh said, a photograph is only a moment in time."

"It's more than that. Maybe it is all the moments up to that time."

"I especially liked the driftwood geese flying across the ceiling of her studio. She said you had carved them."

He raised long-fingered hands and stared at them as though he wondered who they belonged to and what they had done. "About my wife—I'm not sure she will agree to have you come and work with Jody for even a week. She's still badly shocked and cries easily. I don't want to upset her any more than I can help."

"Have the doctors decided what injuries prevent her walking? Is there any hope?"

He hesitated. "Three specialists have told me there's no reason at all why she can't walk as soon as she makes up her mind to try. Her inability to move her legs may be psychological because of her emotional state. She's easily shattered right now. I think she may feel that if she tries to walk, and fails, that will be worse than not trying. After her own attempt on her life last night, I'm doubtful about having you see her. But Ruth has insisted. She wants to deal with you herself."

"Deal with" sounded ominous, but if Kelsey was to find any way to help Jody, *she* might have to deal with Ruth.

"I saw two wonderful photographs of Jody today," she said.

"One was taken with you at the Hawk Tower. In the other, Jody was modeling a head of his mother."

Tyler's expression seemed to darken even more. "The boy in those pictures is gone—gone forever."

"I keep hearing that about him. Forgive me if I'm too frank. I know nothing helps the way you feel, but perhaps those pictures are just what you need to hold on to. There *has* to be a goal. Something to work toward one step at a time."

His look seemed to suggest that his contempt for her notions had returned. He stood up without answering. "We'll see Ruth now. All I ask is that you disturb my wife as little as possible."

A flight of uncarpeted stairs rose from a corner of the living room to a landing a few steps up, then turned steeply to the floor above. Tyler led the way to a dark upper hall, with doors opening off along one side. Ruth's was a corner room.

When Tyler knocked a small, plump woman let them in. She wore a white dress that resembled a uniform, and Kelsey remembered that Dora Langford had once trained as a nurse. She seemed constantly hurried and harried, and moved with little grace. Her skin had wrinkled from too much California sun, and her white hair was a curly mass about her face.

She nodded to Kelsey without smiling, her concern evident. "Ruth is waiting for you."

"This is Mrs. Langford," Tyler said. "Dora, Mrs. Stewart."

The little woman held out a soft, uncertain hand. Kelsey thought of the things Denis had told her about his father, the General, and returned her handclasp warmly. Ruth's mother probably deserved a lot more credit than she ever got.

The bedroom was large and bright, but not a particularly quiet room. The carpet glowed ruby red, and there were crimson squares in the draperies and the upholstery of one chair. An urge to hush the room and tell it to be still stirred in Kelsey. It seemed not at all a room for a woman who needed healing.

Though a wheelchair stood in one corner, Ruth lay in the

bed, propped against pillows, and even though Kelsey was prepared, she felt shocked by the contrast between the happy, guileless face of Marisa's portrait, and this apathetic woman who had plainly given up. Her short, dark hair was held back by a band of red ribbon. Apparently once her favorite color—the color of life and animation, both of which had abandoned the woman in the bed. Her body, outlined beneath the sheet, seemed almost as slight as Jody's, and her fine-boned hands lay outstretched on either side, motionless, the wrists bandaged.

Tyler moved briskly to the bed and bent to kiss Ruth's cheek. Kelsey sensed his hurry to get through something that might be unpleasant. Ruth made no response. She turned neither her head nor her eyes as Tyler made the introduction, her lack of any interest clear.

Kelsey stepped to the end of the bed where she could place herself in the line of Ruth's vision. The sea-gray eyes seemed to focus, as though Kelsey's effort to make contact had caught her attention.

"You wanted to see Mrs. Stewart," Tyler said impatiently.

Ruth roused herself to an effort, her voice faint.

"My husband says you think you can help Jody."

"I don't know whether I can or not. I'd like to try."

"What can you do for him that hasn't already been done?" Her voice strengthened a little, though her look was still apathetic. "We've been told that Jody's state may be permanent. Even if he comes out of it, the doctors think he'll be in a permanent vegetative state. A vegetable!" For the first time emotion surged into her voice, and Dora Langford moved toward the bed anxiously. "I can't bear that! It would be better to send him where he can be properly cared for and perhaps helped in small ways to be comfortable."

Kelsey spoke quickly. "What if he'd rather stay here? What if he'd miss you? Coma isn't a word you can be specific about, and every case is different. I've seen children who were labeled 'vegetative' recover, even after weeks and months had passed. I'm not even sure that Jody is still in a comatose state. I'd like to test his reactions in several ways."

"And if he has no reactions?"

"He's already shown the reaction of tears, and that means something."

Ruth glanced at her husband for the first time, and Kelsey guessed that she hadn't been told about Jody's tears.

"I didn't want to give you any false hope," Tyler said stiffly.

"Recovery takes time and a great deal of patience," Kelsey went on. "Time to watch for the slightest improvement and use it fully the moment it comes."

Apathy seemed to possess Ruth again. "I really think he'd be better off where various therapists could treat him—if there's anything to treat. There's all sorts of equipment, I understand, in the place where we're sending him."

"I'm sure you're right," Kelsey said gently. "But all that's for later on. I don't think Jody's ready for any rehabilitation yet. In his present state very little can be done for him in an institution. There's never enough time for all those children—never enough staff, even in the best of places. What he needs right now is personal, persistent attention." Fervor warmed her voice to a new earnestness. "Someone needs to *make* him come back to the world. Or at least try."

"Ginnie Soong is giving him that sort of attention."

"I've met Ginnie, and I'm sure she's very good with him. But she also believes that more could be done than she can manage alone."

The woman in the bed raised one hand helplessly and let it fall—as though too wearied to continue.

"If Jody's brain is as seriously damaged as they say," Tyler put in, "what use is there in helping him physically? He'll never be able to talk again, or walk or enjoy his life as—" he broke off and turned away.

Kelsey thought of those photographs in which Jody had been so alive, so eager for life. It was Jody she must give all her sympathy to, and she was growing impatient with these two negative parents who had given up.

"Nobody can say that for sure!" she cried. "If Jody can understand enough to cry, I truly believe there's something—some intelligence there."

"Do *you* think he'll ever talk again?" Tyler demanded.

"I can't play guessing games, Mr. Hammond. But I'd like to try a few things this coming week before you send Jody away. Though it's far too little time for a real test."

Ruth moved her shoulders restlessly and spoke to Tyler without looking at him. "Oh, let her come. I suppose it can't do any harm. I'm tired now, Mrs. Stewart. I want to rest."

Nevertheless, her eyes opened for a single direct look before Kelsey turned away, and there seemed an unspoken appeal in their gray depths. Ruth, too, was asking silently for help. Next time, if she returned, she would try to see Ruth alone. She knew now what Denis meant about Tyler's presence.

Dora Langford accompanied them to the door, and when they were out of Ruth's hearing, she took Kelsey's hands in both of hers. "Please do something for my grandson—*please!*" Then she threw a nervous look at Tyler, and hurried back to her daughter.

Without comment, Tyler walked toward the stairs, and Kelsey followed.

"So the decision has been made. For now at least. You can come tomorrow morning, if you like." He spoke in what seemed to her a studied indifference. "Give Ginnie time to get him ready for the day. Ten o'clock should be all right."

"Let me stay with him for a little while now," Kelsey urged. "There's some afternoon left, and I'd like to use every moment I have."

"If you like." Tyler still sounded coldly indifferent, and the indignation Kelsey had been trying to restrain began to rise.

"Don't throw your son away!"

They stood in the big living room, and her words echoed. She expected his anger to lash out at her, but instead he spoke quietly.

"Do you really think I want to do that?"

"I hope not," she said.

He left her abruptly, and she found her way to Jody's room. As she reached the open door, she heard sounds of pain and fear, and she stood for a moment watching.

Ginnie and Hana, the maid, had lifted Jody out of his bed, and were supporting his stiffened body between them. They held him for a few seconds in an upright position, his feet flat on the floor, encased in lamb's wool supports. The boy's head lolled forward on his chest, and he made small animal sounds of distress.

"We'll try the chair now," Ginnie said, and Kelsey went to help.

Padded with blankets, an armchair with a high back stood near the bed, and they carried Jody to it and set him down gently. Straps were fastened to hold him in place, and the back of the chair supported his head. Once his head was raised, Kelsey could see the scar the trach tube had left at the base of his throat. That scar belonged to the hospital time, when he'd needed help at first with his breathing.

Ginnie bent to place Jody's feet in their supports, carefully on a stool. The right angle of the foot must be preserved if Jody was to stand and walk again with his feet flat on the ground. If they "froze" so they were permanently pointed he would be in trouble.

Ginnie thanked Hana and when she'd gone, looked questioningly at Kelsey.

"Mr. Hammond said I might start this afternoon, Ginnie. If Jody's not too tired. What exercises do you do with him?"

"So far, just range of motion—a couple of times a day to keep his muscles and joints working."

Jody sat upright in the chair, held in place, his eyes staring at nothing. His arms turned inward in the familiar spastic stiffening that was always disturbing to see, though these very movements would help to keep his muscles from atrophy. His mother, in her bed upstairs, whether willfully or neurotically unable to move, might be in even more danger of permanent damage.

"What would you like to try?" Ginnie asked. Her attractive wide-cheekboned face expressed her own anxiety about her young patient. Ginnie Soong would never be uninvolved.

"Nothing very drastic." Kelsey pulled a straight chair next to Jody's and sat down. She took his right hand and removed the terry washcloth around which his fingers were curled—to keep them from turning into stiff claws—and straightened them gently. This small boy's hand had once been talented and creative, but now the fingers were without life.

"Listen to me, Jody," Kelsey said, her words slow and distinct. "I know you can hear me and understand. I want you to help me. Can you press my fingers, Jody? Just a little?"

There was nothing, no response.

"Can you move one finger—only one finger?"

Again, nothing. Kelsey leaned so close that she could feel his breath on her cheek, and it seemed that some awareness looked out at her. No one could tell how far Jody could see, or if he could focus at all, since he didn't respond to signals. Yet she was sure something was there.

"I want you to try very hard to help me, Jody," Kelsey said. She put her hands on his shoulder, covered by the thin hospital gown, and pressed gently, stroking downward. "Think about my fingers, Jody. Feel them as they move. Think about following them. Make your thoughts flow right down to your arm—into your fingers."

Kelsey had taken a few classes in what was called "therapeutic touch"—a more scientific development of the "laying on of hands"—and she stroked downward slowly, gently, firmly, murmuring to him in a voice she knew was soothing, unfrightening. Almost anything could hurt him now, and he couldn't tell anyone where the hurt might be. Her hands moved the length of his arm, pressing his wrist lightly, the back of his hand, and then into each separate finger, letting her own energy flow from her mind, her own fingers, into his.

"The strength will come, Jody. I know it will. Think your way down your arm with me. Let's try it again—all the way."

His spasticity seemed to lessen just a little.

"See, Jody—the feeling is beginning to come. You probably think you've lost your hands because you can't feel them. But you haven't. They're right here where I'm stroking. Let me show you."

His arm had relaxed enough so that she could bend it at the elbow and raise his hand to the level of his eyes. When a patient could become aware of his own hands and make the necessary eye contact with them, sometimes voluntary movement became possible.

She lowered his hands and spoke to him again. "Now move this first finger, Jody. I can give you some of *my* energy to help, but you have to use your own too. Move your finger just a little, so I can tell that you're listening."

Nothing happened, and once more she began at his shoulder, pouring her own healing force into him as her hands moved. Praying a little as well. This time more of the stiffness seemed to be released, so that his fingers began to go limp.

"That's wonderful, Jody. You're doing it! I knew you could. Now if you can, make this finger move in any way at all. Think hard, Jody—make it move."

As his hand rested in hers, two fingers twitched slightly, and Ginnie, who had been watching closely exclaimed in triumph, "You made your fingers move, Jody—you did!"

Nothing more happened, and Kelsey knew that so great an effort had tired him. Now she would attempt a different form of stimulation.

"Ginnie, do you have any picture books that you've been reading to Jody—anything with animal pictures?"

Ginnie went to a shelf and picked out a book with large colored illustrations. Kelsey opened it to the picture of a roaring lion, and held the book before Jody's face.

"Can you see this, Jody? Do you know what it is? If you do, just blink your eyes once."

He blinked several times, and Ginnie shook her head. "We've tried that so often, but he can't control the blinking. So we don't know whether it's a reflex or an attempt to answer. Though I *think* he's trying to tell us."

"It doesn't matter," Kelsey said. "It will come, Jody. Look at the picture again. You know what it is, don't you? It's an elephant, isn't it?"

An almost visible struggle seemed to be going on inside Jody. His mouth moved soundlessly, as if in pain, and his eyes seemed to stare at the picture. A sudden explosive sound burst from his lips—a discernible "No!"

She hugged him and kissed his cheek. "I knew you could tell us. It's a lion, isn't it?"

Jody's tongue tried to touch her cheek. The gesture was spastic, but it was nevertheless a response.

"I understand what you mean, Jody. You'd like to kiss me back. One of these days you will. Right now, your tongue is the easiest part of you to move. Let's go back to the picture. It *is* a lion, isn't it?"

Jody produced three more "no's" quite clearly, and Kelsey laughed. "Yes is a lot harder to say than no. But this time I think you mean yes. You've made a big step ahead today, Jody. You *are* going to talk again. Jody, do you know what happened to you? Do you know why you haven't been able to move and talk?"

Ginnie shook her head. "No one's told him because they thought he couldn't understand. And I was afraid to upset him if he did."

Kelsey picked up his hand again and found the fingers once more stiff. "It's better to know, isn't it, Jody? You must have been wondering inside your head—wanting to ask questions. After a while, if you work at it, you'll be able to speak all those questions out loud yourself. Right now, I'll try to guess at some of them. You want to know, don't you?"

"No!" Jody agreed.

"All right. I'll tell you what happened. You were out at Point Lobos and you had a bad fall onto some rocks, Jody. Your mother was with you and she fell too. But she's going to be all right. Your head was hurt so that it's hard for you to think, hard to make words come or any of your muscles move. But these are things you can learn again, and you will. I know how scary it's been for you there inside, when you couldn't make anyone understand. But that's over now. You've started on the way back. Haven't you, Jody?"

"No, no, no!" Jody cried.

Kelsey and Ginnie fell into each other's arms. The sound at the door made them look around. Tyler Hammond stood watching, and the mask he usually wore had slipped a little. He too had seen and heard.

"Show your father, Jody," Kelsey urged. "Say your word."

But the hint of expression had vanished from Jody's eyes, and they no longer held any focus. It was as though his father's very presence had ended the tremendous effort he'd just made.

"It's all right," Kelsey assured him. "You can try another

time. I know you're tired now. I'll come to see you tomorrow, and we'll do this again. We're going to do a lot together, Jody. You aren't alone. So I'll say good-bye for now. Think about that yes word too—think about how to say it, and one of these days you'll say it in the right places too."

She kissed him again on the cheek, but this time he didn't reach out with his tongue. Her eyes shining, Kelsey went into the hall to face his father. "Did you hear what your son managed? The 'n' sound is easiest. Saying no will do something for his confidence next time."

"What good will that do?" Tyler asked. "I mean, what if he comes back to the mind of a three-year-old, and that's all he'll ever be for as long as he lives? My God, what's the use?"

He looked so tall and made of granite, and he was dark with true despair, but Kelsey felt almost impatient enough to shake him.

"Nobody knows that, including you. So do you have the right to make the choice you seem to be making? Tell me something—has Jody been outside his room at all in the month he's been home?"

"Ginnie has carried him onto a balcony a few times, so he could sit in the sun."

"That's something, but I'd like to try more. He needs stimulation, change, interest. Something to wake up his mind. Have you any idea how boring it must be for him there inside his head when he can't communicate at all? No wonder he drops into nothingness!"

Tyler was staring as though her words had startled him. "I suppose I hadn't thought of that. I'm not sure it's even true."

She wouldn't argue with him about that. "This is probably the first case of this kind you've ever seen. I've worked with a great many. They're *all* different, and we don't take anything for granted. Is there a place where Jody used to like to go with you? Something that was special for him—a treat?"

"I suppose so."

"Then let's get him there tomorrow. I'll tell him in the morning so he'll know something interesting is going to happen. Whether he's one year old, or nine—he's not a vegetable. We can take him anywhere you choose. I'd like to come too, of course, to see what happens."

"I'll think about it," Tyler said woodenly.

"Of course he really ought to have a wheelchair. One with a special back that would support his head. I can give you the specifications, if you'll order one."

This time Tyler showed his exasperation. "Look, Mrs. Stewart—you're forgetting something. The place where Jody is going next week will provide a wheelchair and anything else he needs. I'll see you tomorrow."

He turned and strode off toward his study. She heard the sound of a door closing.

Ginnie had come into the hall and had listened to the exchange. "*I* know how much you accomplished today," she said. "I've hoped for this all along, but it's been hard trying alone, and my skills are different. Kelsey, there are really three sick people in this house—not only Jody. Two of them have the sickness of despair. I think it could even kill Ruth, and it's already damaged Tyler. So all we can do is concentrate on Jody." She hesitated for a moment and then went on. "How is Denis?"

"I think he feels shut out. Tyler won't let him see his sister right now."

"Perhaps that's for the best—I don't know."

"Why do you think that?"

Ginnie turned back to Jody's room. "It doesn't matter. All that trouble was a long time ago. It hasn't anything to do with Jody. I'd better go back to him now. I'll see you tomorrow."

Kelsey found her way to the front door, and as she climbed the steps to the garage area, she paused to look down upon the steel-blue walls and red tiles of La Casa de la Sombra. It was indeed a house of shadow. But Ginnie was right. She must concentrate on the boy. If she could help him to come back, even a little, perhaps that would begin to heal his mother and father too.

Movement at an upper window caught her eye. Someone stood behind glass, watching her. She recognized Dora Langford's fluff of white hair, but when Ruth's mother saw that Kelsey had discovered her, she disappeared from view.

Kelsey wondered who might tell her what was really going on in this house. There seemed to be even more tension here than the tragedies themselves could explain. Tonight she would talk to her aunt again, and perhaps even to Denis. Something terribly disturbing must have happened, even before the accident. The photograph she'd seen of Tyler had been taken several years before, and Marisa had caught the torment in his face.

VII

THAT NIGHT at dinner in the cottage, Denis seemed at first more cheerful and hopeful. He listened—and so did Elaine—to every detail that Kelsey related. But then he revealed some of the same doubts Tyler had expressed.

"I don't know. . . . If you keep Jody there and he remains a small child mentally, and if he's still helpless physically, won't that be more cruel to Ruth and worse for her to deal with? And harder for Tyler as well? He's being beastly enough as it is."

"Beastly's a good word for him," Kelsey agreed. "He's an impossible man to deal with, and it's not fair that he can dictate a sort of death for Jody if he pleases."

"I finally got through to my mother this afternoon," Denis said. "She thinks Ruth is more interested in your coming than she wanted to show while Tyler was there, Kelsey. Perhaps you could slip upstairs to see her sometime when he's not around."

"I'd like to do that, but I'd better move cautiously. Jody has to come first. I keep wondering why Tyler Hammond is the sort of man he seems to be. What can have made him so hard and cynical?"

Elaine and Denis exchanged looks.

"He's afraid of good fortune," Elaine said. "He counts on the worst to happen."

"But why?"

"It's not a pretty story, though it may explain a few things about him. Tyler grew up in a small town in Illinois. His father was president of the local bank—very respectable and conservative. His mother was younger than her husband, and I've heard Marisa Marsh say that she was a beautiful and unusual woman. Who knows how it happened, but she fell in love with another man—who probably appreciated her. Tyler's father found out about the affair. He shot her and then killed himself. Tyler's mother died a few hours later. Tyler was only a little older than Jody, and the awful thing was that he saw it happen. He was *there.*"

Elaine's stark telling made the story all the more terrible. This was enough tragedy for one lifetime—too much for a small boy to endure. And now as a man he must suffer still more. With some people awful events made them stronger, better able to deal with whatever happened. Others could turn inward and brood, unable to forget, even when they made themselves seem tough and hard. For the first time, sympathy stirred in Kelsey, but not forgiveness for the way he was behaving toward Jody. "Mrs. Marsh told me that she and her husband raised Tyler. She said he always went his own way."

"I'm sure he did." Elaine sounded grim. "I gather that he was bright and talented, but he always had a black temper like his father. All that horror back there in the past must have kept eating at him. Now he has a fatalistic turn of mind. It's as though this accident to his wife and son were somehow inevitable. In some ways he's a strong man, but inwardly I think he might crumble if the pressure got too great."

"I don't think he's anywhere near crumbling," Kelsey said. "But he's having a bad effect—especially on Jody."

"Everyone's afraid of him, including my sister," Denis said.

"I felt that about your mother too," Kelsey agreed.

Elaine shook her head. "Don't underestimate Dora. I've known her for a long time. She skitters around as though she were afraid of her own shadow, but there's more going on than you'd think."

"Right!" Denis's grin was rueful. "After all, she put up with the General for all those years without becoming a total doormat."

Kelsey remembered her glimpse of Dora Langford looking down from an upper window, and her entreaty to help her grandson. If Kelsey needed an ally in that house—someone close to Ruth, perhaps . . .

Denis seemed to read her mind. "Don't count on Dora. She's no doormat, but the only one who matters to her is Ruth —Ruth's happiness. She'll be against anything she might think would be bad for my sister, even though you think it might be good for Jody."

Kelsey heard the bitterness in his voice, and suspected that there could have been times when Dora took her daughter's side against her son.

When they finished dinner, Denis went off on an errand, and since Elaine had to attend a meeting, Kelsey walked over to Ocean Avenue to explore the village on her own.

Some of her inner soreness and aching had lessened a little. It would still come in stabs for a long time, but it was a distraction to become so deeply involved in Jody's plight. This was something she could throw herself into with all her heart and strength. Mark was gone, but Jody was alive. Even though the probability of failure was immense, and might be very hard for her to deal with, she knew she had to try. A debt might be paid. Then a little of her own useless guilt could be lifted.

She walked along, enjoying the fairytale aspects of the village. One of Carmel's charms was that it had remained small. Since plots of land were limited in size, individual shops were often tiny, and they all bore that touch of imagination that distinguished Carmel from more prosaic towns. It might be theatrical, but it was fun. Everywhere trees abounded. There were so many that one couldn't see the mountains from village streets, and as Denis had said, they had the right of way. A tree might grow out of the middle of a sidewalk, its roots tilting bricks or cement, or branches might poke through a wooden fence built to accommodate its eccentricities.

Wandering along a street of art galleries, she paused before a window display of small sculptured heads that reminded her of the photograph she'd seen at Marisa Marsh's today—Jody working on his portrait head of Ruth. Tomorrow she must ask Tyler if the clay head was still around. She might have a use for it.

When she returned to the cottage, her aunt was still away, but Denis sat outside on a bench under the twisted branches of an oak tree, waiting for her.

"I'd like to talk with you for a minute," he said. "I couldn't bring this up in front of Elaine."

"Of course." Kelsey led the way into the cottage and sat in a rocking chair while Denis paced the small sitting room restlessly. Finally he paused before a window, looking out absently as he spoke.

"I know you need to concentrate on Jody, but *please* try to see Ruth when Tyler isn't there. I must help her, too, and to do that I must know how she really is, and why she's being forced to say she doesn't want to see me."

"I can't promise," Kelsey told him. "It will depend on whether an opportunity offers itself. Your sister isn't yet convinced that I can help Jody—I don't even know that I can myself. She just gave up, gave in, because she was too weak to fight. More than anything, she seemed apathetic. Perhaps no one's shutting you out deliberately. Right now I don't think your sister cares about anything."

"Well, I care about seeing her get well—even more than Jody. Jody's already lost. But how can I help Ruth, if I'm shut out?"

"You shouldn't even think that. Besides, Tyler told me the doctors say Ruth can walk again if she really wants to. After lying in bed all this time, she's probably very weak, and the way back will be hard for her."

Denis looked disturbed. "No one's told me that. I thought her spine was permanently injured. That's what they suspected at first. If it isn't, and she's giving up, not trying, someone has to *make* her want to live again."

"Don't count on me, Denis. Ruth isn't my patient and she doesn't want to be. Though Ginnie said something that I've wondered about. She spoke of some old trouble that happened a long time ago. Do you know what she meant? Could it have anything to do with the present?"

Denis turned from the window and sat down abruptly—sat very still. "What else did Ginnie say?"

"That was all. Is this anything I need to know? If it has nothing to do with Jody, then I'd rather not hear about it. La Casa de la Sombra is already haunted enough without adding anything more."

Denis made a gesture of dismissal. "Don't worry. Ginnie's right—it's history best forgotten. Kelsey, I've been thinking about something. Wouldn't it help if you could move in up there? Live in the house for a while? Then you'd be in a better position to help Jody, and you could see Ruth as well."

"That's the last thing I want!" Kelsey cried. "This case is going to be pretty intense, and I want to see Tyler Hammond as little as possible. My living there would be too hard on everyone."

"This *case!*" Denis said bitterly.

"I'm sorry. You should know by now that Jody's already a lot more to me than a case. Maybe you can tell me something. I've been thinking about that photograph I saw at Marisa Marsh's today. The one of Jody and the clay head he was making of his mother. Do you suppose it's still around?"

"I wouldn't know. What does it matter?"

"Everything matters. Anything that might stir a memory in Jody can matter. We don't know what's going on inside his head, or how much can be brought back—how much he's able to remember. No one had even talked to him about the accident! But from what has happened today, I know there's something going on in him. Don't you care, Denis?"

He looked shocked, and she knew she had hurt him. "Of course I care. But my main concern right now is still for my sister."

"Perhaps whether she can get well or not is going to depend a lot on what happens to Jody. Denis, at first you didn't want me to go to see Jody at all. Why did you change your mind?"

"Maybe I was wrong. When I talked to my mother she said Ruth had seemed to come to life for a few moments while you were there. In that house she needs a friend."

"Her husband isn't a friend? He seems to care about her."

Denis looked depressed, and Kelsey sighed. Ginnie had said there were three sick people in that house. Now she wondered if Denis made a fourth. The "walking wounded"!

They were both quiet for a time, thinking their own none-too-cheerful thoughts, when the ringing phone startled them.

Denis went to answer. "Mother . . . yes, I'm here with Kelsey Stewart. Elaine is out. . . . Sure, of course you can. Shall I pick you up? . . . All right, we'll wait for you here."

He set the phone down, looking puzzled. "Dora was calling from the village. She wants to see me and she'll be here in a few minutes."

"Then I'll go up to my room," Kelsey said. "You'll want to see her alone."

"No—she wants to talk to you as well, so do stay."

At the sound of a car outside, Denis went to the door to meet Dora Langford as she came up the walk. She seemed upset as she came into the sitting room. Her small, plump hands had a tendency to clasp each other tensely, and she looked uncertainly from Denis to Kelsey, as though she didn't know how to begin. The mass of curly white hair about her face looked windblown, giving her all the more an appearance of distress.

Denis brought her to the sofa and sat down beside her. "Would you like some coffee?"

"No—nothing." Dora made an effort to keep her fingers still. "Things are growing worse all the time. I know Ruth is deathly afraid of Tyler, though I don't know why. She won't talk to me at all. She lies there pretending not to care about anything, and all the while she's terrified. She'd rather die than go on living like this—and she's already tried to die."

"Not very hard," Kelsey put in gently. "I think what she did was probably a call for help. That's not to discount the danger of suicide. What do you think can be done?"

"Denis, we need to get her away from that house, away from Tyler. What I'd like is to take her with me back to the desert. I could take care of her there and help her to get well. She'll never recover where she is. Then, if Jody can be helped, she could return later when everything is better. That is, if she ever wants to return."

"How will you persuade Tyler to let her go?" Denis asked.

"That's the problem! I think he wants to keep her there—in her prison. He wants something from her that she can't give, and I don't even know what it is. Denis, can't you talk to him, persuade him to let her go?"

Denis stared at her despairingly. "You're pretty desperate to suggest that. You know he won't even let me see her right now. Does she ask for me—say anything about me?"

Dora didn't answer, but looked uncertainly at Kelsey. "Something has to be done. Tyler has allowed you to do more than he has anyone else. Could you talk to him? . . . perhaps . . ." Her words trailed off helplessly.

"I wish I could," Kelsey said gently. "But Jody's father isn't likely to listen to me. I'm only being allowed to work with Jody for a few days, and I can't interfere anywhere else."

"What happened to bring you here now?" Denis asked his mother.

"Well—there's what Ruth tried to do last night. If it was a cry for help, what are we to do about it? There's no one to hear except Tyler, and that's like asking the—the hangman to save your life."

"What else?" Denis urged. "It isn't only that, is it?"

"No—it's something Ginnie told me this afternoon. Something I didn't know until now. On the morning of the accident, Ruth and Tyler had some sort of furious argument. Jody was there at the time. Of course I was still at the Springs, but Ginnie was in a nearby room, and she heard the raised voices, though she didn't catch the words. Ruth came out of Tyler's study looking terribly upset, and Jody was hysterical. Ruth told Ginnie she would have to get Jody quieted, and she would take him out to Point Lobos for a picnic. You know the rest."

"But what has that to do with now?" Denis asked. "Ruth and Tyler had fights enough in the past, God knows."

"Ginnie thinks whatever happened is part of what's making Ruth give up. If I could just get her away from the house— from Tyler. Even for just a little while."

Denis raised his hands and let them drop.

Kelsey felt sorry for Dora Langford, who seemed caught on the horns of the whole tragedy. "Maybe we can leave everything open," she suggested. "There's no telling what may happen in the next few days, and if there's any sort of opening that would give me a chance to talk to Ruth, I'll try. But I can't promise."

Dora began to cry quietly, and Denis put an arm about her. "Something will happen, Mother. Kelsey's our rescuing angel."

"Don't put that on me! A rescuing angel I'm not!" Kelsey felt exasperated. She was getting tired of all these enervating emotions swirling around Jody's hapless head.

Denis spoke to his mother. "Do you want me to come back to the house now and try to talk to Ruth?"

"No, dear." She patted his hand and smiled through her tears at Kelsey. "Thanks for listening. I feel a little better just for talking about this. There's so little I can do except take care of Ruth's physical needs."

She seemed to pull herself together as she spoke. Perhaps her years with the General had taught her to accomplish in roundabout ways what couldn't be done head-on. What it was she really wanted, Kelsey still wasn't sure. Nor could she forget the way Dora had watched her from a window of the house.

When Denis went out to the car with his mother, Kelsey returned to her room, feeling that she'd had enough of nearly everyone here right now. No "case" was simple, and often there were tugs-of-war going on around the bed of some small patient, but this seemed grimmer and more desperate than most. As if they all lay under some dark shadow in the past. And she hadn't a glimmer yet of what the real trouble was all about.

In the morning, when she arrived at the Hammond house a little before ten, Hana met her at the door, and she had no glimpse of Tyler on her way to Jody's room.

Ginnie seemed glad to see her. "I've been telling him you were coming. What would you like to try first?"

"Do you ever get Jody dressed?" she asked.

"I wanted to do that when he first came home from the hospital, but Tyler didn't think it was worthwhile to disturb him."

"Then let's start right now. Do you have any of his clothes here?"

While Ginnie brought jeans, a shirt, socks, and shoes from a closet, Kelsey spoke soothingly to Jody, telling him what they meant to do.

"Dressing every day is part of getting well, Jody. We know it won't be comfortable in the beginning, but you can try to help in any way you can."

Jody's eyes seemed to focus on her face—again a hopeful sign. He stiffened as they started to dress him, and made sounds of complaint, so that the process was a struggle. In the end, they got everything on, and all his tubes adjusted. When he was dressed, they lifted him into the same chair where he'd sat for a while yesterday, and strapped him into it. Kelsey repeated her stroking down one arm and then the other, coaxing him to relax until his fingers could be more easily moved. Ginnie joined in praise for the slightest success.

Next Kelsey showed him pictures in the animal book, and talked about the bears and tigers, and the lion that wasn't an elephant. She tried by various means to get him to say "no" again, but Jody was silent and unresponsive. Though not, she felt, uninterested. At least something less boring was happening in his dreadfully restricted world.

She worked on an "m" sound—which would lead to "Ma"—pressing her lips together, putting her face close to his, and trying to get him to imitate the movement of her lips. Jody's mouth twitched slightly—and since anything at all was encouraging, she praised him again, and went on to other exercises. Range of motion, which Ginnie did with him twice a day, helped, but he needed still more, not all of it physical.

Such children, as she knew all too well, required a lot of simple affection—gestures of love readily given. This wasn't hard for Kelsey. Jody's silent appeal was so great that she could easily pour out her own child-starved love to him. She looked down at his stiff, unmoving body and thought of Mark as she'd last seen him in the stillness of death. At least Jody's heart was beating.

"We'll let you rest now," she told him after another effort. "Then I may have a surprise for you. I'll bet you like surprises. Ginnie, where can I find Mr. Hammond?"

"He could be anywhere. I don't think he works regularly anymore, but he's often in his study. You might look for him there."

Kelsey patted Jody's arm. "I'll be back soon, and I hope I'll have something to show you."

She found her way around the jog in the corridor and saw that the door of the room that looked out over pine trees stood open. Tyler sat at his desk writing a letter, and when she tapped on the door he looked up.

"Good morning, Mr. Hammond. May I speak to you for a moment?"

He gestured toward a chair, unwelcoming, but resigned. He wore jeans this morning, and a pullover white sweater with a crew neck. His dark hair, still damp from a shower, had been combed indifferently with his fingers.

"I'm sorry to interrupt," Kelsey said. "Perhaps you could set a time for me every day so I could talk with you about what I'm doing with Jody. We've dressed him this morning—just getting dressed puts a better front on the way he meets the day. And we've done some exercises with him."

She hesitated, since she needed to move into tricky territory, and when he didn't comment, she went on.

"One of the things every sick child needs most is love. I'm a stranger, and he needs it from his family. Ginnie gives it in everything she does for him, but he must want it from you and from his mother. Just because he can't give anything back doesn't mean that you can't pour it into him, once you understand his need. Was Jody close to his mother?"

"Of course." Tyler spoke curtly. "As any small boy would be."

"And to you?"

He stared at her bleakly, his guard up, and she knew her words must have wounded him. He could remember the old Jody very well, yet be unable to relate to the changeling at the end of the corridor. Often she felt indignant with parents who were afraid to search for what might be there—afraid of more hurt. She must be patient with this father, as well as with the son.

"Jody can't do much of anything yet, but you can, Mr. Hammond. You need to talk to him cheerfully every day. You need to make him believe that *you* think he can get well. It doesn't matter whether you believe it or not—you need to show him affection, encouragement."

He seemed to be considering this thoughtfully. "What else do you need to have done?" he asked.

"Have you decided where we might take him this afternoon?"

"There is a place. . . ." he said grudgingly. "You'll have lunch here with Ginnie, of course, and then we'll see. Now, if you'll excuse me. . . ."

She could excuse him for very little, but once more she spoke carefully, remembering his own suffering. "There's one other thing. When I visited Mrs. Marsh's house yesterday, I saw a photograph she made of Jody when he was modeling a head of his mother. Do you still have that head?"

He was so still that for a moment she thought he might not answer. Then he rose from his desk and said, "Come along and we'll see."

There were stairs nearby dropping to a lower level that followed the hillside, and she went down with him to a large, pine-paneled workroom. There was a sawhorse, a workbench, various power tools, as well as tools for hand carving. A chair seemed to be in the making and she recognized the style.

"You do beautiful work. I saw the set you must have made for Mrs. Marsh."

"Sometimes it helps to work with my hands," he said indifferently.

"I know," she said, understanding very well. "It always helps to think about something else."

"Or not to think at all," he countered. "That was Jody's worktable over there. Sometimes we did things down here together. His interest recently was in clay, and he made some rather good pieces. His mother has a bowl upstairs that I had fired . . . unless she's had it taken out of her room."

A strange thing to say, and Kelsey risked a question. "Why doesn't she want to be reminded of her son?"

"Why should she—the way he is now? Don't you think it's killing her? She must learn to let him go and save herself."

"At Jody's expense? Do you think any mother would want that?"

Tyler gave her a dark look and picked up a clay dove from Jody's table. The piece hadn't been fired, and it crumbled in his fingers. For a moment he stood looking at the bits, and then threw them into a trash bin at the end of the table.

Something in the bin caught his eye and he pointed. "Is that what you're looking for?"

There in the trash beside the broken dove was the clay head Kelsey had seen in Marisa's photograph. No one but Tyler could have put it there, and that seemed shocking—as though, symbolically, he really had thrown his son away.

She lifted the head out carefully and turned it about in her hands to give herself time to recover from her own mingled indignation and pity. She might understand the gesture, but she hated Tyler for making it. As long as this was his attitude, it might be impossible for Jody to recover.

"This really is very good," she said, even as she recognized that this happier likeness Jody had created bore little resemblance to the stricken woman in the bed upstairs.

"I didn't want to look at it anymore," he said bleakly.

She let that go. "May I borrow this for a while?"

"What do you want it for?"

"Come and see," she challenged. "We can't be sure what will work and what won't. It depends on how much Jody can remember, and what he can see and recognize. Those are the things we need to find out. We need to know where to begin with him."

Carrying the head carefully, lest it too crumble, Kelsey walked out of the room and up the stairs, leaving Tyler to follow or not as he pleased. At least she must have made him curious, because he came with her.

At the door of Jody's room she paused. "Please go in and speak to him as though you understand that he can hear. He can, you know. Tell him something pleasant. Something kind."

Tyler was so tall that she had to look up to meet his eyes. In a sense, he was like Jody—giving nothing away in his expression. Yet there was a slight response—almost the twitch of a smile on that grim mouth.

"Yes, Mrs. Stewart," he said mildly, and she knew he spoke partly in mockery, and partly because she had reached him just a little.

For an instant she felt almost as triumphant as she had when Jody had said his first "no." She stood aside, out of Jody's range of vision, and let his father approach the bed alone.

"Hi, Jody," Tyler said.

The boy's eyelids blinked rapidly, and his father went on.

"This afternoon we'll take you out for a while. Is there any place you'd most like to go?"

Jody's head moved slightly, and Kelsey knew he was looking at his father. This time the movement wasn't a spastic jerking. She hoped that Tyler realized that this too was a triumph.

"It's okay, Jody," Tyler said. "I know you can't tell me yet, but Mrs. Stewart says you'll begin to talk again one of these days."

She hadn't told him anything of the sort, but that was fine—this was what Jody needed to hear, and she felt almost proud of her new pupil, his father.

"This afternoon," Tyler went on, "we're going to Tor House. You always liked to go there with me. You liked to climb the Hawk Tower . . ." Tyler broke off, remembering that this time there'd be no climbing. "Do you want to go there today?"

The wild blinking occurred again, and this time Jody pressed his lips together and produced a grunting "mm" sound. Kelsey spoke quickly, lest Tyler spoil what had happened.

"That's very good, Jody. You're telling us you want to go, aren't you?"

Jody said "mm" again, and Kelsey looked at Tyler. He seemed a bit shaken. It would be chastening for him to remember the careless things he and others had said in front of his son since the accident. Even doctors weren't always thoughtful about what they said in the presence of patients they believed were unconscious.

Tyler, however, was not one to reveal his own feelings readily, and when he spoke to Kelsey his tone was cold again. "What are you planning to do with that clay head you've brought with you?"

Kelsey had set the head on a table, and now she picked it up and carried it to Jody's chair. She took his right hand and moved the fingers so they could touch the clay face, all the while talking to him.

"Do you remember this head, Jody? You made this at Marisa Marsh's house, and it's really beautiful. It must look just like your mother. Can you feel the face under your fingers, Jody?"

There was no telling how much he could sense since coma and stroke victims often lost connection with their hands.

Kelsey handed the head to Tyler. "Hold this for a moment, please." Ginnie came closer so she could watch as Kelsey bent Jody's elbow and held his right hand up close to his own face. She touched Jody's cheek with his fingers, let the fingers stroke his lips, tap his nose, and once more Jody put his tongue out, this time to touch his own fingers.

"There!" Kelsey cried. "You see—you do know that's your own hand. Can you feel it a little now? When you touch this beautiful head you made, can you feel it with your fingers?"

Tyler brought the head close, and Kelsey touched the face again with Jody's fingers as she had made them stroke his own face. A sound like laughter burst from him—a sound of satisfaction.

"Keep thinking about your hand, Jody. This is *your* right hand. It's the same wonderful hand that formed this clay. Remember that it's there, and one of these days it will do what you tell it to—the way it used to. Tomorrow we'll work on the other hand."

Tyler handed the clay head abruptly to Ginnie and almost fled from the room. He had had all he could take.

Kelsey ran after him and caught up with him in the hall. This was the moment—while he was still moved and perhaps blaming himself for a number of things.

"You saw how he responded," she said. "Now perhaps you can come to see Jody and talk to him every day. He needs you. He needs for you to touch and hug him. And there's another thing—he needs his mother too. When we take him out this afternoon, perhaps you could carry him upstairs first to see his mother. When she understands that it isn't as hopeless as she thought, perhaps—"

Tyler broke in. "I don't think that's a good idea right now."

"Then do you mind if I take him to her? You've given me so little time."

"Do as you like."

As he walked off she recognized the thin wire she balanced on. One bad slip, and Tyler would be against her all over again —this time for good.

Ginnie was waiting for her eagerly when she went back to Jody's room, and they spoke together softly.

Ginnie, however, shook her head when Kelsey mentioned taking Jody to see his mother. "She's still too sick. *She's* damaged, and she needs to mend before she sees him. If she says the wrong thing to him, or turns away, it could stop the progress you're making."

"There are always setbacks, and we have to deal with those too. Perhaps I could talk to her first, and if she's too negative, we won't do it."

Hana appeared with their luncheon tray, and Ginnie and Kelsey went across the hall to a small room where a table had been set. Ginnie had turned on the television set to keep Jody company. They could see him through the open door, and hear him if he made any sounds of discomfort.

As they ate soup and salads, Ginnie returned to what Kelsey had said, speaking softly.

"I don't know if it would help him to see Ruth now. I knew her when we were in college and roomed together. We were good friends for a while. I saw a lot of Denis too, and visited their house near Palm Springs on weekends. I even met the General once when he came home from the wars. That background helps me to understand Ruth a little better now. At least, I try to understand. You never saw such a doting father as

General Langford was toward his daughter. I don't think he even liked Denis, who tried so hard to please him. Dora knew how to get around him indirectly, but Denis never learned that. I suppose Ruth was protected and spoiled, and had everything her own way. That doesn't make a person strong and able to deal with trouble when it comes. I feel sorry for her, Kelsey. I feel sorry for Denis too—and even for Tyler. Ruth, especially, needs to face what's real. Perhaps she'll never be the way she was before, and neither will Jody. But she's not accepting that and trying to build on it."

Ginnie had more good sense than anyone else in this house. "What would you try with her?"

"She needs to learn how to forgive Jody, and forgive herself. He was only being a heedless little boy, but the truth is that they fell because of his wild behavior. So that's all mixed up in the feelings his mother and father have about him. I think Tyler has turned everything off inside himself so he won't feel at all. He's lost his son—for good, he thinks, and his wife may be a permanent invalid. Sometimes trouble strengthens, and sometimes it destroys. It depends on the person it happens to."

"Thank you for saying these things, Ginnie. I do need to understand. But at the same time, I have only a few days in which to show Tyler that Jody should have a chance. *They* need to help him."

"I don't know if they can until they help themselves," Ginnie said. "Be careful."

"I will—I'll really try. Mr. Hammond told me that Ruth could learn to walk again, if only she would attempt it."

"How do you get her to believe that?"

"If we could get her started thinking about that little boy in there, and what he needs. . . . Ginnie, was she a loving mother? I asked Tyler that, and he said that of course she was."

Ginnie nodded, and the black wings of her hair moved

against her cheeks. "The most loving. Jody was devoted to her too."

"Does Jody understand why she doesn't come down to see him? I mean that she can't walk?"

"I don't know. I've tried to talk to him sometimes, but he's never given any sign of understanding until now."

"Anyway," Kelsey repeated her theme resolutely, "Jody has to come first with me, and let—"

"The chips fall where they may?" Ginnie said sadly.

Kelsey knew all about how tough recovery was—she hadn't made it fully herself yet. But all she could do now was work with Jody, fight for him.

Ginnie glanced across the hall toward Jody's room, where the boy sat motionless, strapped in his chair. There were no little animal sounds now, and perhaps he was listening to television.

"I wonder—" Ginnie said. "If you could understand a little more about the way things were when Ruth and I were finishing college. . . . There was a time when I even thought I was in love with Denis, and perhaps he was a little in love with me. That was around the time when Ruth first met Tyler, and *they* fell in love. Tyler always said he'd never marry, but that didn't make any difference to Ruth. She wanted him and she went after him—just as the General had taught her to do about anything she wanted. She mapped a real campaign to get Tyler. In a way she was a complete innocent. She thought things had to come her way, because that's how it had always been. So she got what she wanted, and they were married about a year after her graduation. I went off to nursing school, and I didn't see much of them after that. Not until I came to work at the hospital in Monterey. When Ruth heard I was there, she invited me to come for a visit. So I was here when it happened. I took care of Jody in the hospital, and then Tyler asked me to come here and look after him for as long as he was at home."

Ginnie was silent and her own sadness came through.

"So we go on from here," Kelsey said. "Thank you for telling me."

"Kelsey, there's a man in San Francisco I'm going to marry one of these days—when I'm no longer taking care of Jody. He'll wait, and I think it will turn out all right. He's Chinese-American, like me, and a businessman. Denis and I are friends, and that's fine. It was never all that serious for either of us."

"What about Dora Langford in all this? I think she's watching me, and I don't know what to make of her."

"Don't be fooled by her fluttery manner. She learned that while the General was alive. If she thought you were a threat to Ruth, she'd certainly watch you. Though I don't see why she should think that."

"Last night she came to the inn to see Denis."

Ginnie, spooning soup, looked up quickly, and Kelsey went on.

"I was there when Dora told Denis that Ruth is afraid of Tyler. She said you overheard a quarrel between them the day of the accident. Would it help me any to know about that? She said Jody was present and became hysterical. That's why they went out to Point Lobos—a treat for him to calm him down."

"Yes, I saw Jody afterwards, and he was almost out of control. Ruth managed to get him quiet enough so they could go on that fatal picnic. I had a feeling that Tyler pushed the quarrel, whatever it was about."

"Have you any idea why Jody was so upset?"

"He was—is—a sensitive little boy, and it must have been terrible to witness all that anger between his parents. They should have had better sense. But I suppose a fight can come on pretty fast."

They finished their lunch in silence. Kelsey had the feeling

—as she'd had once before—that Ginnie, for all her seeming openness, held something back that troubled her.

Now, however, Kelsey decided to talk to Ruth, since Tyler hadn't actually rejected her suggestion. Though this wasn't a task she looked forward to.

"Good luck," Ginnie said, and went back to Jody, while Kelsey went determinedly upstairs. At least, determination was the outer shield she had to wear.

VIII

DORA LANGFORD met Kelsey at the door. Looking past her into the room, Kelsey could see Ruth lying against pillows with her eyes closed. Once more, the room seemed to quiver with color—much too invigorating color. At least Tyler was absent.

"Is she asleep?" Kelsey asked.

Dora didn't move out of the doorway. "I don't think so, but—"

"Could I speak with her for just a moment?"

Dora Langford looked toward the bed before she stepped aside. "I suppose so. Please try not to upset her."

"I have some good news to tell her," Kelsey said, and followed Dora toward the bed.

"Company, dear," Dora told her daughter gently.

Nothing about Ruth's empty face changed, but she opened her eyes—those great gray eyes that were so much like Jody's, and even trimmed with the same long lashes.

Kelsey sat down in the chair near the bed. "I'd like to tell you about what we're doing with Jody, Mrs. Hammond."

Ruth's unblinking stare was disconcerting, but Kelsey

sensed that this might be her one means of protection, just as her husband had his own guard up against more wounding.

"Jody is trying to talk," she went on. "He has started trying to form one or two simple words, and that's a beginning. A wonderful beginning.

"Ginnie and I will get him dressed every day now—to bring him back to a world he can live in again. We've heard him laugh, and I'm sure he understands some of what we say. How much he can remember, or even how much he sees, we can't be sure yet. He did recognize the picture of a lion, and he said a very strong 'no' when I called it an elephant."

At least Kelsey had caught the attention of the woman in the bed. "Do you really think Jody can recover?" she asked listlessly. "My husband doesn't believe that."

"Your husband may have changed his mind—just a little. This afternoon we're taking Jody out for a while—to Tor House, Mr. Hammond said, and I think your son wants to go."

"Tor House!" For the first time there seemed feeling in Ruth's response. "Tyler was always obsessed with Robinson Jeffers."

Kelsey went on quietly. "Jody must feel terribly alone, not being able to communicate in any way. Only Ginnie Soong and the television set talk to him. He needs new experiences to catch his attention, to stimulate new interest."

"His doctors say he probably can't hear us, or understand anything. So what on earth can you possibly accomplish?"

"He's already proved them wrong. All we can do is try—just try. That's better than giving up and doing nothing."

Ruth reached a thin hand to a table near her bed. Her fingers rested on the rim of a small, blue-glazed bowl with a pattern of flying birds etched into the clay. The birds were crude, yet they had a certain grace of form that suggested flight—like those geese that flew across the ceiling of Marisa Marsh's studio.

"Is that Jody's work?" Kelsey asked.

As if her hand had moved absently, without her being aware, Ruth drew it back and hid it under the sheet, rejecting her own gesture.

Of course she'd be remembering the small son who had made the bowl, and was now lost. Kelsey went on quickly.

"Perhaps he'll be able to work like that again, Mrs. Hammond. This is what you need to work toward, to believe in."

Ruth spoke to her mother. "Take that bowl away! I can't bear to look at it. You should never have put it there. I don't want to remember. Do you understand, both of you? I don't *want* to remember!" Her voice had risen in desperation.

It was always hard to be cautious with despairing parents, and Kelsey seldom kept quiet at the right time. "That's giving up!"

Again Ruth turned gray eyes upon her. "Why shouldn't I give up? It's better than false hope that only means more pain. Don't you see how cruel it is—to hope? That's all you have to offer. Sometimes all that's left to do is give up."

Ruth Hammond had made her own choice, but no one had the right to choose that for Jody.

"Brains can heal," Kelsey said. "I've seen remarkable recoveries. Anything can happen. He's *not* a vegetable!"

Ruth turned her head away, as though this effort had wearied her. She had gone back to her own clouded inner life, and Kelsey wanted to cry, *Wait, don't go away—Jody needs you!* But Dora touched her arm and motioned toward the door. She had already removed the bowl from Ruth's sight.

Kelsey looked about the bright room with its exclamation points of red. Obviously Ruth had done this room to suit her own lively tastes, but now the room was much too strident and demanding. These were the wrong colors for healing. Marisa understood about such things.

Nevertheless, in spite of Dora's hand on her arm, Kelsey had to make one more attempt. "There is a way you could help, Mrs. Hammond. If you could have someone bring you down to see Jody once in a while, or even bring him up here. . . . He must miss you, and he doesn't understand why you don't come to see him."

That brought Ruth's attention alive again, and she looked at Kelsey, her eyes swimming with tears. "Tyler did take me down, and it was awful. The way he couldn't move and didn't know me! I won't go through that again!"

"You're upsetting her," Dora protested. "Please go."

Ginnie had spoken of Ruth's protected life—a life in which she'd been given whatever she wanted. Nothing terrible had ever happened to her until now. That sort of self-indulgent life had only made her weak and practically helpless. How could she help Jody, when she couldn't even help herself? But this wasn't Kelsey's problem to solve. She accepted the pressure of Dora's hand and moved toward the door.

"Besides," Ruth said, her voice a little stronger, "if Jody should understand fully what happened, do you think that would help anything? He would only blame himself, on top of everything else."

"Have you thought that he may understand that right now?" Kelsey asked. "If no one talks to him about it and takes away the blame, that's pretty awful. What if he thinks you and his father hate him?"

Ruth stared at her in dismay. The happy innocence of Marisa's photograph was gone and this woman was experiencing new emotions she didn't know how to handle. Whether she could learn to cope with them was something else.

Tyler spoke suddenly from the doorway. "You seem to be upsetting my wife, Mrs. Stewart."

Kelsey faced him, and tried to speak calmly as he came into the room. She might as well throw herself into this—she was in more trouble than she could handle anyway.

"I've been telling Mrs. Hammond about Jody's progress. Perhaps you can bring her down to see him today or tomorrow. That might help toward his recovery, and it might help your wife too."

"Anytime she likes," Tyler said.

Ruth had given up completely. She closed her eyes and turned her head against the pillow, retreating from everything.

Tyler spoke to Kelsey again. "Are you ready to leave now, Mrs. Stewart? Shall we get Jody ready and start this foolish expedition on its way?"

Tyler folded up the wheelchair beside the bed and carried it out of the room, leaving Kelsey to follow as she pleased.

She caught up with him in the hall, filled with an indignation she needed to put into words, whether they were diplomatic or not.

"Why is your wife so afraid to live?" she demanded. "Why has she given up?"

He marched ahead of her as far as the stairs, and then turned to face her, his anger barely restrained. "Mrs. Stewart, have you any idea of the amount of gunpowder that is lying loose around this house? Do you want to be the spark that blows us all up?"

This sounded worse than anything she'd considered. "I'm sorry. You've given me a week to accomplish what I should have months to do. So I suppose I push everyone. I don't think Jody's parents are doing much to help him right now—if you must know. I can't promise not to snatch at every bit of rope that comes my way."

The faint quirk that almost resembled a smile touched his mouth. "I'll accept your apology," he said, and started down the stairs.

She hadn't meant to apologize—just to explain. But he was right about her upsetting Ruth. Whether she liked it or not, she needed to step with a little more caution—though caution had never been her strong suit. If she didn't speak out, how could anything change? Someone had to.

When they reached Jody's room to prepare him for the trip, there was a problem at once with the wheelchair, as Kelsey had known there would be. The back wasn't high enough to support a patient who couldn't hold up his head.

"Perhaps you could put a board in the back?" Kelsey suggested.

"I'll get something." Tyler went off to his workshop on the lower floor. While he was gone, Kelsey held Jody's hand. Anxiety already showed in the stiffening of his arms as he turned them inward.

Ginnie busied herself with his various tubes in order to move them with him to the wheelchair.

"It's going to be all right, Jody," Kelsey told him. "Your father will make you comfortable, and the trip will be fun. At Tor House you can show me some of the things you like there."

Jody said, "Um," which was a slightly new sound.

"How about a smile?" Kelsey said.

His lips quivered and she knew he was trying. But he gave up at once as his father returned.

Ginnie helped to move him into the chair, and since he was accustomed to her lifting him, he only moaned a little. They bound him into place with the straps used to secure him in his regular chair. At first his head fell forward on his chest, and then, before anyone could lift it, he raised his head himself and let the pillow and board take its weight.

"That's wonderful, Jody!" Ginnie cried. "You've never done that before."

When they'd wheeled him out to the courtyard, Tyler carried him up the steps toward the garage area and the street above while Ginnie followed with the wheelchair. She wasn't coming with them since she'd suggested that there might be too many people looking after him, which would only make him feel confused.

When Kelsey was in the front seat of the car, Tyler lifted Jody onto her lap. She held him with his head against her shoulder and spoke soothingly so that he began to relax.

When they were on the way, Tyler, as usual, was silent. Kelsey wanted him to talk in order to hold Jody's attention, and keep him from being afraid of strange movements.

"Tell me about where we're going," she said. "Jody knows, but I don't. I mean, I've read some of Robinson Jeffers's poems —I remember 'Roan Stallion,' and 'Tamar,' but I know only a little about him. Aunt Elaine told me that you're doing a short biographical film on Jeffers."

Tyler let that pass, but he was willing to talk about the poet.

"Robin and Una, his wife, lived in Carmel most of their lives. They met at the University of Southern California, and she must have been exactly the right woman for him—as he was the right man for her."

"Wasn't she married first to someone else?"

"Yes, when she was seventeen. But when she fell in love with Robin, that was it, though they couldn't marry for years. As a young man Jeffers had the usual fling, and he never expected to settle down. Una and Tor House changed all that. She helped to give him a purpose and a direction in his life."

"What about her?"

"She was pretty special in her own right, and she recognized his genius and nurtured it."

An interest that Kelsey had never heard before had kindled in Tyler's voice, and she sensed that Jody was listening too.

"Wasn't he pretty much of a recluse?" she asked.

"Yes, and Una wasn't, so she had to make up for that side of him. She dealt with the outside world, and gave him the quiet and peace he needed for his work."

Kelsey remembered what Ruth had said about Tyler's "obsession" with Jeffers. Perhaps Tyler Hammond had found a kindred spirit in Robinson Jeffers, and surely a creative obsession was not necessarily a bad thing to have. She felt the weight of Jody's head against her shoulder, and wondered if she too might be growing obsessed by the needs of this broken little boy. A *creative* obsession, if only she could help him.

Tyler went on without being urged. "They built Tor House on a prominence that juts out above the beach at Carmel Point. A daughter was born to them before they built the house, but she died on the day of her birth. Later, there were twin boys, Garth and Donnan. They must have all loved the solitary life, with the sea and mountains, and an unspoiled countryside to explore. There weren't many houses out there then. Una used to search out local legends, and she'd tell her stories to Robin, so that some were used in his narrative poems. You've read them, so you know how strange and even frightening they could be. Mystical and sometimes hard to understand. He was an original, and people weren't used to what he had to offer, so he had a long struggle before he became famous."

"He didn't think much of humanity, as I recall."

"It was more that he *despaired* of humanity. He longed to see men save themselves, but he didn't believe they would." Tyler glanced at his son, relaxed now in Kelsey's arms. "I think he's listening." He spoke softly, as if afraid to hope.

"Of course he's listening—aren't you, Jody?" Kelsey said, and Jody made his new "um" sound. If only this trip would work for Jody. . . .

They drove up a narrow turning road and left the car in a small parking area.

"Family still lives in one of the houses," Tyler said. "The main house is open to the public only on tours. Since I've been working on a Jeffers project, I have a key and permission from the Foundation to come when I like. There are docents who take people through and they're remarkably knowledgeable and dedicated."

When the wheelchair was ready, Tyler lifted Jody into it with all his paraphernalia, and he was once more secured into place. Kelsey wheeled him through the gate and up a brick walk. On their left stretched a square of well-watered green lawn bordered with plantings. Low stone walls abounded, and there were two stone houses besides the main house and the striking Hawk Tower. One had been a garage, Tyler said, and now housed the visitors' reception room.

The air smelled wonderful with its scents of sea, pine resin, and the perfume of sweet alyssum growing in what had been Una's English garden. There were rose beds as well, and the bright colors of cosmos and other flowers. From the direction of the beach could be heard the endless sound of waves rolling in below the cliff on which the house stood.

Tyler went ahead to the foot of the tower, and it seemed to Kelsey that Jody was aware of both the tower and his father.

The great stones rose up almost forty feet—massive, with narrow windows, and a narrow door at the foot. Precarious outside steps built into the stone wound up to a room at the top of the tower.

"In one of his poems," Tyler said, "Jeffers spoke of the 'silence of stone' as 'insolent.'"

"How could he have built it all alone?" Kelsey asked.

"While the main house was being built, he learned masonry. Una wanted a tower like those she'd admired in Ireland, and he set about to build it for her. He brought all those boulders up from the beach himself, and he rigged a pulley and a slanting plane on which he could roll stones up as the tower grew. There's a tremendous view of the Pacific coast from an oriole window in Una's room at the top. I've seen a picture of Jeffers standing in that doorway, dressed in his usual open-collared shirt, with gray pants tucked into boots, and a pipe in his hand.

He fills the whole doorway, and you can see the letters carved into the keystone over the door."

Kelsey looked up at a "U" set over "RJ." These two who had lived here were coming to life for her, growing so real that it seemed as though they must appear and speak to the intruders.

"Tones," Jody said, suddenly and distinctly.

Tyler looked startled. "Yes—stones. You remember the stones, Jody?"

"Um," Jody said.

His father pressed his shoulder. "That's very good, Jody." Tyler looked hopefully at Kelsey who nodded her agreement, and then went on to explain. "Robin and Una were great stone collectors. They brought home special stones from all over in their travels, and friends brought them more. There are hundreds of them, all noted and identified. Jeffers set some of them into the tower inside. There are stones from Ben Nevis in Scotland, from Croagh Patrick in Ireland. Stones from Tintagel in Cornwall, and one from Cecil Rhodes's tomb in Cape Town. There's even a bit from the Chinese wall, and from the Great Pyramid of Cheops."

"Tones," Jody said again.

"Right, Jody—you're doing fine." Tyler choked on the words, moved to a loss of control by the effort his son was making, and Kelsey began to feel encouraged. This might really work. Oh God, it had to work!

"At the top," Tyler went on, steadying his voice, "there's a Babylonian tile set in a niche. Jody used to know most of the special stones and where they came from."

Jody made a slight, wriggling movement in his chair, and Kelsey saw that he was smiling, his eyes no longer blank and empty, but really looking at the tower and his father. Even if they were a blur, he could see them. His smile was so special that Kelsey found herself praying that nothing would happen to spoil this new reaching between Tyler and his son. And then, unwittingly, Tyler spoiled it.

"I remember the last time we came here," he said. "I remember the way Jody scrambled up those steps—a lot faster than I could manage. I remember—" He stopped, and Kelsey saw that Jody's smile was gone.

"You'll climb them again," she said quickly. "Think about it, Jody. See it in your own mind. Think of every step in the tower and the way you're going to make your legs carry you clear to the top. You can't climb the tower yet, but I'll bet you can count the steps. You can go up it in your own mind over and over again. After a while you'll really do it. I believe that."

Now he was looking at her, and she knelt on the brick path and began to stroke one leg gently, all the way down to the foot, concentrating on her own healing energy and his need. "It's this foot—this pair of feet—that will take you up the tower. So think hard, just as you did with your arm. Think all the way down. Can you see my hand—even if you're not sure you feel it yet. Move your foot just a little, Jody. Stay relaxed. Try, Jody."

Her hand moved again along his leg, pressing. His feet in their sneakers were placed against the footrests of the chair, and when she reached his ankle, one foot moved slightly—a barely discernible twitch. The foot she was touching.

"You did it, Jody!" Kelsey cried. "You've made a beginning. It will take a lot of work, a lot of trying, and sometimes you'll get tired and discouraged. But you'll keep doing a little better all the time. We'll *make* it happen." So much of healing was in the mind, and if Jody could think, he could help himself.

She looked up to see that Tyler was watching her strangely, but now there was no way to tell what he was thinking—or whether he fully understood what had happened.

When Kelsey stood up, he led the way beside the stone wall that was a continuation of the west wall of the house. From the wall, they could look over at grasses and wildflowers growing to the edge of the steep dropoff to the beach. The air had grown cooler, and the day was turning gray.

Tyler noted the change and looked up at the sky. "Jeffers liked gray days, stormy days. He must have felt a kinship with dark weather. I've been here during a storm, and I know how the waves crash in and send spray clear to the windows of the house. You can hear it spattering on glass when you're inside. He *listened* to the sea—no one has ever written about it more stirringly than Robinson Jeffers. Carl Sandburg said once that Jeffers, like Balboa, had discovered the Pacific."

Tyler's voice could be mesmerizing in its deep tones. Kelsey found herself listening to its sound, as well as to the words, remembering what Marisa had said about his voice.

They leaned together on the stone wall that Jeffers's hands had built, and looked out at a distant ship floating past on rolling gray water, barely visible now in thin fog. Kelsey wished Jody could see the vast spread of view, but his chair was too low, and he might not be able to focus on the distant scene anyway.

Beside her, Tyler stared at the water, still lost in the Jeffers legend, wind stirring his dark hair.

"One of the poems I always liked was called 'Night,' " he said. "I remember a few lines especially.

" 'The tide, moving the night's
Vastness with lonely voices,
Turns, the deep dark-shining
Pacific leans on the land. . . .' "

The words seemed to quiver on the air, and she wondered if a ghostly presence heard and relished them. All those "lonely voices" that must still echo in this place!

Once more she felt a stirring of liking and sympathy for the man beside her. He had known horrible tragedy as a boy, so that scarring memories must linger forever in his mind. Now, with what had happened to his wife and son, his distrust of life would have grown still more. Even to the point where he might be afraid to hope. Because of Kelsey's absorption in the boy, colored by her own loss, she might have been too hard on the father. The force of this man moved her as nothing had done for so long. Was she, too, coming back to life?

They walked around to the front door of the main house, and Tyler unlocked it, then hoisted Jody and his chair up the few steps into the living room. A low beamed ceiling and redwood walls made the room seem dark until Tyler switched on a few lights. The furniture was old and comfortable and unstylish. The family who had lived here pleased themselves and their own tastes. There were many pictures on the walls that must have held special meaning for the family. Una and Robin's books crowded shelves set behind grillwork—the volumes no longer to be handled lovingly. On the western side, small-paned windows looked out at the ocean.

"They used kerosene lamps and candles for years," Tyler said. "Stoves kept them warm and did their cooking, so no electricity was put in until the fifties. There wasn't even a telephone. That's Una's desk over there—it used to be a captain's desk—where she sat doing accounts and writing letters to her many friends. Though they traveled a bit, they had very little active social life. Only a few choice friends came to see them. They were always enough for each other, and the driving force in Robin's life was his work. Of course when he became famous, Una had to protect his need to be solitary."

The "lonely voices" were not only of the sea. And being alone was not always sad. Kelsey had a sense of intrusion into very private lives—as though those two strong spirits must be here still, whispering somewhere in the shadowy room.

"I can almost feel them here," she said softly. "It's as though we have no right to be in this house, intruding."

He glanced at her quickly as if she'd surprised him. "I have a sense of their presence too sometimes when I come here. That's one reason I wanted to do a film that might bring them to life again. Impossible now, of course."

Jody summoned them back in his own way. "Tones," he repeated, enjoying the word.

His father heard. "Right you are, Jody. You mean the stones over the fireplace, don't you? Let's tell Kelsey about them. That black lava set into the cement plaque is from Mount Kilauea in Hawaii. The white lava is from Vesuvius. I know there are lots more, but you should be the one to explain them, Jody. You will one of these days. For now, let's show Kelsey the rest of the house."

It was the first time he'd called her "Kelsey," and she knew that Tor House and all it held for him had relaxed Tyler a little, just as it had his son.

"I really want to hear about the stones, Jody," she told the boy, "as soon as you can tell me. Don't worry—the words will come. It just takes a little time."

Time—the element about which Jody had lost all recognition. It must slide by for him monotonously in a way others could never understand. At least his father had begun to see that far more improvement was possible than he'd accepted before.

Across the room stood a splendid bronze bust, and Kelsey walked over to it, caught by the face. This was Robinson Jeffers in his mature years—the lines in the cheeks strong, the mouth solemn and sensitive, the wide forehead one of intellect. The sculptor had caught the look of eyes that saw farther and more deeply, perhaps more sadly, than most men.

"This must be a wonderful likeness," she said.

"I believe it is, judging from all the photographs I've seen. Jo Davidson did the original, and it's in the National Gallery in Washington."

"I remember photographs of Jeffers that I saw a long time ago," Kelsey said. "He must have been as tall as you are, and built rather the same way—long and thin."

"That's been remarked," Tyler said dryly. "It even gave me an idea for the film I'd planned to do."

She waited, hoping he would go on, but he walked into the dining room and adjoining kitchen, leaving her to follow with Jody's chair. Standing in the kitchen, he took up his narrative again.

"The primitive life must have suited them. They never really gave it up until Una was ill, and electricity became a necessity. Of course in the beginning they were very poor. It was a long time before publishers were willing to bring out poems with rhythms that seemed strange, and which presented dramatically so much tragic beauty. Often friends helped keep them going, and Jeffers went unrecognized, unappreciated, for a long time."

"Where did he do his writing?"

"There's a big loft room upstairs where there were compartments for the family beds, and where he had his desk and all the solitude he wanted. They used to hang a sign on the gate out there: 'Not at home.' Here's another room for you to see."

This was a bedroom with a window that faced the ocean. Kelsey wheeled Jody into the room after his father, and the boy still seemed attentive. At least he hadn't gone off into his own mists.

"They always called that the 'sea window,'" Tyler said. "Jeffers wrote a poem called 'The Bed by the Window.' From the beginning he had a special plan for this room."

"You said they slept upstairs."

"Yes. But from the first he said this was the room, the bed, in which he would die. And that's the way it was. Una went first, and he never recovered from her loss. He died in 1962, just ten days after his seventy-fifth birthday—eleven years after

Una's death. There was a raging storm that day. A *snowstorm*
—though it never snows in Carmel. Robinson Jeffers was born
in a snowstorm in Pittsburgh, and he died in one here in
Carmel."

There was undoubtedly a presence in this room too—nothing ghostly, but a sense of lives that had been lived richly in
these small spaces. Lives that had left a special imprint on all
they'd ever touched.

"I should think a biographical film about Jeffers would be
very hard to do," Kelsey said. "I mean, would you use actors to
represent the people?"

"Not exactly. That would intrude a false note. I'd thought of
doing the narration myself—I was roughing out a script for
what I wanted to say, since I always work from a script. I don't
like doing haphazard shots and then trying to piece them
together with some sort of story. That's what's wrong with a lot
of documentary filmmaking today. I thought of using a shadowy figure dressed the way Jeffers used to dress in the days
when he was building the Hawk Tower. But the camera would
see him only in soft focus, or from a distance—just to suggest a
presence."

"The sort of presence I can feel here now," Kelsey said
dreamily.

Again he looked at her as though she had surprised him.
"Yes, exactly. I wanted to hint, rather than spoil the feeling
and the reality of the place with actors playing the roles in
false dramatics. What I was after was the spirit of Tor House—
its appealing history that grew out of the man who lived here
and worked with his head and his hands. I even thought of
reading lines from the poems myself. The only professional
actor I'd want to read them would be Judith Anderson, and
that probably wouldn't be possible for so small a project."

"Why Judith Anderson?"

"She performed his *Medea* to all sorts of acclaim for them

both. And after she persuaded him to adapt his *The Tower Beyond Tragedy* for the stage, she played his Clytemnestra as well. A few years ago, Anderson herself was honored here at Tor House for all her splendid work in Jeffers's plays. She has the right majestic harshness for Jeffers—"

He stopped, lost perhaps in regret for a dream he'd forsaken. After a moment, he began to speak again.

"Of course there were all sorts of problems I hadn't begun to solve. A film isn't the work of one person. In my type of short documentary, I use a small crew for sound, lights, camera. The cameraman is all-important, of course. I'm a combination of producer and director, and I take a hand in those endless hours of editing where we splice together the final film from thousands of feet of footage. As I'm sure you know, the editing really makes the final version of any film."

This was the first time Tyler had really opened up like this, and she wanted to keep him talking. "Don't you do any of the camera work?"

His attention returned to her sharply. "I take a hand sometimes. But I'm not an expert. I was considering my wife's brother, Denis Langford, for cameraman. He worked on two other films of mine, and he was very good. He had the sensitivity to understand what I wanted. So there was a time when we were discussing possibilities."

This was surprising. Denis had spoken deprecatingly of his many jobs, but he'd never mentioned his work with Tyler Hammond. Nor had Marisa when showing her own photographs.

"This sounds enormously worth doing," she said thoughtfully. "And you certainly have the voice for it. You could even be that 'presence' you want on the film. So why is it all in the past tense, Mr. Hammond?"

He answered with sudden irritation. "I should think you'd

know the answer to that." He glanced at Jody, very still in his chair. "The fire's gone out. I don't care anymore."

When had she ever had the sense to retreat in time? She couldn't now. "But you haven't lost your feeling for Robinson and Una Jeffers, and Tor House. It's come through in everything you've told me here."

"Mrs. Stewart—" he began ominously.

She broke in recklessly, knowing only that more than a film hung in the balance—even Jody's life could be affected by whether his father tried to save himself. "Maybe you need to rekindle that fire, Mr. Hammond."

He stood at the sea window looking out at fog that had begun to wisp its way into crevices of rock, drifting past small panes to blur the view.

She went on more quietly. "It's important, since your voice seems so right. When I visited Marisa Marsh yesterday she mentioned an interview. An interview with—what was her name?—Francesca Fallon. Marisa spoke especially about your voice and mentioned how good it was on that broadcast. She hoped you'd do the narrative for your film yourself."

He turned from the window. "Francesca was a vicious woman! That interview was anything but a success!"

His anger seemed out of proportion to what had been said, and Kelsey gave up at once. The only thing she could do now was to stop feeding an anger that she didn't in the least understand.

A choked, desperate sound from Jody caught her attention. For a moment it seemed as though he were struggling to speak. He had turned pale, and was shaking all over, gasping for breath, hyperventilating. She dropped to her knees beside his chair and put her arms around him, soothing and quieting.

"It's all right, Jody. You'll be fine. You're tired now. We'll get you home and into your own bed. Breathe slowly and deeply,

Jody. Easy, Jody, easy does it. Breathe with me, very slowly. That's it. Now you can get your breath."

His breathing eased, but he was still shaking.

"This trip wasn't good for him," Tyler said roughly, loosening the straps that held Jody in his chair. He picked his son up in his arms and spoke to Kelsey over his shoulder. "Bring the chair."

She folded the wheelchair and found that her own hands were shaking. Though she could hardly point it out, it was probably Tyler's angry tones that had frightened his son and brought on this attack.

When they reached the car, Tyler said, "Get in the back seat, Mrs. Stewart. Then Jody can stretch out and you can hold his head in your lap."

So it was arranged, and during the short drive home the boy quieted a little. Something else happened as well. The fingers of his right hand, usually stiff or limp, pressed her own faintly —as though he wanted to hold on to her.

She pressed back and spoke to him softly. "I understand, Jody. Don't worry. Your father is angry about something else. He's not angry with you."

At the house, Tyler lifted Jody out of the car and Kelsey went around to the trunk to lift out the chair. He stopped her at once.

"Leave it there, Mrs. Stewart. I'll send somebody up for it. We won't need you to come in with us. I'll get Jody to his room, where Ginnie can look after him. He's been upset enough for one day. You must see how bad this trip has been for him!"

Just like that he had wiped out all the good things that had happened. She'd met unfair parents before, and she recognized Tyler's contrary emotional drives that she was in no position to deal with. But there was one more thing she needed to say. Somewhere under all his defensive anger, Jody's father was experiencing greater despair than ever. She remembered the moments at Tor House when for a little while he had seemed a different man—excited and alive. She had been drawn to him then, and she felt what was almost a sense of loss because he had fallen back into the old, ugly pattern.

"Don't worry about what just happened," she told him gently. "There are always setbacks to deal with. Jody made some big steps ahead today, and there'll be more. Don't be afraid when he's upset." She walked toward her aunt's car. "I'll see you tomorrow morning, Mr. Hammond."

"I don't think so," he said. "We don't need setbacks. He could have died back there. I don't want any more experiments."

A door had been slammed in her face, and she stood watching, stunned, as he carried Jody down the steps toward the house. The red tiles on the roof seemed anything but cheerful under gray skies, and no one stood at the windows looking out. Strange—the air of desertion she could sense about the place. As though all that was good and hopeful had fled its walls, leaving an inhuman shell. Tor House had a spirit in residence. There was no one really living here at La Casa de la Sombra.

When Tyler had gone through the door, carrying his son, Kelsey got into the front seat and sat for a moment, her hands grasping the wheel tightly. She felt utterly discouraged and depressed. For all she could tell, she had been dismissed for good.

As she drove back toward Carmel, more fog blew in from the water. Mist already snaked through the folds of the mountains, though on the road it was still thin and didn't obscure her driving.

She went directly to Elaine's cottage, ready to give in to her own despair at last. The day had destroyed her newfound belief in life. Such discouragement could lead to helplessness unless it was fought. The very feeling of Jody's body in her arms had heightened her own personal loss, and once more she was ready to dissolve into the tears she was forever holding back. She'd done enough crying in the past. Weeping could be a release, but after a while it could also weaken you.

Just as she dropped limply onto the sofa, the phone rang, and she reached for it apathetically. When she said, "Hello," Marisa Marsh answered.

"I won't ask about your day," she said. "That some of it went badly is in your voice. I want to see you, Kelsey—we need to talk. Alone. Let me pick you up at the inn around eight tomorrow morning, and I'll take you to my favorite place for breakfast in the village."

"Thank you," Kelsey said, and could hear her own relief. Here was a hand just when she'd felt herself sinking. "I want to talk with you too. I'll be ready at eight."

The call made a difference. Marisa was the one person to whom she could tell all that had happened at Tor House—the only person she might look to for help. Her aunt would give practical advice, but Marisa possessed the gift of a special sensitivity. Besides, thanks to her relationship with Tyler Hammond, she might still carry influence with him and be able to affect what happened to Jody from now on.

One thing Kelsey knew. She didn't mean to give up this struggle. Somehow she had to get back inside that house and do whatever it was that some fate seemed to be pushing her into. She might have to make a few people furious, but though Tyler Hammond didn't know it yet, he still had a fight on his hands.

"I'm coming back, Jody," she said aloud, and felt better for hearing her own words.

IX

In THE late afternoon, Kelsey returned to the beach. Just walking at the water's edge, listening to the hypnotic sound of the waves rushing in, might help her to order her thoughts a little. She breathed deeply of the faintly fishy smell of seaweed and the sea. She wanted to talk to no one but Marisa—only to walk here on the sand, with fog blowing in from the Pacific. All reality seemed blurred and distant sounds were subdued by white mist. A lonely feeling, yet not disturbing.

Now she could live over what had happened at Tor House, and think about it more quietly. She remembered the lines Tyler had quoted about the great Pacific leaning on the land. Robinson Jeffers had understood about "lonely voices."

She had heard so many lately. Tyler's, perhaps, most of all. What was it he tried to escape from in his own desperate way? And of course there was the loneliness of that sad, defeated figure of his wife lying in her bed, unable to recover her zest for life. Denis's voice too had seemed to cry out at times from some despair of his own. Something he often tried to hide with his cheerful, smiling manner.

Saddest of all was Jody, who could only whisper silently in his mind with no means to vent his fears and pain. This afternoon at Tor House, just before he'd frightened them so badly, she'd had the feeling that he'd wanted terribly to tell them something, and that his own frustration over thoughts he couldn't express had brought on his attack. She tried without success to remember what they'd talked about just before.

The world around her had nearly vanished in the thickening mist. Sometimes a wave sent a curl of white foam to lap at her sandals. The silence seemed intense. In the muffled distance there were no houses, no people, no cypress trees, or pines, or village streets—but only this white, smothered world through which she walked. A world that offered a certain peace because of its very isolation.

The sound that reached her suddenly from far down the beach was eerie. She recognized it, and knew it was impossible —incongruous. Her scalp prickled as she stood still to listen, unbelieving. The shrill music came slowly closer until she was sure. Bagpipes were skirling off there in the mist—bagpipes on a Carmel beach! There was Scottish blood on Kelsey's family tree, and she knew this sound.

She stood still and waited, while the ocean lapped across her feet, and in a few minutes the mist thinned. Out of it came the piper in full regalia. A jaunty Glengarry, its ribbons fluttering, topped his head, and the green tartan of his kilt swirled at his knees. A fur sporran bounced as he moved, and a dirk handle showed in one knee-high sock. At his shoulder, clasping the plaid, was a cairngorm pin. As he followed the firm sand directly toward where Kelsey stood, his feet moved in the proper step of hesitation that should accompany the playing of the pipes.

She moved back out of his way, and watched as he went past, with the drones against his shoulder, the blowpipe in his mouth, and the chanter carrying the melody. The wild, mournful tune of a lament rose to meet the sound of gulls and sea, and the piper stared straight ahead, stepping carefully, never looking her way. She might have been no more than a shadow in the mist as he walked slowly on until fog swept in to blot him out, and the music faded into that hushed world that seemed not to exist away from the beach.

Kelsey hugged herself in the chill air. What had happened was a gift—a splendid moment out of time. Pipers had always walked the shores, walked by the waters of their own land. It didn't matter that this ocean was the Pacific.

Strangely, she felt better. Nothing had happened, nothing was changed or solved, but this small gift she'd been awarded lifted her spirits as she turned back to town. She had a feeling that she would remember this moment and use it when the need came.

For the rest of the evening, Kelsey saw nothing of Denis. He didn't drop in to find out how her time with Jody had gone. Perhaps he already knew. Elaine, of course, wanted to hear everything, but Kelsey left out what was most disturbing in her account. Shrewdly, her aunt didn't press her. She liked the idea that Kelsey was to see Marisa Marsh in the morning, even though Marisa occupied a different kind of space than Elaine's.

That night, Kelsey's sleep was restless, her dreams uneasy and troubled. Yet when she awoke in the morning, she couldn't remember them. Instead, she lay for a moment thinking of the piper on the beach, trying to recapture the lift his appearance had provided to push her out of her bell jar. But all too quickly, she remembered that she wouldn't see Jody today, and that only a little while remained before he would be sent away. This must be a day of figuring out how to get back to that house when his father didn't want her there. Marisa must be the one to help.

She dressed in jeans and pullover, and was ready outside

when Marisa pulled up in her bright yellow car. Kelsey might have expected turquoise. Today, Marisa had shed her gold and blue for a white skirt and cardigan, and a dark red blouse with a gold chain shimmering against the red. Her long braid had been looped into a coil at the back of her head, held in place with tortoiseshell pins. She looked as striking as ever, and again Kelsey sensed the vitality in this woman. Sometimes she seemed to sparkle, and being near Marisa Marsh made one feel more alive. Yet there was some inner quality that never quite reached the surface. Kelsey had a sudden realization that she would not like to become this woman's enemy. There might be a fighter here.

"I don't quite pass the test, do I?" Marisa asked as she opened the opposite door for Kelsey.

But she was smiling, and Kelsey smiled back. "I have to watch my face," she admitted. "It's always giving me away."

They drove the few blocks to the restaurant, and since it was early, found a place to park. A side path led to the door. Katy's Place had just opened for the day, though tables were quickly filling. They were given one near an arched window that looked out upon greenery. Overhead the white ceiling was beamed with wood, curtains at the windows were of lace, and brass lamps hung above the tables. Old baskets graced the walls, and there were old-fashioned pictures as well. The atmosphere was of the past, and there was a comfortable hominess.

Katy herself was big and beautiful. Marisa said she had once been in the theater—as was true of a good many Californians who had found more profitable lines of work. She certainly knew how to run a restaurant and had made a popular success of this and her Wagon Wheel out in Carmel Valley. She came over to their table to greet Marisa, who was an old friend, and presented Kelsey with her warm smile.

"Now then," Marisa said when she'd gone, "decide what you want to eat and then we'll get to work."

Marisa's brisk manner was reassuring. Points would be made, and problems would be solved.

The menu was imaginative and Kelsey ordered raspberry pancakes and a slice of melon. When the waitress had gone, she gave Marisa a full account of her morning with Jody, her disturbing visit to Ruth, and the afternoon experience of visiting Tor House. Marisa listened intently, her clear involvement with Tyler and Jody evident.

She responded with special pleasure over the small advances Jody had taken. "This is practically a miracle. And whether Tyler appreciates it or not, he has you to thank."

"He's not thanking me. He doesn't want me back."

"Pay no attention. I know he's allowed himself to turn bitter. The accident must seem all the more unbearable after what happened to him as a child. Do you know about his background?"

"Aunt Elaine told me. But if he goes on like this, he'll damage Jody, and maybe Ruth too."

"I have someone in mind I want to have see Jody. She's a doctor and a very special woman. I've been waiting for the right moment to bring her in. Tyler's been too occupied with all his high-priced specialists to listen. Now he may. Dr. Norman has done some interesting research on brain damage, and it's just possible that she can help. We'll see. At least it was a good idea to take Jody out to Tor House. He used to love that place."

"I'm not sure. Tor House depressed Tyler all the more because his own drive to work is gone. For a little while he seemed to catch fire, and from what he said, I thought he might have made a wonderful film about Robinson Jeffers. One thing seems strange—that Denis never mentioned working with Tyler Hammond on past films."

"They parted badly after the accident. Everything blew up then. It's a sore point with Denis. He really wanted to do the camera work on the Jeffers documentary, and it troubles him that he'll never have the chance now. It's difficult for him to talk about."

"Denis told me that you found them, Marisa—out at Point Lobos. How did it happen?"

For a moment Marisa looked as though she might refuse to answer, but then she went on reluctantly. "I don't much like to discuss that. I really hate it when this sort of thing happens to me. I'm afraid of it, in a way, and I'm never sure I should follow such prompting. Though this time it seemed to pay off, as Denis told you."

"You *did* save them," Kelsey said gently.

"I suppose I played a part in saving them, but sometimes lately I ask myself for what. Would Tyler have been better off with a clean break, instead of being left with a damaged wife and son to take care of, with little hope that they'll recover? Perhaps there's a natural war going on inside him because part of him only wants to escape from this impossible situation."

"There isn't any escape," Kelsey said quietly. "We have to bring Jody back as far as he will come."

Marisa seemed to study her for a moment. "I was pretty close to where they lay when I heard a weak voice calling. I climbed to where I could look down and see Ruth and Jody caught on a shelf of rock, just above the water. I tried to reassure her and went for help. A park ranger called an ambulance, and I went back to stay near them until they were rescued. I talked to Ruth—just talked, to help with the pain."

"Did she tell you anything about what happened?"

"She was out of her head some of the time. What little came out didn't make much sense."

The waitress brought their orders, poured coffee, and when she was gone, Kelsey said, "What did Ruth tell you?"

"She was almost crazy with pain and fear. She was worrying about how badly she might be hurt, and whether Jody was dead. He didn't move, and the wound on his head was still bleeding."

Something was missing in the account—perhaps something else had happened that Marisa chose to be silent about. There was no use asking more questions.

Kelsey spread creamy butter on steaming pancakes. Marisa had ordered Katy's wonderful whole wheat bread toasted, the slices thick and generous.

They ate for a little while in silence, while Kelsey troubled over the question in her mind. She still needed to know, for Jody's sake, what the missing pieces might be.

"What are you leaving out?" she asked bluntly.

"Nothing you need to know about now. You might as well get prepared, Kelsey. Tyler's coming in the door. I asked him to meet us here."

Kelsey looked around, stiffening. Tyler stood at the desk, talking to Katy. "Why didn't you warn me?" she cried.

"And have you so worried about seeing him that you couldn't think about anything else? Relax. Just let whatever happens happen."

He came toward them across the room, looking grim and anything but friendly. When he reached their table, his "Good morning" was grudging, and he managed a mocking smile for Marisa. The portents were as ominous as ever.

"What are you up to?" he asked Marisa.

She smiled cheerfully, though it seemed to Kelsey that her eyes were watchful, measuring. "Plenty. What would you like to eat?"

He ordered coffee, and when it came he took a few swallows, black and hot. "All right," he said, "you might as well start talking. Since you brought me here to listen."

"First," Marisa began, "I want you to know that I'm on

Kelsey's side. And Jody's. Kelsey has told me about your visit to
Tor House, and about the effort Jody is making for the first
time."

"Did she tell you how he fell apart and couldn't breathe?"

"Yes, she told me. That's why I'd like you to listen to a
suggestion I want to make. I have a friend—Dr. Jane Norman
—who lives in Pacific Grove. I'd like her to see Jody."

"Never heard of her."

"Probably not, but that's hardly important. She's been working mainly in research these days, and off the orthodox beaten
track. Her subject happens to be brain damage. Jane doesn't
practice much anymore because she's too absorbed in her
research. But Jody's problem is her main concern, and she'll
come to see him if I ask her to."

"I suppose it can't matter, one way or another," Tyler said
glumly.

"I like your positive attitude. I'll see if I can get her there
tomorrow."

He only shrugged and drank his coffee.

"How did Jody do after you took him home yesterday?"
Kelsey ventured.

He looked directly at her—a cold, appraising stare that
promised nothing, and she wondered how she could ever have
been drawn to him for that little while at Tor House.

"My son was sick most of the night," he told her. "The night
nurse had a bad time with him, as Ginnie did too, earlier. He
was vomiting and crying and moaning. We had to have our
doctor in to get him quiet."

Kelsey wanted to say, "Maybe *you* upset him," but that was
hardly the way to win another chance. "How is he this morning?"

"Still too excited. But at least not sick. He's making a lot of
strange sounds."

"He's trying to talk," Kelsey said.

"But he can't, can he?"

"What if he has something he wants terribly to tell you? Not being able to would make anyone ill."

Tyler gave her a look of distaste. "He keeps repeating something that sounds like 'Elly.'"

Quick tears came into Kelsey's eyes. "He's trying to say my name!"

"That's what Ginnie claims."

"Give up, Tyler," Marisa said. "You're fighting for the wrong goal. Let Kelsey come back and see what happens." She put her hand on Tyler's arm in a gesture of affection.

He didn't surrender at once, however. He was a man who would never surrender easily—perhaps that was what had kept him going. Though, as Marisa said, he was now on the wrong side.

"All this has upset Ruth as well. We had to tell her what had happened, and she couldn't sleep last night either. She's asking to see you again, Kelsey. And she wants to see Jody too."

"You really have stirred things up, haven't you, Kelsey?" Marisa sounded pleased.

Kelsey stared at Tyler, waiting.

He set down his cup and rose from the table. "Come at your usual time, Mrs. Stewart. Though I'm not promising anything. I'll be talking to you, Marisa."

He went off with his long stride, his shoulders a bit more hunched than usual—as if he had warded off more blows.

Marisa released the breath she'd been holding. "Whew! That was touch and go for a while. You did pretty well, Kelsey. You hardly snapped at him at all. Tyler doesn't know how to handle what's happened. He's always hurled himself at stone walls, no matter how much he bruises."

"I suppose I should thank you," Kelsey said uncertainly. "If you hadn't done this, I might never have been able to go back."

"Jody did it. He's asking for you!"

Kelsey glanced at her watch. "Breakfast was very good, but I can't finish these pancakes. Too many lumps all the way down my throat."

Marisa put a light hand on her arm, as she had done with Tyler, and it was as though some force flowed into her. "Finish your breakfast and the lumps will go away. You have plenty of time."

She could feel it happening—the relaxing of tense muscles allowing a sense of quiet to flow through her until her mind grew peaceful. This was what she tried to do for Jody.

Afterward, they discussed no more troubling matters, and Kelsey told Marisa about the piper on the beach—that "gift" that had been so unexpected.

"That's good," Marisa said. "You can use it. Hold that experience in your mind. When things get bad, switch over to your piper. Go down to the beach in your thoughts and see him again. Though maybe you'd better turn off the sound—pipes can be a bit *too* stirring!"

As they finished breakfast, Kelsey asked the question that always returned to trouble her. "Why does Tyler set himself in opposition to everyone who's trying to help? I don't think it's because he doesn't love Jody."

"He's in such a state of painful confusion right now that almost any direction seems dangerous. And maybe it is."

The last seemed an odd thing to say. "Even though he cares, he seems determined to send Jody out of the house and out of sight," Kelsey added bitterly.

"It's not quite like that, but I don't have all the answers to unlocking Tyler. Even though I know him so well."

"It seems as though everyone is afraid of him. Dora Langford is nervous around him. And she seems convinced that he frightens Ruth. Denis certainly isn't comfortable, even talking about him."

"Comfortable will never be the right word to use about Tyler. The gifted are often hard to get along with. Their drives are different, and perhaps more selfish. But they give more to the world in the long run. All I could do for Tyler was try to provide him with a climate he could grow in."

"You're still doing that," Kelsey said. "I was upset at first about the way you managed this today, but I'm glad you pulled it off."

"It's not pulled off yet," Marisa reminded her. "Now it's up to you."

When she'd paid the check, they told Katy good-bye and returned to the yellow car.

"Reminds me of the sun," Marisa said as they got in. She drove back to the inn, and before Kelsey left the car she held her arm for a moment, as though there might be something more she wanted to say. Apparently she didn't find the right words, for she only patted her and let her go. "Just look out for *you,*" she said as she drove away.

Kelsey told her aunt that she was going to see Jody after all, and hurried to change from her jeans. Once she was on her way, anxiety set in again. She hated this situation in which she could be sure about nothing, and whose complications kept her from giving all her thoughts to her patient.

Again Hana waited for her at the front door of the house, and she looked upset as she hurried Kelsey in.

"They're waiting for you, Mrs. Stewart. Maybe you can help him."

In Jody's room she found the boy lying in bed, while Ginnie attempted to calm him. He lay rigid, his arms turned stiffly inward, and he was grinding his teeth. Dora Langford stood on the other side of the bed, her nursing skills helpless in the face of whatever demon Jody was fighting. Both women glanced around in relief when Kelsey walked in.

"Here's your Elly," Dora said.

Jody's eyes found Kelsey and tried to focus. She sat on the bed in order to be close to him, and took one stiff hand in her own. Slowly she began to stroke down his arm, relaxing each finger while she talked to him.

"Your father told me that you can say my name, Jody. That's wonderful, and I'm happy that you wanted to see me again."

She pressed his hand, and in response he made a slight movement with his fingers. The wild look seemed to quiet. Kelsey changed her position so she could lean against the head of the bed, and raise him in her arms. Then she sat quietly, holding him with his head against her shoulder, talking to him softly, offering the pressure of her arms. Offering love. Slowly she coaxed the stiffness from his body, and his teeth stopped grinding.

Dora, still insensitive to the fact that Jody could understand, said, "I've never seen him as bad as last night. I think he was afraid you weren't coming back."

"That's what Tyler told us," Ginnie said grimly. "But you've given Jody a lifeline to hold on to, and he's not going to let anyone take it away from him. Are you, Jody?"

Looking down, Kelsey could see Jody's lips curve in what was almost a smile. The machinery in his brain that would enable him to speak must have time to be retrained. But it was working to the extent that he could understand much of what went on around him.

"You *will* talk, Jody," Kelsey assured him. "It may take a while, but it will happen. I know there is a lot you want to say, so you'll have to work hard—as you did today when you started saying my name. It's not an easy name, but they tell me you've managed very well."

Jody said "Elly" clearly and distinctly, and Dora gasped.

Ginnie said, "See?" triumphantly.

"I'd better get back upstairs," Dora said. "Ruth sent me down to see how he was. She'll be happy to know what you've done." Jody's grandmother started toward the door, and then stopped. "Oh, dear," she said and came back into the room.

Kelsey looked up to see Tyler pushing the wheelchair that Ruth, until now, had refused to use. Sitting in it limply, Ruth looked exhausted, yet keyed up and tense. Once more she wore a red ribbon in her short, dark curls, and Kelsey suspected that Dora had tied it there. The gray eyes that were so much like Jody's were fixed upon her son.

Quickly Kelsey released the boy and stood up, watching Jody's parents out of her own anxiety. In Tyler's face all expression, all feeling had been ironed out; he was holding himself under a tight rein. Kelsey remembered again what he had said about explosives lying loose around the house—"gunpowder!" —and wondered if he were the one who sat on the powder keg with a match in hand.

She watched uneasily as he wheeled Ruth close to Jody's bed. The boy appeared to struggle inside himself. His body stiffened again and he grimaced as if in pain. A great deal would depend on what his mother did—on what Tyler did.

Dora, equally anxious, spoke to her daughter. "Ruth dear, Jody is saying Kelsey's name in his own way. He's trying to *talk.*"

Carefully, Ruth reached out to touch Jody's hand where it lay outside the sheet—as carefully as though it were made of glass. Her anxiety was evident, but at least she tried.

"Jody, darling, do you know who I am?"

The struggle intensified in the boy, and when Dora would have spoken, Ginnie touched her arm lightly and shook her head. At least the "m" sound was easier to achieve than "k," and in a moment Jody said "Ma" clearly. When he'd managed the one syllable, he began to cry, tears running down his cheeks.

Ruth picked up his hand and pressed it to her face. "That's

wonderful, darling! It's all right—don't cry. I do understand. You must have worried a lot. I was afraid to come to see you because it might upset you all the more if you began to remember. But everything's fine now. What happened wasn't your fault, Jody. You must never think that." She looked up at her husband, standing impassively beside her chair. "Tyler, you can't send Jody away. Please! Let Kelsey come to help him, and help Ginnie. You really must do this."

Tyler continued to look blank, his dark eyes empty, as though nothing that had happened had moved him in the least. "Whatever you wish," he said dully.

Ruth gave him a bright, tearful smile. "We have so much room in this house. Can't we ask Kelsey to come and stay for a little while? If she could be here all the time, then what happened last night might be prevented. Jody, would you like Kelsey to stay here with us?"

"No!" Jody cried with great enthusiasm.

"It's all right," Ginnie told Ruth quickly. "He means 'yes.' I do think it would be a real help if Kelsey could move in and be on call."

"Would you, Kelsey?" Ruth cried.

She looked at Tyler. "I'll come if Mr. Hammond won't send me away, along with Jody, at the end of the week."

Tyler thought for a moment, his dark face still expressing nothing. But when he spoke to Ruth his words were mild enough. "We can try it and see how her staying in the house works out. But if she upsets Jody, we'll return to the first plan. Let me know when you want to go upstairs, Ruth. Don't wear yourself out."

He walked out of the room, his back reminding Kelsey of one of those granite slabs below Tor House. Yet now and then she'd glimpsed a chink in the rocky armor. Perhaps his guard was extreme because he feared the emotion that might break through. Once more, she felt touched by sympathy for him, but she resisted it, lest it weaken her resolve to help his son.

She spoke reassuringly to Jody. "I'm going to the inn now so I can pack some of my clothes. If a room can be fixed for me, I'll come back in an hour or so. I have some things in mind that we can try together, Jody, and that might be fun. So I'll see you very soon."

"Thank you, Kelsey," Ruth said, still tearful. "I know you can help Jody. If you happen to see Denis, please tell him I need him. He mustn't stay away any longer."

"I'll tell him," Kelsey promised, but a question was growing in her mind. Somewhere along the way, she had been allowed to think that *Ruth* wanted to send Jody away, and that she had refused to see her brother. Who had been trying to deceive her? Tyler? Denis? Ginnie? Dora? By this time she wasn't sure, but it could very well have been Tyler.

She went outside quickly, and ran up the steps to the upper level, feeling relieved. Tomorrow Marisa's Dr. Norman would probably come, and possibilities would open up to speed Jody's healing. It might even be good for her to live at the house where she could see him whenever she wished. Then she could do much more for him. Through this little boy, her own healing had begun, her own grief had been assuaged a little.

When she climbed to the garage area, she found a second car parked beside her aunt's. Denis Langford sat at the wheel, and the moment he saw her he got out of the car.

"Hi, Kelsey. I've decided to storm the fort. I won't let them keep me away any longer. Even if Ruth doesn't want to see me, I've got to see her!"

"She does want to see you," Kelsey said. "But you can't go barging in like a white knight, sword in hand. Come back to the inn first so I can tell you about what's happened. Away from this house." She glanced over her shoulder as she spoke, and saw Dora once more at an upstairs window, watching. Denis saw her too, and for a moment she was afraid he would do what he'd geared up his courage to do—assault the house. Then he grinned sheepishly and got back in his car.

X

AT THE INN, Denis was called to the desk, and he showed
Kelsey the way to his office along a wooden gallery built above
an inner courtyard.

"My rooms are at the end, Kelsey. Wait for me there, and I'll
be with you in a minute."

She enjoyed the rambling galleries and courts that made up
the Manzanita Inn. It had grown over the years as new owners
added on, and she stood for a moment looking down at a small
fountain lined with Spanish tiles—a touch of old California.

Where the gallery ended, she found herself at the open door
of what was apparently both Denis's office and his living quarters. From a big central room, stairs mounted to a gallery level
of bedroom and bath. There were no windows at this lower
level, but skylights in the roof banished shadows. A walnut
desk held a prominent position, and there were files and a
place for a stenographer to work. There were also armchairs,
lamps, and a bookcase to make this a living room as well.

Kelsey went to look at two framed photographs on Denis's
desk. One was a studio portrait of his sister—a lovely picture

that must have been taken when she was much younger. The other was an enlarged snapshot of a young, pretty Dora standing beside a man in full dress uniform. The General, of course. Dora wore the same air of uncertainty that was characteristic of her now. There was nothing uncertain about the man beside her. The rugged, rather ruthless face seemed to indicate all that Kelsey had learned about him. General Schuyler Bridges Langford must have done his part to cripple whatever lives came close to him. And probably without ever realizing it —because *his* way would always seem right and best to him. Looking at the picture, she felt even more sympathy for Denis.

On the desk pad lay three loose black beads, placed close together, as though to prevent their rolling. They looked unusual and Kelsey picked them up. Each bead had a different face carved in black ebony—tiny, grotesque faces done in amazing detail. On one side of each bead was a miniature face, the features carefully etched, so that piercing eyes, distorted mouths, and elongated ears were shown. On the other side, intricately braided strands of hair had been carved in the wood. The work was beautifully executed, and undoubtedly African. Nevertheless, the beads repelled and chilled her because the little faces had an evil look. Somewhere recently she had seen a strand of black beads, but she couldn't recall where.

She replaced the beads on the desk pad, and moved on around the room. What was surely a Marisa Marsh black and white photograph dominated one wall—a splendid interior shot taken at Tor House. She recognized the bedroom with its sea window—the bed in which Robinson Jeffers had died peacefully in a snowstorm. Marisa had managed to convey a brooding sense to the scene. It seemed intensely real, as though Jeffers himself might walk through the door at any moment.

She turned as Denis breezed in, and was struck once more

by his youthful look. He had managed long ago to put on a guise of cheerfulness that stood him in good stead, though she knew by now the sadness that existed underneath.

"Now we can talk without interruption," he said. "How do you like my place?"

"It's perfect."

He shrugged. "I'm always living in borrowed homes. One of these days I'll move into something of my own. Sit down, Kelsey, do, and tell me what happened this morning."

She glanced again at the Tor House photograph. "When you were telling me about the jobs you've tried, you never mentioned that you'd worked on some of Tyler Hammond's films. He said you were very good with a camera."

Denis dismissed the subject. "It didn't seem worth mentioning. Let's talk, Kelsey. Then I can get back to the house and try to see Ruth."

She sat in one of the armchairs, and told him about Jody's attempt to form words, and even trying to say her name; about Ruth's unexpected appearance when Tyler wheeled her into Jody's room. And of how Jody had managed to say "Ma."

Denis was silent, as though this might be a lot to absorb. He'd lost his cheerful look, thoughtfully sober as he asked a question.

"How did Ruth seem? How did she respond?"

"Very well, I thought. She reassured Jody and told him that the accident wasn't his fault. If he can remember, he may have been brooding about this. Then she sprang a surprise by asking Tyler to have me move into the house so I could work with Jody on a regular basis. I told them that I would if they didn't plan to send Jody away in a week or so."

Denis looked astonished. "Will he allow that?"

"He'll let me move in and try. Ruth wants to see you. She asked me to tell you—so now you needn't storm the fort. There's still an uneasy atmosphere, and I guess we'll all have to move carefully. I didn't think you should go in there until I'd had a chance to tell you what's happening."

Denis was roaming about the room in his usual restless way, but now he sat down at his desk. "I wonder what's happened to change things. You, maybe? Perhaps Ruth will start to get well herself now."

"I hope so. The only person who isn't responding naturally is Tyler. He's holding on to himself for some reason, and he's said strange things about the situation at the house being explosive. He doesn't yet dare believe that Jody will improve enough to matter. He doesn't appreciate what an achievement small things can be at this point. Anyway, I'm going to move up there for now. If you'll wait till I pack a few things, I can go back with you. I'll let Aunt Elaine know and join you in a few minutes."

"She's at the cottage now, so let's go see her and I'll wait while you pack."

Denis put his hand on the desk pad as he stood up, and the little black beads rolled. He saw them for the first time and stood staring down in something more than surprise. It seemed to Kelsey that he looked shocked.

"Where did these come from?"

"They were there when I came in. Why?"

"Tyler must have been here."

"I don't see how he could have been, since he was at the house. Unless he came earlier. What's wrong, Denis?"

He sat down again at his desk and stared at the three tiny faces, grinning maliciously up at him from the pad. When he spoke, it was as if to himself and almost by rote.

"Marisa has a theory about evil. She thinks it's more than just an absence of what's good. She thinks it's a force in itself— maybe even a necessary part of life. Because there are always opposites. Dark and light. Happiness and grief. Goodness and wickedness. Poles that attract and repel—and balance the universe. When there's real wickedness, rationalization can be carried to an extreme. What happens is always someone else's fault. The owner of these beads was that sort of person."

He stared now, not at the beads, but at the picture of his father and mother.

"You're thinking of your father, aren't you, Denis? Did the beads belong to him?"

He looked startled, but he didn't answer. Gingerly, as if they revolted him, he picked up the little black beads, folded them in a bit of tissue, and stored them in a brass box on his desk.

"I'll get to the bottom of this later. I'm sorry, Kelsey. I didn't mean to carry on."

As they walked to the door together, he put an arm about her for a moment, and she knew he was thanking her for listening.

At the cottage, Elaine approved the new move at once. "Yes, of course you must do this. Take her up there, Denis. I'll look in on the girls at the desk and keep an eye on things."

Kelsey went upstairs to pack some things in a suitcase. If she stayed, she could come back for more.

They left as soon as she rejoined Denis. On the way he was silent, thoughtful, more than a little anxious. When they reached the House of Shadow Hana let them in at the front door and Denis asked for his mother. Hana said she'd gone out some little while before.

"Mrs. Langford had some shopping to do, and I think she went to the Valley."

"Then I'll see my sister," Denis said, and Kelsey sensed that he braced himself.

"Mrs. Hammond is on the living-room balcony," Hana told him. "This is the first time she's been there since—since what happened."

"Thanks, Hana. I'll look for her there. Kelsey, will you come with me for a few moments? This seems a good sign, but I'm afraid of upsetting her, saying the wrong thing. It might help to have someone else there at first."

"Of course," Kelsey said, and put down her suitcase.

Hana picked it up at once. "Mr. Hammond chose a lovely bedroom for you upstairs, Mrs. Stewart. I'll take your bag there now, and when you're ready I'll show you where it is."

She went off and Denis crossed the foyer to the big living room with its beamed ceiling and great limestone fireplace. They could see Ruth's wheelchair through the open balcony door, so Tyler must have carried her down here. She sat motionless, her back toward them. Beyond her, the mists had cleared and sun was coming through to bathe the splendid view.

For a moment, Denis hesitated. Then he spoke softly to Kelsey. "More than anything else right now, I want to help my sister. This may not be a comfortable meeting. She may not understand why I've had to stay away. So help, if you can, Kelsey."

She wasn't sure what she could do, but she followed him through the open door. Denis stopped beside Ruth's chair, and she looked up at him with the same emptiness in her eyes that Kelsey had seen before.

"You were long enough coming, Denis. Kelsey, I'm glad you're moving in. No matter what Tyler thinks, I believe you can help my son." But she spoke in a monotone, and Kelsey wondered whether *she* believed.

"I'm going to try," she promised.

Even though she had asked for him, Ruth seemed guarded toward her brother, blaming him in some way. Kelsey stepped to the balcony rail, looking out toward the water, giving the two behind her a chance to make their peace.

They were talking softly now, so perhaps she wasn't needed. She gave her attention to the hillside, dropping steeply away below the house. Only a few nearby pines rose taller than the roof. The rest grew down the hillside, so that one looked out over a billowing sea of dark, whispering green toward the blue of the ocean. Surf creaming in, trimming the waves with white lace, marked the edge of the continent. To the right Point Lobos cut into the water, with the village of Carmel visible beyond. This was a view from the opposite side from the Carmel beach. On the left, where the land curved around the water like an enclosing arm, she could see again the long ridges of the Santa Lucia Mountains.

The two behind her were silent now, and Ruth wheeled her chair closer to Kelsey. "There's a path down there near a stream that runs through the woods to the sea. Dogs who've belonged to this house are buried down there in a small enclosed space. And you'll find a little marble statue hidden among the trees. There's even a gate and some green steps—though we don't know why, because they lead nowhere. You'll enjoy exploring, Kelsey, but stick to the path and watch out for poison oak."

"I'll walk down when I have time," Kelsey said.

Ruth looked up at her brother, her lips suddenly trembling. Tears came into her eyes and rolled down her cheeks. It was part of her weakness that she cried so easily. At once Denis dropped to his knees beside her chair and pressed his cheek against hers. The ice jam had broken, and Kelsey was no longer needed for moral support. She slipped away and neither brother nor sister seemed to notice her going.

She thought of what Denis had said about evil. The General had probably left his indelible stamp on both of them, and made their lives difficult enough without this further blight that had been set upon them. Perhaps those wicked little beads were just the sort of thing that would have appealed to him. Though why they'd been placed on Denis's desk now she couldn't guess.

Ginnie Soong met her at the door of Jody's room. "I'm glad

you'll be in the house now, Kelsey. I'm so busy with Jody's physical needs that there's never enough time for anything else. So you can help a lot. Right now he's sleeping. He's had a pretty exciting day, so we'd better let him rest for a while. Why don't you get settled in your room and come back in a couple of hours?"

That was fine with her, and Kelsey found Hana waiting in the hall to show her upstairs. Her room was big and comfortable. Windows seemed to let in the outdoors, and again there was a small balcony, its painted white floor strewn with pine needles.

"They get into everything," Hana said. "Somebody's always sweeping them away, but they blow in again with every breeze. I love it here—it's so beautiful. You should see the woods in springtime. The hill along the stream is white with calla lilies, and there are wildflowers everywhere."

"Where are you from, Hana?" Kelsey asked.

"I grew up around here. I'm saving to put myself through school, and Mr. Hammond says he'll help. Someday I'm going to open my own Japanese restaurant in Carmel."

"I think you will," Kelsey said, glad of Hana's friendly presence in a house that sometimes showed its hostility.

"I just hope the peanut shells won't bother you," Hana said from the doorway.

"Peanut shells?"

"This is the haunted room. Of course there has to be a haunted room, doesn't there? A gentleman ghost who eats peanuts visits this one, and he leaves shells around on the floor. So don't mind if you find them."

"I hope I will," Kelsey said. A peanut-eating ghost seemed rather pleasant to have around.

When Hana had gone, Kelsey moved about the room, getting used to it. There was an enormous old-fashioned walnut bed with a heavily carved headboard, the bed covered by a green and white patchwork quilt. On a bureau, dark with more carving, sat a small lamp with a china globe strewn with pink and green flowers. It had been an oil lamp originally, for a chimney rose above the globe, but now it shed an electric yellow glow.

Kelsey hung up the few things she'd brought in the big wardrobe, and set her toilet articles in the adjoining bathroom. She already liked what might be a welcome retreat in this house. The scene out the window, curving shoreline, blue water, and green trees, would always hold her. She was already discovering that the time of day and state of weather could paint different scenes. That this was also a house of turmoil and pain could be shut away to some extent up here.

Since there was time before she returned to Jody, perhaps she could do as Ruth had suggested and explore the hillside below the house. She put on low-heeled shoes and went in search of a lower door.

One opened near Tyler Hammond's workroom. Since she had no wish to see him, she walked past quickly and found stone steps that led down to a springy carpet of pine needles. Now she could hear the sound of the stream, and remembering Ruth's warning about poison oak, she found her way cautiously to its rocky bank. There she stood for a few minutes watching the hypnotic movement of water swirling over wet stones as it plunged toward its goal of the ocean.

The path was at hand and she started down through the woods, sliding now and then on loose needles, and coming at last to a fallen giant of a tree across her way. When she'd climbed over, she sat for a while on the rough trunk, sensing the hush around her. There were no human sounds, except for a distant car now and then. Birds sang in high branches, seemingly miles away up there against the sky. A squirrel darted out to look at her, and then hid himself behind a pile of wood someone had been chopping. In the distance she could hear the curious barking of sea lions.

The time for renewing herself had come. She used her favorite method and closed her eyes, let everything turn gray behind her lids, waiting for whatever pictures might come. Almost at once, she was walking on the Carmel beach again, hearing the sound of bagpipes—faint in her mind, and no longer shrill—watching the piper come out of the mist and walk slowly past her. It was healing to experience again that moment on the beach when she'd been able to let all unhappiness flow away from her, and just *be*.

High sunlight slanted through the trees in bands of gold, warming the shady portions of the grove. She raised her face to the warmth and felt a stinging spatter on her cheeks. A breeze had touched branches overhead, scattering needles like beads across the brown carpet.

She was quiet, completely relaxed, waiting for whatever might come. Whatever thought, whatever feeling. The thought that emerged was strange, unexpected, and not of her choosing. Pine needles scattered like *beads*. . . . Recent memory flashed a scene before her closed eyes, flashed a picture. And an answer was there—though it wasn't a question that had seemed urgent. She knew now where she had seen a strand of black beads—only the day before.

In Marisa Marsh's studio there had been a portrait of that woman with the large eyes and pointed chin. Francesca Fallon had worn a full chain of black beads in Marisa's picture—the woman no one seemed to have liked, and whom someone had hated enough to kill. Of course the tiny carved faces hadn't been visible in the photograph, but Kelsey felt sure they were the same beads. Now new questions replaced the old. When had the strand broken, why had three beads been placed on Denis's desk, seeming to disturb him so thoroughly? Where was the rest of the strand, and why had Denis thought immediately of Tyler. There were no answers, and she rose from the fallen tree to wander farther down the hillside.

She came quickly upon the small headstones that marked the enclosure where pet dogs had been buried over the years. This brought another idea. A pet would be good therapy for Jody, and she wondered if he'd ever had a dog. She would ask Tyler.

Below the small white stones, crudely painted with the names children had given their pets, she found a flight of wooden steps leading to the gate that led nowhere. The sound of the ocean seemed closer now, and if she went clear down the slope, she would come eventually to the beach. But then there would be a long climb back to the house. So, instead of going on, she turned and looked up at La Casa de la Sombra crowning its portion of the hill directly above. Across the road that she couldn't see from here rose the even steeper hills of Carmel Highlands, and higher roofs.

Red tiles and steel-blue walls stood out among the green of pines. There were many windows across this face that looked toward the ocean, some decorated with little red awnings that matched the tiles. She could locate Ruth's room, and Tyler's study on the floor below. She even found her own window along the upper hallway. All the balconies were empty now, but at one of the windows of Ruth's room Dora Langford once more stood watching. So she had come home and was again giving herself to this strange activity directed at Kelsey. Why this intense interest in everything she did? Kelsey wondered. She must talk to Dora Langford and get behind this watchfulness that began to seem disturbing.

Where the hill was steep, Kelsey had to pull herself along by means of small bushes, avoiding anything that looked like poison oak. Once undergrowth parted when she pulled at it, and she glimpsed something white almost hidden by small pines growing haphazardly around what must once have stood free.

She went around concealing brush and found the little marble statue Ruth had mentioned. It was perhaps a fourth life size—old, weathered marble, with bits broken away, the wounds no longer fresh. Two small children stood together, naked and innocent. The girl was smaller, and frightened. The boy had his arm about her, protecting her from harm. For Kelsey this was an unexpected delight to come upon half-hidden on this hillside. It was too bad that no one cared enough anymore to keep the growth cut away, so it could stand in the open to be enjoyed.

She went on, and by the time she reached the rear steps of the house, Dora had disappeared from the upper window. Kelsey knew what she wanted to do before she returned to Jody's room. Too many questions were churning inside her, and there was one place where she might find answers.

Inside, she made her way to the front hall, where she'd seen a telephone. Marisa's number was in the notebook in her pocket, and she dialed it quickly. When Marisa answered, Kelsey said, "I need to talk with you again, please. So many things have happened just since breakfast this morning. May I take you to lunch tomorrow? Somewhere quiet where we can talk?"

"I'd like that, and I know just the place." Marisa sounded calm and sure. "You haven't been out in Carmel Valley yet, have you? It's beautiful, and we can drive a bit, if you're free."

"I'd love that," Kelsey said. "I can get away when Jody is resting."

"Good. Jane Norman has agreed to come tomorrow. I'll call Tyler and let him know."

When she'd hung up, Kelsey went to Jody's room and found him dressed and in his chair again. Ginnie's smile told her that all was well for now.

"Hi, Jody," she said, and he managed a sound that might

have been a greeting. She sat in a chair beside him, while Ginnie made up the bed, and began to talk to him.

"This morning I saw Marisa Marsh. I wonder if you call her Grandma. We'll have to work on that. I had breakfast with her, and I know how much she wants to help you and see you get well."

Jody made a grunting sound, and she knew he was listening intently. How long his attention span might be was still a question.

"Marisa has asked a friend who is a doctor to come to see you tomorrow. Dr. Jane Norman has been working in research on the sort of trouble you're having now, Jody. She'll have some ideas that will help you. This is something you can look forward to, and I hope you'll help her when she comes."

Jody seemed to listen, and his eyes had begun to follow Kelsey when she moved. Sometimes stimulation, an awakening of interest could make a difference. She went through several exercises with him, and he really tried to cooperate. Eye tests weren't very successful, since he couldn't respond clearly as yet. He seemed to look, but who could tell what he saw? The hearing tests were clear enough. Any sudden sound made him jump, and he now turned his head slightly toward whoever spoke to him if that person spoke clearly and strongly. He paid no attention to softer sounds.

When Kelsey had explained what she and Ginnie would do next, and how Jody could help, she unstrapped him from his chair, and between them they held him on his feet. Jody moaned, since any movement alarmed him, promising pain, but Kelsey soothed and reassured.

Ginnie had been getting him on his feet once a day, but it was hard to do alone. Now they would try this oftener so they could accustom him to taking a little weight again. This was the only way that his feet could be saved from the terrible dropping that would freeze the whole foot into a position where the toe pointed permanently, and he could never stand.

When they'd held him for a minute or so, they stretched him out on his bed, and Kelsey went through a more elaborate series of range-of-motion exercises. This was always painful to muscles unused to doing their proper work, so this was a struggle, accompanied by sounds of protest, and sometimes tears. But it had to be done. To help a little, Ginnie worked to distract him, turning on the tape recorder to music Jody had liked, and even dancing a bit so he would watch her as Kelsey moved his arms and legs.

When he was in his chair again, Kelsey fed him a spoonful of water, and he swallowed it without difficulty. Even though nourishment was being given through a nose tube, he must learn to take food and liquid in his mouth, learn how to chew and swallow solid food again. First, they would start with baby food.

Ginnie brought a dish of apple sauce from the adjacent kitchen, and Kelsey put a little in his mouth. He promptly spit it out and made a face. Anything would taste awful to him at first, but Kelsey coaxed him and tried again.

"You do want to eat properly, Jody, and get rid of that tube. It's not comfortable, and it's a nuisance, but until you start eating, it has to stay in. So you'll just have to put up with the bad taste. After you've tried for a little while, everything will taste right again, and you'll be hungry. Remember how much you liked to eat, Jody? Now see if you can try this apple sauce again. Chew it a little and swallow it. Don't spit it out."

He wanted to please her, and though he made a face, he kept the bit of apple sauce in his mouth and actually swallowed it. That called for enthusiasm from Ginnie and Kelsey. They didn't push him any further, but stopped for lunch and gave him a rest. Then, for the rest of the afternoon, Kelsey tried alternating exercises and distractions, with times of rest, and the day passed with a reasonable feeling of progress, however slow.

Near dinner time, Hana came with word from Tyler. "Mr. Hammond would like you both to have dinner with him tonight. When the night nurse comes, please join him in the small dining room. In about half an hour."

Kelsey hurried upstairs to change. Just as she reached the door of her room, she heard a telephone ringing. The phone sat on a small table down the hall, where she hadn't noticed it before. No one seemed to be answering so she picked it up and said, "Hello?" No one spoke on the line.

The silence had the sound of someone waiting. A crank call *here?* She spoke again, and this time a voice that had been deliberately lowered to a hoarsened level answered, "Don't ask so many questions. It's bad for the health."

The caller hung up, and Kelsey put the phone down with a thump. That hadn't sounded like some unknown crank caller. It had come from someone who had recognized her voice. This was unsettling, and she would ask Tyler about it at dinner. There'd been no telling whether a man or woman had been on the phone. It was difficult to imagine the person who would do this. Not Tyler, or Ruth, or Denis, if he were still in the house. Certainly not Ginnie. Dora seemed unlikely, in spite of her watchfulness.

As she dressed, Kelsey tried to throw off her uneasiness. The one dress she'd brought was a wheat-colored silk with a rose suede belt. A string of rose and white onyx beads that she clasped about her neck made her think again of the three black beads she'd seen on Denis's desk. But that particular question would have to wait until tomorrow when she saw Marisa Marsh.

Of course those unexpected words on the phone might

mean that she was getting too close for someone's comfort. But comfort for what? If she knew anything dangerous, or was about to find out anything, she had no idea what it could be. Or what questions she was supposed to stop asking.

XI

WHEN Kelsey went downstairs to Jody's room, the night nurse had arrived, and Ginnie was ready. She hadn't changed from her uniform since she kept no other clothes here.

"Jody just threw up the water and apple sauce," she said. "Though that little bit shouldn't have upset him."

"Maybe it didn't. I think he's worried about something." Kelsey sat beside Jody's chair and took his hand. His eyes seemed to widen, and the spastic stiffness increased. There was something he wanted very much to put into words.

"I know you want to talk, Jody," Kelsey said. "And you will. Just give yourself time."

He blinked rapidly.

"Is it about the accident? Nobody blames you, Jody. Everything's all right."

He merely stared at her fixedly, and she couldn't tell whether she had comforted him or not.

"Did Ginnie tell you that we're invited to have dinner with your father tonight? I put on the only dress I brought with me. How do I look? Do you approve?"

At least he was easily distracted, and he managed his quivery smile. Then he opened his mouth, drew in a breath, and blew out a word. It sounded like "Hi," and Ginnie laughed.

"That's good, Jody," she told him. "You remembered what Hana taught you. Kelsey, he isn't saying 'hi' in a greeting. The Japanese word for 'yes' is *'hai.'* It's an easier word for him than saying yes."

Jody blew out another *"hai"* in agreement, and Kelsey hugged him.

The night nurse, Mabel Smith, was pleasant and middle-aged, and she seemed fond of Jody. When Ginnie had reported his latest successes—and failures—she led the way to the living room and its adjacent dining area.

"There's another dining room that's practically baronial," Ginnie said, "but it isn't used these days since there are no dinner parties. I remember Ruth told me once that this was a house that loved people. But I expect that depends on who is living in it. I don't think it's true anymore. I don't think there are many lovable people left here now."

She was probably right, though this was the first time Ginnie had made a critical comment.

An oval table had been set before big arched windows that looked out above pine trees toward the sunset. The reflected light brightened linen tablecloth and napkins. The silverware and dinner china gave a formal touch, and there were silver candlesticks and a crystal bowl of chrysanthemums.

Tyler hadn't appeared, but Hana hovered anxiously. "I made it look special," she said.

"It's lovely," Ginnie approved, and went on to tell her that Jody had produced the word she'd taught him. When Hana went off, pleased and happy, Kelsey and Ginnie stepped outside on the white balcony where Ruth had sat earlier. They watched the sky and waited for Tyler.

"Except for the cook, is Hana all the staff there is?" Kelsey asked. "How can she do it all?"

"She doesn't. Outside help comes in a couple of times a week and takes care of scrubbing and cleaning. Hardly anyone has big staffs these days. Help is too hard to find, and there are companies whose services can be hired. Besides, Tyler hates to have extra people around. Dora usually eats upstairs with Ruth, since Ruth doesn't come down for meals. Whoever happens to be free carries trays up and brings them down again. Sometimes Dora, sometimes Hana, or even Tyler. Denis took their lunch up today, and I expect he'll take up dinner, since he's still here. It would be a lot easier if Ruth would let herself be brought downstairs."

Out on the water, a yacht in full sail was gliding past, white against rosy orange and the delft blue of low clouds. But Kelsey's thoughts were far from the sunset sky, and she couldn't stop asking questions.

"Ginnie, I keep feeling that so much more than the accident is troubling everyone in this house. What is it?"

Ginnie was plainly upset by the question. "Please leave it alone, Kelsey. Just concentrate on Jody. That's all you're here for."

"Why am I always put off—told to leave everything alone? Maybe this albatross, whatever it is, makes for so unhappy an atmosphere that Jody can't mend. If that's it, he'll keep slipping back."

Tyler joined them on the balcony to stand between the two women, looking out toward Point Lobos, where the rocky headland thrust into the water. The very existence of that "Point of the Sea Wolves" must be a constant reminder to everyone in the house.

"I walked down through the woods this afternoon," Kelsey told him. "I found the green gate and steps your wife mentioned to me, and the little marble statue. What a shame that it's hidden in brush where no one can see it."

Tyler wore his usual repressive manner. The statue didn't interest him, and he gestured them inside to the table. This probably wouldn't be a cheerful meal. She must wait for the right moment to bring up the matter of the phone call. Hana turned herself into the perfect, unobtrusive waitress, serving them with a grace that was practically an art form. Once when she caught Kelsey watching her, she lowered one eyelid in a wink that no one else saw. She would do fine with her restaurant.

Shrimp and sea scallops were fresh and perfectly broiled. The salad greens were also California fresh, and the Roquefort dressing homemade. Vegetables, lightly steamed, had been seasoned with herbs. Mrs. Preston, the cook, had a talent, and was apparently enjoying a company meal for a change. The guests, however, ate with very little enjoyment because the man at the head of the table seemed so far away, so uninterested in either the food on his plate or his two guests. Why in the world had he invited them to dinner in the first place? Kelsey wondered.

Since no one else was going to talk, she broke the silence rebelliously. "Would you like to hear the latest report I can make on Jody, Mr. Hammond?"

He seemed to drift back from some distant place, looking a bit startled, as though he'd forgotten they were there.

"All right—tell me," he said.

She went through an account of the exercises she'd done with Jody, and described the way they'd stood him on his feet for longer than usual, and without too much protesting. Jody had listened with interest to a story, and he'd swallowed some water and apple sauce by mouth. Unfortunately, she had to relate the aftermath as well.

"That's risky." Tyler was negative as usual. "He might choke. You shouldn't take that chance."

"But he has to learn!" Kelsey cried. "He *is* teachable, you know. And I don't think it was entirely the food that upset him. I have the feeling that something is worrying him. If that's so, it must be awful not to be able to tell anyone what it is. Can *you* eat when you're unhappy."

His smile was grim. "Don't we all do that?"

"Well, Jody can't. He's a frightened little boy, closed in behind a wall he can't climb and doesn't understand. Who would? He needs to believe he can get over that wall and change everything for himself. He needs to have something hopeful happen every day. When he can talk again, I think everything will be better."

"You're always so sure, Mrs. Stewart. Sure that he'll eat, talk —I suppose even walk. I wish I could share your confidence."

Ginnie had known him for a long while, and she broke in frankly, "You're part of the problem, Tyler, and you'd better see that. You can't glower at Jody and expect him to be happy. Maybe *you* have to snap out of it first. I understand what you're feeling, but—"

"You couldn't possibly understand!" He looked so exasperated that for a moment Kelsey thought he might throw down his napkin and leave the table. Then, to her surprise, he laughed. "Just the same, you may be right, Ginnie. I can see you're both against me, so I'll try to put on a better face with Jody. Okay?"

Ginnie smiled back at him, and some of the clouds lifted.

This seemed a good moment for Kelsey to make a suggestion. "You're a filmmaker—so why not record Jody's progress from day to day, even if it's small? This would show you what may happen."

Tyler looked so doubtful that she went quickly to another matter.

"Mr. Hammond, we haven't talked about what hours you'd like me to work. Jody will need to rest in between whatever we do. Do you mind if I go to lunch with Marisa Marsh tomorrow?"

"That's fine. You're not tied to any regular hours. Play it by ear. This is all experimental anyway. Just so you're here at night in case he needs to be calmed down. You seem good at that. The night nurses change, and he may want someone here whom he knows when things go wrong."

"Of course I'll come down whenever I'm needed," Kelsey said. "But if it's the middle of the night, who will let me know?"

"There's a phone in the hall near your room that can be used as an intercom," Tyler said.

"A house phone?" Kelsey repeated carefully.

"It can be used for outside as well. Why do you sound surprised?"

"Someone called me a little while ago on that phone in the hall. Anonymously. A disguised voice that told me not to ask so many questions."

Tyler stared at her. "What did you say to this person?"

"I didn't have a chance to say anything. Whoever it was hung up right away."

"Do you know anything about this, Ginnie?" Tyler asked. She shook her head. "How should I?"

"I'll look into it," Tyler said.

"Why should anyone worry about questions *I* might ask?"

He was beginning to look aggravated again. "I've said I'd look into it. In the meantime, you'd better curb your curiosity."

Kelsey flushed, but it was pointless to defend herself. Let him think what he liked.

"Now," he said, "I'd like to know from you both whatever

suggestions you may have for helping Jody. You've told me some of what you're doing, but there must be more."

If this was the reason for inviting them to dinner, it was fine, and it gave Kelsey an opening she wanted. "When I walked down through the woods, I came to the little dog cemetery down there. Children who've lived in this house must have had a number of dogs. Has Jody ever had one?"

"His mother doesn't like them," Tyler said. "So it hasn't seemed wise."

Kelsey persisted. "It might mean a lot to Jody."

Ginnie spoke gently. "Tyler and I both know what happened. When Ruth was a little girl, her father brought home a big brute of a police dog. *His* kind of dog. From the first, Ruth was terrified of that animal, and her very fright got her into trouble because fear was the one thing the General could never stand in his own children. She tried to make friends with the dog, but the animal knew she was afraid, and when he jumped at her, Denis tried to intervene. So the dog bit them both. Ruth on the hand, and Denis on the arm. Denis got over it, and Ruth didn't. Their father shot the dog then and there, and the whole episode was traumatic for both children. Ruth has never stopped being afraid of dogs."

The General again. He sounded a thoroughly terrible man. But under the circumstances of Jody's need, she had to try once more.

"This could be a little dog. The size that could lie across Jody's knees. He could be kept out of your wife's sight, and he might be very good for Jody. They're doing more and more therapy with pets these days in all sorts of situations. He might even accept discomfort in order to touch a dog that would be his very own. He'd want to feed him, pet him."

"I'll think about it," Tyler said. "I don't want to add to Ruth's unhappiness right now. Besides, who's going to look after a dog—feed it, walk it, keep it happy—when Jody can't?"

"Maybe we could all pitch in," Ginnie said. "He needs a friendly little dog who wants to love and be loved. That shouldn't upset Ruth."

Hana removed their plates and served the pecan pie Mrs. Preston had baked for dessert.

Once more, Tyler seemed to retreat into his own distant place where he was unaware of the presence of others. When they'd finished, Ginnie excused herself and left for her apartment in Monterey—perhaps to give Kelsey a chance to talk to Tyler alone.

When she'd gone, he seemed to return. "You appear to have made friends with Marisa Marsh, Kelsey. She called me today to say that Dr. Norman is coming. Marisa likes you."

"I hope she does."

"What do you talk about?"

"With Marisa, I like to listen, as well as talk."

"You're evading the question. Anyway, she thinks I should pay attention to what you advise."

"I'm grateful if she feels that way."

But there was more on his mind, and when he spoke again his tone had hardened. "She says you want to hear the tape she made of my interview with Francesca Fallon. Why?"

"It sounded interesting."

"It wasn't. It came closer to being a brawl. I told Marisa not to bother playing it for you."

"Why did you do the interview if you didn't like Mrs. Fallon?"

"Maybe your anonymous caller was right. Maybe you do ask too many questions."

"I'm sorry." She dropped the subject quickly. "It must have been interesting growing up in Marisa's care. She's involved in so many things."

"She kept me going when I needed somebody," Tyler said.

"The way Jody needs you now."

At once the look of not-so-distant thunder was back. One of these days, the lightning would strike, and she'd be out of the house again, but, no matter what, there was one more thing she had to say. She managed to speak quietly.

"Your son is alive, Mr. Hammond."

He looked shocked, perhaps even ashamed. "I'm sorry, Kelsey." Obviously he wanted to say more—and could find no words. "Good night," he told her as they left the table, and went quickly out of the room.

In a way he was like Jody—living too much inside himself. Except that Jody wanted out, and she wasn't sure Tyler did. He'd built his own protective cover—though from what she couldn't tell. There was more troubling him than the terrible happening of two months ago. His marriage to Ruth? Yet he always seemed concerned for her, and considerate.

Before she went upstairs, Kelsey looked in on the boy again, and since everything was fine, she didn't stay.

The phone down the hall was silent as she opened her bedroom door, though she glanced at it uneasily.

Right now she needed distraction, and she regretted that she'd brought no books with her to read. Nor did she feel like writing to anyone. She had sent her parents a note when she arrived, and she would write again soon. But not now. They had their own quiet lives, somewhat removed from the real world, and they had a right to that. The painful troubles their daughter had experienced had hurt them deeply and it was kinder to let them alone. They were relieved that she was supposedly living safely with Elaine, and that was enough for now.

When someone tapped on her door, she opened it to find Denis. His smile seemed genuine this time, and not put on as a front. When she invited him in, he surprised her by enveloping her in a hug, and whirling her about the room.

"You've stirred up my sister, Kelsey," he said, as he dropped into a chair, laughing. "Maybe she'll try a little more now. Though she still has the idea that she'll never walk again. If Dora can at least get her into her wheelchair, as she did today, it will be something. She's even thinking more positively about Jody. I only wish—" He broke off and left the thought unfinished.

"Tyler's the obstacle, isn't he?" Kelsey asked.

"It's always Tyler. Did you ask him about those beads I found on my desk?"

"I never thought of it, and I wouldn't have asked anyway. I don't even know why you think he put them there."

"Because he's the one who had them."

"At least I've remembered where I saw such beads before, Denis. It was in Marisa's studio—in that photograph of Francesca Fallon. She was wearing a long strand of black beads in that picture. Are they the same ones?"

"Ask Marisa sometime. She knows."

Clearly he didn't want to talk further about the beads. "I'm meeting Marisa for lunch tomorrow," she told Denis. "She said we'd drive into the Valley."

"That sounds good. I always feel better about everything after a visit with Marisa. At least most of the time."

She caught the hint of reservation, but let it go. Whatever had happened in Ruth's room seemed to have relieved some of Denis's own worry, so that he was willing to sit quietly and listen.

Kelsey told him about the phone call she'd answered, but he looked more puzzled than disturbed.

"I don't know who it could have been, Kelsey. It wouldn't be Ruth, or Dora, or Ginnie. Or me."

"You mean that leaves Tyler?"

"Who knows? He's not the most open person in the world. And he can do some pretty strange things."

"But there'd be no reason. If he wanted to warn me about

anything, he'd tell me straight out. And I've come here at his request." She couldn't even consider Tyler.

Denis stood up. "I wanted to let you know that everything is fine now between Ruth and me. So I'd better get back, since I'm on duty at the inn tonight. I don't want to push Elaine too far by being late."

As she came to the door with him, the phone rang again. Denis looked at her, and then went quickly to answer it. After a moment of asking who was there, he just put the phone down.

"Whoever was on didn't want me, Kelsey. Maybe you'd better not answer after this."

At least it wasn't Denis who was doing this. "I have to," she said. "I might be needed with Jody."

For a moment longer he stood looking at her. Then he touched her cheek affectionately. "I'm sorry if this has upset you, but it probably doesn't mean much. Just lock your door at night, Kelsey. I'll see you."

His walk was almost jaunty as he went off down the hall, and now the phone stayed silent.

The need for something to read was still strong. Tomorrow she must certainly see if there was a library in the house. If not, there'd been books on the shelves in Tyler's study, and she would find something to read there.

Though it was still early, she got ready for bed. The day had been long and emotionally strenuous, so perhaps she could fall asleep. It seemed the right choice, and she slept almost as soon as her head touched the pillow.

At two in the morning, by the small clock on her bedtable, she came wide awake, feeling much too tense and wakeful. Early morning hours were always the worst. These were the mournful hours when all her sorrows were her own. Missing Mark. Always that sudden stab of pain; thoughts of the husband who hadn't cared enough to give her his support; the emptiness of her personal life—all these were churning in her now, with no way to make the hurting stop. In the daytime, Jody's needs could absorb her, but in these night hours she was totally at the mercy of her own thoughts.

When she could bear it no longer, she got up, put on a robe, and went to stand on the balcony, looking out over dark tree-tops toward water that shone like rippling satin under the stars. A few lights gleamed here and there, but most of the area toward Carmel lay asleep. The quiet was intense, broken only by the occasional hooting of an owl, and the sound of an ocean that never slept.

Closer among the trees, something caught her eye—a flash-light moved on the dark hillside below the house. Was Tyler up at this hour wandering about, as unable to sleep as she was? She went back inside and made up her mind. Books were as important as food, and somewhere in this house she'd find something to read. She couldn't endure her own thoughts, and she couldn't sleep. Nor could she make plans for Jody in her present state.

She took her small flashlight with her into the hall. One light burned near the stairs. Otherwise, everything was dark and still. The far door to Ruth's room was closed, and she had no idea where Tyler slept. Using her light and moving softly, she found the stairs and went down into the living room that seemed to stretch into a black, empty cave.

When she shone the flashlight around, paintings on the walls stared at her briefly, and disappeared as the beam moved on. The balcony door was closed, and the room felt clammy. She suspected it would echo with its own voice if she stumbled into furniture. There seemed to be no bookshelves here, and it was probably a room no longer used very much. However, if there was a library, it ought to be close by.

Her light picked out a door that stood open to the right of the big fireplace. Cautiously, she crossed the room, avoiding chairs, and turned the beam inside. The light spotted book-shelves, and she stood in the doorway for a moment, seeking a light switch. A small rustling sound reached her.

"Is anyone here?" she asked. The living room behind her threw her voice against its walls, but there was no further sound in the quiet library.

A window stood open, and the rustle could have come from trees outdoors. She found the switch and turned off her flash-light as she started down the room. It was probably half the size of the living room, but still large, and filled satisfyingly with bookshelves.

Another time she would explore titles and learn what was here. For now, she chose a shelf at random, and found a row of old novels, smiling as she pulled down a well-worn copy of *The Prisoner of Zenda*. She hadn't read Anthony Hope's old chest-nut since she was twelve. The adventures of Rudolf Rasendyll seemed exactly right—another place and time, pure escape, was what she needed.

She turned to leave with her prize and saw the woman who sat curled into a great wing chair. The back of the chair had hidden Ruth Hammond as Kelsey walked into the room. No wheelchair stood nearby, and it was unlikely that she'd been carried here and left alone. Shock held Kelsey dead still, and as they stared at each other, she saw the challenge in the very set of Ruth's head, yet at the same time an uncertainty in her eyes.

"So now you know," Ruth said. "What are you going to do about it?"

Kelsey had no idea what she was going to do. Obviously, Ruth had been living a lie. Her presence in this room at this hour could mean only one thing—that she could walk, and that this further misery that had been thrust upon her husband was needless. Unexpectedly, a sudden warm sympathy for Tyler—a feeling she hadn't experienced as strongly as this since Tor

House—rushed through Kelsey. As though some floodgate had opened and let in something she couldn't welcome.

Ruth watched her sadly. "I can see what you'll do. Tyler has that effect on women, so now you'll condemn me without a hearing."

"I don't want to condemn anyone," Kelsey said, trying to recover her own composure. "I'd like to sit down and talk a little."

"It's time," Ruth said. "Pull over a chair."

Kelsey drew a leather chair to where Ruth sat wrapped in her fleecy white robe, and sat down, still shaken, not only by what she'd discovered about Ruth, but even more because of the flash of warm emotion she'd felt toward Tyler. And must not experience—not to this extent!

"So what shall we talk about?" Ruth's tone held mockery again, though Kelsey sensed that this might be a shield, and that a terrible insecurity might exist underneath.

"We needn't talk at all, unless you want to," she said.

Ruth uncurled her legs and stretched them out in front of her, slippers dangling from her toes. Then she stood up, stretched her arms over her head, and moved easily about the room, to come to a halt in front of Kelsey.

"As you can see, there's nothing wrong with either my back or my legs—as of course the doctors have told me all along. As soon as I'd recovered a bit, I made Dora help me out of bed when no one was around. I didn't want to become weak and helpless—I needed my strength to fight with. Though to *seem* helpless has been a necessary protection. I exercise in my room, with Dora on guard. Sometimes I roam around the house in the middle of the night. When the nurse wasn't looking I've stood in Jody's doorway watching him sleep. It's better to stay quiet during the day and pretend to be weak and ill, while I move about at night. I heard you on the stairs just now, and turned out the light, hoping you'd go away."

"Why?" Kelsey asked. Her wave of revulsion toward Ruth's pretense and her strong sympathy for Tyler had both subsided a little.

The quiet of the library, the waiting, grew long. Then Ruth threw off her guard. "Because I'm afraid of what Tyler will do if he knows I'm well! You haven't any idea of the fury that can take hold of him. Do you think my husband really wants Jody to get well? Do you? Though he would like *me* to be well again. Then he could get the divorce he's threatened me with. This way I'm dependent on him for everything, and he can't walk out."

Ruth's words were devastating in their sad bitterness. She flung herself into the big chair and burst into tears. The wildness of her weeping was frightening, but it was better to sit quietly and let Ruth cry herself out. Besides, Kelsey needed time to get over her own shock and dismay. She remembered all too well the vulnerability and innocence of Marisa's portrait of Ruth. Innocence was gone, but the vulnerability was there, and with it the danger of emotional damage. Who was acting the greater lie—Ruth or Tyler?

Such a freshet of tears couldn't last for long, however, and in a little while Ruth sat up, wiping her eyes. "All right," she said, once more mockingly defiant, "are you going to tell him? Of course it's your duty to report to the man who hired you."

"My concern is for Jody," Kelsey told her quietly, trying to reassure herself as well. "I'd like to do whatever is best for him."

Big gray eyes considered her for a moment. "Yes. And I thank you for that. I wish I could explain. I wish I could tell you all that's happened, but some of it would only sound as though I were defending myself. It wouldn't serve any purpose to start pointing fingers of blame."

Kelsey's first condemnation of Ruth had weakened a little. "I could help Jody more if I understood what is troubling him."

"Do you mean he can really remember what happened?"

"We don't know yet how much he remembers. But the signs are hopeful."

"Tyler told me this, but I didn't believe him. Now Denis is claiming the same thing. If it's true that his mind will come back, that's wonderful, Kelsey. This is why I wanted you in the house—so you could help Jody—and perhaps let me know directly. Tyler tells me what he pleases, and no more."

"There's a long way to go," Kelsey said carefully. She wanted to offer Jody's mother hope, yet there was always the danger of expecting too much too soon, and then being destroyed by repeated disappointment. A difficult line to walk. "We can't be sure how far Jody can be brought, since the damage was serious. That's why I thought it might help if I knew a little more about what's worrying him. Something is. Sometimes it seems to surface when your husband is near."

"I'd expect that. If Jody is at all aware, he must sense the blame Tyler feels toward him. Anyway, Kelsey, it's better if you don't get too involved. Then no one will try to harm you."

A strange thing to say. "What if someone is already trying?" Kelsey asked, and told her about the ringing telephone near her room.

Ruth curled up again into a small, defensive knot. "Don't tell me any more! I can't bear it—I don't want to know!"

"You know who was on the phone?"

"I don't even want to guess. Just be careful, Kelsey. You're dealing with monsters. *I* know monsters—my father was one. So don't be fooled by disguises."

"Including your disguise."

"Mine's gone, as far as you're concerned—and I can't blame you for judging me."

"I don't want to judge anyone."

Ruth spoke more quietly, a little wistful. "Maybe you're the one person in this house who doesn't need a disguise. And you've been good to my brother. Denis is the real innocent, Kelsey, and he leads with his chin most of the time. So someone is always clipping him. He likes you, and he thinks you can work a miracle with Jody."

"But you don't believe in miracles?"

"I lost that ability when I was pretty young. The General taught me about grim reality. He thought he was arming Denis and me, but sometimes I wonder. Maybe I turned out to be the foolish one. Denis is gentle—and good."

She covered her face with her hands, and Kelsey was afraid she might cry again. However, when she raised her head after a moment, though she looked sad, there were no more tears. She seemed to make an effort to thrust ugly thoughts behind her and speak of the inconsequential.

"What will you do with yourself, Kelsey, when you're not with Jody?"

"I expect to read a few books." Kelsey held up the copy of *Zenda*, and Ruth almost smiled. "And I'll explore a bit around Carmel. Marisa Marsh and I are having lunch together tomorrow, and she's driving me into the Valley."

This seemed to startle Ruth. "Do you like Marisa?"

"I don't feel that I know her very well, but I find her interesting."

Ruth closed her eyes. "She means so much to Tyler that I've always wanted to trust her. But sometimes I'm not sure. Marisa never does anything without a purpose, so I wonder what she's up to with you tomorrow."

"I invited her to lunch."

"Of course she claims that it's her voices—or whatever—that tell her what to do. A bit weird, it seems to me."

"Denis says that she found you and Jody after you fell—that it was this instinct of hers that saved you."

"Anyway, that's the story. I suppose we should be grateful. But sometimes—when I think of Jody—I'm not."

Kelsey heard the desolation in her voice and spoke quickly. "He *will* improve."

"Improve isn't enough. Will he talk and laugh? Will he run and play and climb? Will he read books and play games and grow up to be a useful, happy man?"

No one could promise any of that, and Kelsey could feel Ruth's terrible pain as a mother. Pain she herself knew very well because her Mark would never do any of those wonderful things. She put away remembrance quickly, needing to be strong for another small boy.

"Can you take this one step at a time, Mrs. Hammond?" she pleaded. "Little things will seem remarkable if you don't look too far ahead. Perhaps all this really will happen in time. We don't know that it won't."

Ruth's guard seemed to lower, and she looked at Kelsey as though she saw her as a person for the first time.

"I know what happened to you," she said. "I admire you for behaving with a courage I don't have."

"I'm taking one step at a time. I'm glad your son has a good chance, Mrs. Hammond. Tomorrow Mrs. Marsh is bringing in a doctor friend, and she may be able to help Jody."

"Yes, Denis told me. I'll try to hope. Come and talk to me sometimes, Kelsey. I need a friend."

"Of course I will," Kelsey said.

With an effort, Ruth seemed to rouse herself. "Tell me what else you'll do to keep from going mad in this house. I know what it is to be bored crazy here. I knew it long before the accident. I could have been so happy—I thought I had everything I'd ever wanted. I was wrong."

"Jody will keep me busy most of the time," Kelsey said. "I like to walk, and today I went down through the woods, though not as far as the beach."

Ruth sighed. "It's so beautiful around here. I miss going out.

I used to love to take Jody on hikes. But now I might be seen, so I don't dare go out of the house on my own."

"I found the marble statue you told me about."

"I had it put there. My mother found the little marble girl and boy on one of her trips with my father. She brought it home from France, though I like to think its origin was Greece. Denis and I used to play around it when it stood in our patio in the desert. I always said the statue was *us*. Denis was my big brother in those days, and he always protected me when he could. Now I feel older, and I'm the one who has tried to protect him. Or used to."

"What do you need to protect him from?"

"From monsters, of course, Kelsey. You've already met them, but you're like Denis—you don't want to see."

"That's a pretty strong word. I've met sad people who are struggling with appalling problems, but I don't believe in monsters."

"You'd better start believing!"

It was hard to understand such bleakness, no matter how great the cause, and Kelsey had to prod. "How can you live like this? You shouldn't play this charade—life has so much more to give you. How long can you keep it from your husband that you can walk?"

"As long as necessary."

"Do you mean days, weeks, years? What sort of life will that be for you."

"Better than if he thought I was strong and able to take care of myself. Then he'd have no mercy. Dora wants to take me back to the desert. Then I could be out of the way since Tyler doesn't really want me around. I could seem to recover gradually. I do need to recover, Kelsey. Just because I can walk doesn't mean that I'm healed. But Tyler will never let Jody go. He can hardly bear the sight of him, though he'll spite me and keep him here. Watch over Jody, Kelsey. Help him." The fear in her voice had a deep and genuine ring.

"I'll do my best," Kelsey said.

Suddenly Ruth sat up, listening.

Someone was coming, hurrying on the stairs. There was no way for Ruth to escape, but it was only Dora who ran through the door.

"I thought I'd find you here!" She threw an alarmed look at Kelsey and then went on. "Tyler's been walking through the woods, and I've seen his flashlight coming back toward the house. If he sees lights on in the library, he'll come to investigate. And he's probably already seen them. So do move, Ruth —hurry!"

This was a new Dora, taking charge frantically. Ruth got out of her chair and started for the door.

Dora stopped her. "What about Mrs. Stewart?"

"She won't say anything," Ruth assured her mother.

Kelsey hadn't promised this, yet she knew that for now she was bound to silence. Telling Tyler the truth about his wife might really result in an explosion. It was hard to order her thoughts and choose a right course, so she must wait, at least a little while.

Dora had no time to dispute Ruth's confidence that Kelsey would keep still, and just before she hurried Ruth from the room, she looked back.

"Stay right where you are, Mrs. Stewart," she ordered. "Then if Tyler comes, there'll be a reason for lights in the library."

Dora seemed one of the unexpected pieces in this puzzle, inconsistent and contradictory in her actions. But Kelsey had no time for Dora now. She didn't want to face Tyler with this new knowledge about Ruth sharp in her mind. Or with the memory of that betraying warmth she'd experienced earlier. She'd been told all too often that she had a face that could never keep a secret, but now she must try. She returned to the shelves and took down another book to leaf through, while every bit of her tensed with listening. Perhaps he wouldn't notice the lights. Perhaps he'd just go upstairs to bed.

The house was so big that sounds at the other end couldn't be heard in this secluded room behind the fireplace. She didn't know whether Tyler had come in until she heard him crossing the living room. At once she pretended absorption in the pages of whatever book she'd picked from the shelf. When he stood in the doorway, the sounds stopped, and Kelsey knew he was watching her.

"So you're not sleeping either, Mrs. Stewart?" he asked.

She turned to look at him. He wore jeans again, with a pullover sweater, and his dark hair had been ruffled by the wind. The all too physical impact of this man struck her as it had before, but now she knew the danger—recognized her own lonely susceptibility.

"I woke up around two," she said quietly. "I can usually read myself to sleep. So I came downstairs to find some books. I'll go back to my room now."

"Considering that phone call, I wouldn't go wandering around the house at night," he said.

"I'll be sure to keep books in my room after this," she told him meekly, her one desire being to escape from his presence without betraying all she needed to hide.

He came toward her. "Let's see what books you've picked."

Reluctantly, Kelsey handed him *Zenda* and the book whose title she hadn't noticed.

"Good old Rudolf," he said. "But Lewis Carroll—*Through The Looking Glass?*"

"Sometimes I think that's where I've gone—through Alice's looking glass," she said desperately.

"What's troubling you, Mrs. Stewart? It's more than being sleepless, I think."

She hated to feel trapped, and tried once more to improvise. "Of course I'm troubled. I think of Jody all the time. I hope Marisa's Dr. Norman can make some helpful suggestions." All this was true, and safe enough ground.

He had come close to take the books from her, and he was so near that she could catch the scent of pine needles and leafy earth that clung to him from the woods. It was all she could manage to keep her hands from shaking as he returned the books. For a moment his own hands touched hers, and she shivered.

"You really do care, don't you, Kelsey? Jody matters to you."

He spoke with unexpected gentleness, and she looked straight into his eyes—a terrible mistake because she saw the hidden fires that burned there, and was afraid. Tyler himself might be the "gunpowder" that could explode if a spark were touched. If that happened, Kelsey Stewart might be the first one to be consumed by the conflagration.

She almost snatched the books from him and fled toward the door.

"Good night, Kelsey," he said behind her, and the very timbre of his voice made her shiver again.

She used her flashlight to find the stairs, and ran up them as though pursued. Yet she knew very well that the only immediate danger lay in her own starved emptiness. It was dangerous to long for arms around her—to want to be held and comforted, kissed by a man. *This* man. There could never be anything more with Tyler Hammond. Not when she thought of Ruth.

This time she remembered Denis's warning, and locked her bedroom door. For the rest of the night she neither slept nor read.

XII

SOMEHOW, in the morning, Kelsey pulled herself together, and was waiting in Jody's room when Marisa and Dr. Norman arrived together though in separate cars. Tyler was summoned, and at once Jody's room seemed full of people. Marisa wore her favorite color again in a turquoise blouse with a long white skirt trimmed with antique eyelet embroidery. Her gray hair hung down her back in a thick braid, and her eyes shone with quiet excitement. As usual, she exuded vitality, but today she sat in a corner out of the way, willing to watch and not participate.

Tyler remained a dark, skeptical presence near the door. After a first glance, Kelsey didn't look at him again. Her own reactions the night before were something she dared not think about. She only hoped, for Jody's sake, that Tyler would do nothing to interfere.

Dr. Norman was younger than she'd expected. Perhaps around Kelsey's own age. She looked slim and tanned, her short hair cropped close to her head, and Kelsey sensed the positive energy she seemed to radiate.

In spite of the fact that both Ginnie and Kelsey had tried to prepare Jody for Dr. Norman's visit, he had stiffened all over—a sign of anxiety and resistance. Once more, Kelsey wondered if it might be his father's presence that disturbed him more than the doctor's.

Jane Norman sat by his bed and began to talk to Jody quietly, explaining that she was going to try him with a few tests—nothing that would hurt him in the least. She used her stethoscope, examined the condition of the tube in his nose, asked Ginnie about various standard records she kept from day to day, and went through a general examination. Jody's eyes seemed to be tracking better when she tested them, and he could certainly hear her.

"Do you know what acupuncture is, Jody?" she asked when she'd finished her examination. "It's a treatment the Chinese have used for thousands of years, and we're finding that it may relieve some of that spastic stiffness you have. It's done with needles, but you'll feel hardly more than a prick. I would like to have someone come in three times a week for a while to give you treatments. Acupuncture is slow, but if it's given time it may help."

Jody made a face, and Dr. Norman patted his hand. "Good—you understand me, and you don't like needles. But this isn't as bad as you think. You want to get well, and you are the one who can help by not fighting what we want to do."

She looked at Ginnie and Kelsey and went on.

"I know you're exercising him, and Marisa tells me that you're using your hands, Kelsey. That's fine. Therapeutic touch is being taught now at Tufts University near Boston. And it's used at Walter Reed Hospital in Washington. I'm glad you're using it, too."

Tyler spoke from the doorway. *"What* is therapeutic touch?"

Dr. Norman smiled at him, unruffled by his tone. "We've

always known about healing done through what was called the laying on of hands. Now we're beginning to understand why it works. It's a way of directing healthy human energy—which we all have in an electric charge around our bodies—through our hands into those who are ill. Those who need help. Like your son, Mr. Hammond. Jody, it feels good, doesn't it, when Kelsey puts her hands on you?"

Jody said "Um" in agreement.

Dr. Norman warmed to her theme. "Everything's important—everything works together, as I've said. Synergistically. Sometimes in medicine we become stuck with our own pet therapy and close our minds to all the other things that are happening around the country. We need to put it all together because every patient is different, and we can never be sure what will work best until we try."

She spoke directly to Jody again.

"I want to give you some special vitamins and other nutrients through your feeding tube. You may wind up with such a big appetite that you'll really want to chew and swallow again. The *right* food will be important then. I'm sure you'd like to be rid of the tube, but we'll begin by using it."

Jody seemed to listen intently. Dr. Norman had brought a wave of bright confidence and hope into the room, and she was affecting them all. Except, perhaps, for Tyler Hammond, who looked as guarded and unconvinced as ever. What on earth was the matter with him? Kelsey thought impatiently. She glanced at Marisa, who merely raised an eyebrow in understanding and smiled.

"I'll come to see you again in a few days, Jody," Dr. Norman told him, "and I'll bring my friend who does acupuncture and knows about spastic problems. The sooner we get started, the better. A lot of what happens now will depend on what you think inside your own head."

Again Jody said "Um," and Dr. Norman nodded.

"Good. Jody, I want you to start now and think about how a lot of people are working to help you get well. You won't feel cheerful and hopeful all the time—nobody does. But *you* can learn how to pull yourself back on the right track. What's happened in the past doesn't matter—it's from now on that counts. There's always a from-now-on. Do you understand me, Jody?"

He made a hissing sound that was almost a "yes," and Ginnie and Kelsey looked at each other, pleased.

Dr. Norman patted him again and left the bed to speak quietly to Tyler. "Is there a place where we can discuss a few matters?"

Tyler motioned toward the small room across the hall, and Dr. Norman beckoned to Ginnie and Kelsey to come too. Marisa stayed with Jody, talking to him, backing up the things Dr. Norman had said.

When they were sitting at the small table, Dr. Norman opened the tote bag she'd brought and took out several small packages.

"I brought some bottles along, so we can get started at once. Are you willing to give this a try, Mr. Hammond? Do you think Jody's mother should be here to hear about this?"

"No," Tyler said quickly. "I can explain what I think she should know. I don't want to raise false hopes in my wife."

For the first time, Dr. Norman looked exasperated. "I'm not sure there's any such thing as false hope. Doctors understand that what goes on in the minds of patients and those around them is one of the best of all healing tools. A lack of hope can kill."

Tyler needed to listen to that, Kelsey thought, and didn't realize that she was staring at him angrily, until he caught her eye and looked startled. Then he almost smiled.

"You may be right, Dr. Norman," he said. "But what I want

to know now is what's in those bottles. If there are any new drugs, I want to consult my own doctor."

"No drugs at all, Mr. Hammond. Nothing that isn't approved by the FDA. This is a different approach. The treatment is being used in a number of places right now. Octocosanol has been found to regenerate brain cells in some cases, and the sooner it's used, the better."

"What is this stuff?" Tyler asked.

"It's a harmless substance concentrated from wheat germ oil, where a lot of life power exists. The oil alone won't do it. This has been refined from the basic oil into something much more complex. We're only beginning to understand how complex and useful it is."

"This is supposed to help Jody's brain cells?" Tyler asked in disbelief.

"It may. The least it will do is to help his general health. We used to believe that brain cells could never be repaired. Now we're learning that sometimes they may be revitalized. No promises, because of all the variables, such as individual reactions. Are you willing to try, Mr. Hammond?"

Tyler looked at Ginnie, and then at Kelsey. Finally he shrugged. "What can we lose?"

"You may even gain," Dr. Norman said. "Of course nothing works alone in nutrition. I'm going to prescribe a number of supporting vitamins and minerals for Jody that will help in this treatment. It's not damage and disease alone that we must deal with. The immune system has to be built up. When that is strong, the body's better able to perform its own repairs. Which is probably what was intended in the first place. Will you let us begin, Mr. Hammond?"

Dr. Norman's own strong conviction must have reached him. He said, "Go ahead," surrendering. "We'll see what happens."

Dr. Norman held out her packages to Ginnie. "These are

what I'd like to start with. I'll have some blood and hair tests done so we can know where he stands chemically. We'll use capsule vitamin preparations where possible because they'll be easy to open and put into fluid in his feeding tube. There are a few hard tablets that you'll need to grind into fine powder so they can be mixed with liquid. All this stuff tastes pretty bad, and when he can start taking it by mouth you'll need to disguise it in apple sauce or something else that he can swallow. He may not be able to swallow capsules for a while."

When she'd made sure that Ginnie understood her instructions, she prepared to leave. "Is there anything else you'd like to ask, Mr. Hammond?"

Tyler looked a bit stunned, as though a world he'd never dreamed of had suddenly opened before him, and he still didn't know what to make of it, or whether he dared to hope. For once, he was almost gracious.

"Thank you for coming, Dr. Norman. Is there anything else you want us to do?"

She nodded at him, not smiling now. "Just pray a lot. Perhaps that comes first of all."

She went back to Jody's room to say good-bye to him and add a few more words of encouragement. Then she told Marisa she would see her soon, and hurried off to another appointment, leaving Kelsey with a feeling that a beneficial summer storm had just breezed through, and that none of them would ever be the same again. She only hoped that Tyler would give Ruth a positive account of what had happened.

Ginnie went to work at once, opening the packages, to find that Dr. Norman had provided a small mortar and pestle for turning the hard tablets into powder.

Kelsey spoke to the boy in the bed. "Interesting things are going to happen now to help you, Jody. Ginnie will explain when she has everything ready."

"Well?" Marisa asked Tyler when he came into the room.

"We'll see," he said.

She shook her head. "I know—'it won't help, but it can't hurt.' That's the phrase to fall back on when you don't understand something. Dr. Norman belongs to a new breed, and you'd better listen."

"I've listened," Tyler said. "I hope you know what you're doing. Anyway, thanks for bringing her here."

He went off, his shoulders stooped again, and Kelsey looked after him, troubled, remembering the terrible things Ruth had said. When she followed Marisa up to the car, she put her uneasy thoughts into words.

"Sometimes I wonder if Tyler really wants Jody to get well."

Marisa gave her a long, searching look as she got into her car. "He doesn't know what he wants. Let's go have lunch. You need a breather, and we can talk more freely away from this house."

They drove down from the Highlands to the fork where the road turned into Carmel Valley. On either hand mountains rimmed the long valley that stretched between steep slopes where shadow and sunlight patterned the land. For Kelsey, the view had a heart-lifting effect—calming, and without the threat that always stirred the ocean.

"We're going to the Barnyard, not far into the Valley," Marisa said. "After lunch we'll take the Valley road for a few miles on. There's something I'd like to show you."

The Barnyard proved to be a center for small shops built on several levels, like a cluster of barns. Creative planning had turned it into something of a garden show as well. Paved walks with rustic steps wound among bright flowerbeds. Outside galleries overlooked the walks, and benches invited visitors to rest. A number of people were moving about, looking as colorful as the flowerbeds, in their California clothes.

Now, however, Marisa had lunch in mind. The restaurant was first of all a bookstore. A wide door opened from the book area into a spacious room with big windows and more book-shelves, so it was possible to eat and read at the same time. Through the windows, walks and flowerbeds and rustic build-ings were visible.

When they'd ordered a light meal, Marisa said, "All right—tell me what's worrying you, Kelsey."

"I give everything away, don't I? But it's not all troubling. Jody's trying hard to say a few words. He *can* understand, and he's frustrated because he can't communicate. I think he's upset by whatever it is Tyler sometimes shows toward him. When we went to Tor House, Jody seemed happier for a time, and interested in everything. Until Tyler got angry, and spoiled the good mood."

"What else?"

Kelsey wished she could consult Marisa about her encounter with Ruth in the library last night, but on this she had to be silent. She didn't want to betray Ruth, who seemed almost as vulnerable as Jody. Marisa might very well tell Tyler if she knew.

"Tell me about Mrs. Langford," Kelsey said. "Ruth's mother seems anxious to please, anxious not to do anything to upset anyone. So much so that sometimes she's ineffectual." Though that hadn't been the case last night, Kelsey remembered.

"Anyone who lived all those years with the General needed to develop an inner toughness. Even though it's well hidden by what sometimes looks like a meek exterior. We've become rather good friends—though when it comes to Ruth, I think Dora'd sacrifice anyone else."

"Did you know the General?"

"I met him a few times. When Tyler went off on his own, he lived at first in the Los Angeles area, and worked for one of the studios. Mostly scriptwriting while he was learning the busi-ness. He met Ruth when he was doing an early documentary on the side—about college young people—and he fell for her hard. So when he wanted me to meet her and her family, I visited Ruth's home near Palm Springs."

"How did they happen to have a home base when the General always moved around?"

"Dora finally put down her foot and insisted on her own place. She liked the desert, and once in a while the General had to give in. Besides, he could always go his own way, which he did. He happened to be there on my first visit, and I felt some very bad vibes when I met him. The only one who really stood up to him was Ruth, though she was eager to escape, and she fell in love with Tyler at the right time. General Langford didn't know how to be anything but a commanding officer, and one with pretty narrow views at that. When he found he couldn't order Tyler around, the way he did Denis, he set himself against the marriage. Of course Ruth knew how to get her own way with him."

"Tyler Hammond doesn't listen much to other people's opinions, either," Kelsey said. "He and the General must really have clashed."

"I wasn't there for all the fireworks, but I hear there were a few. You're right about Tyler. From the time when he was ten and came to live with us, he only listened to his own strange drummer. Which makes it hard for those around him. Brilliant men are often difficult. There can be a ruthless streak. He doesn't want to be distracted by side roads, and he can march right toward his own fixed goal, whether anyone else approves or not. If you oppose him, you can get trampled. Ruth wasn't used to that. But he really loved her, I think—at least in the beginning. He was doing well in his work, happy with his son —and then all this happened. In a single instant, he lost both Ruth and Jody, and perhaps he realized for the first time that they were the foundation under his work. He's lost his direction now, and he feels doomed. That tragedy when he was a child, and now this. . . . He's turned fatalistic. I think he's wrong, but while he's willing to listen to me, he goes his own way."

Kelsey wondered if Marisa knew that Tyler had wanted a divorce. "Anyway," she said, "he's giving Dr. Norman a chance, and I think she may really help Jody."

"As you are helping him," Marisa said. "Don't ever discount the role you've already played in this short time. Ginnie tells me you've made friends with Jody and that he trusts you. That's a big accomplishment right there."

When their salads and soup came, Kelsey remembered the other thing she'd wanted to talk to Marisa about—those three black beads that had disturbed her ever since she'd seen them on Denis's desk. She told Marisa about what had happened.

"I had a feeling that I'd seen similar beads before," she finished, "and later I remembered the photograph you did of Francesca Fallon. Wasn't she wearing a strand of black beads in that picture?"

"Yes. In fact, I was there when the strand broke."

"Denis seemed upset when he saw those beads on his desk. He said that Tyler must have been in his office. Why?"

"I suppose because he knew Tyler had those three beads. You see, the necklace was broken during that radio interview Francesca did with Tyler. They made the broadcast right in the library of his house, since Tyler wouldn't go to the studio. Francesca started in on him hard after a few innocuous preliminaries. Of course she should have known better. She had a way of asking nasty questions that could be taken in the wrong way by listeners. Tyler saw what she was doing, and when he couldn't sidetrack her, he got mad. When *he* gets mad, watch out! He lit into her with a few barbed questions of his own, and the battle was on. She almost lost control, she was so furious. Just before the broadcast ended, she caught at those beads in her anger and gave them a tug that broke the strand. They went flying all over the library. She claimed to have bought them in Nairobi, and apparently treasured them. So when the program was off the air she went down on her hands and knees, picking them up. Tyler had invited me to be there, and Denis had come too. So we all hunted beads.

"I suppose, in a way, what happened when the beads scattered made a good diversion for Francesca. She knew her outburst had been anything but admirable, and she was so upset that she needed a coverup until she could pull herself together. She and Tyler didn't even speak to each other again. As soon as she thought she had all the beads, she got the crew and herself out of the house."

"Tyler asked me not to listen to that interview," Kelsey said. "But I think I'd like to hear it."

"I'm not sure you would. I haven't decided whether to destroy the tape or not."

"The three beads turned up later?"

"Jody found them. He'd been allowed to sit in a corner and watch, and afterwards he found them under a chair. He gave them to his father. But how they wound up on Denis's desk, I've no idea."

"Your inner voices don't answer questions?" Kelsey asked, half joking.

"They aren't to be ordered. They speak when they please, and mostly I like it best when they keep still."

Kelsey returned to the unpleasant scene in the library. "Since Tyler didn't like Francesca Fallon, why would he agree to do the interview in the first place? I asked him once, but he didn't tell me. I'd have thought he'd have avoided it, no matter what."

"It wasn't in character for him to do it. I've never understood that either, and he would never talk about it. In those Los Angeles days they all knew one another, and it could be that she was calling in some debt he owed her. I don't know. I don't much like it that those beads have surfaced again, yet I don't see what they might have to do with Denis. They've always seemed evil little faces to me. Perhaps because objects sometimes have their own energies that I react to."

This was Marisa's mystical streak again, but since Kelsey had experienced an uneasy feeling when she'd touched the beads herself, she could almost accept this concept of objects being evil.

"I wish I could feel more settled in my own mind," she said. "I feel as though I'm being pulled in different directions, and that doesn't help me to be calm and quiet with Jody. He needs serenity as well as stimulation. Serenity in those around him."

"We all do, but it isn't easy to come by. I suppose we try to work toward that ideal—an undivided self. But instead, we go splitting off in all directions. Maybe getting oneself together into one piece is what maturing is all about. Tyler was almost there at one point, I think. At least he'd put behind him the things in his life that he couldn't do anything about, and was really moving ahead in his work. Now he's cracked apart so badly that I worry. He needs patching together as much as Jody does. And Ruth."

After lunch, Kelsey picked up some paperbacks in the bookstore before they drove into the Valley. There was no fog here, and mountains ran along on each side, their tops gentle and rolling against the sky, protecting the stretch of valley between. There were groves of redwoods now, and blue gum eucalyptus on some of the hills. At first there were houses, but not all of the Valley was built up as yet.

Marisa turned the car up a narrow side road that cut into a canyon in the mountains. This was more isolated country as the slopes steepened. They passed one dilapidated shack that had been abandoned, and a small house with chickens in the yard. Higher up, Kelsey saw a third house set against a grove of oak trees.

"That's where we're going," Marisa said. "This is a private road."

The way came to an end at the house, and Marisa got out. "Since Tyler's given me a key, I come out once in a while to make sure everything's all right. He hates the place and won't come here himself. So far he's been unable to sell it. There are too many stories connected with it that people don't like. It's the sort of spot Robinson Jeffers might have written about when he and Una roamed around exploring."

Kelsey joined Marisa on the walk to the house. Log fences, some of them fallen, had once closed off what must have been a grazing pasture above the house. Weeds grew high in front, thrusting through cracks in the cement walk.

"Nature takes over so quickly," Marisa said. "Somebody's got to get out here and clear out the weeds and spruce it up a bit, or Tyler will never sell it."

The gray, shingled roof overhung a narrow porch where oak leaves had drifted into brown piles. To the right, a few yards from the house, stood the gaunt black skeleton of an oak tree. Along one dead arm that reached toward the sky, parasite ivy struggled for life.

"That's the tree I took a picture of when it burned," Marisa said. "That was quite a night. I've told you about it. Afterwards, my friends let the dead tree stand guard, and named the house after it."

As Kelsey went up the steps she saw the plaque over the door, with letters burned into the wood: FLAMING TREE RANCH.

Perhaps there had once been a clearing all around, but now the oak trees grew in too close, darkening the windows, their branches scraping the roof.

"I'd better tell you a little more before we go inside," Marisa went on. "Recently, years after my friends moved out, Francesca Fallon bought this place. She wanted isolation, and she got it. She'd planned to work on it, fix everything up. Instead, this is where she died. You needn't come in if you'd rather not. I'll just run through quickly and have a look. There can be vandals, even out here."

What Kelsey felt was the same disquieting sensation—a feeling that was almost dread—that she'd experienced when she'd held those three beads she'd found on Denis's desk. Again there was a connection with Francesca Fallon. It was as though a clammy wind had touched her skin—not a clean wind from the sea or the mountains, but something that carried with it the smell of death.

Marisa watched as though she waited for some reaction. Kelsey braced her shoulders and walked through the door.

"It's all right to feel it," Marisa said when they were in the living room of the house. "I do too. Perhaps it's only our imagination working overtime because something awful happened here. Or perhaps there's more—some sensing that we aren't wise enough to understand."

"A warning feeling?" Kelsey asked.

Marisa gave her a quick look. "Yes—exactly. The vibes here are especially bad."

The carpet had been removed and the furniture was covered with sheets. A big fireplace dominated one end of the room, though nothing as grand as the one at La Casa de la Sombra. This one was built of brick, with a carved wood mantel, fluted along the edge.

All books and ornaments had been removed since Francesca's death, except for one. A hammered brass mask, fit for a giant, hung over the mantel, regarding the room malevolently through slitted eyes. Francesca seemed to have had an affinity for the ugly and depraved.

"Maybe that's what she was like inside," Marisa mused. "She had a lot of other stuff like that here, but Tyler moved it all out and stored it for the time being." Marisa went over to a covered sofa. "This is where her body was found."

It was best to breathe deeply, to fight the nausea that seemed ready to envelop her. Kelsey spoke in a whisper, not wanting to stir the shadows.

"Tyler owns this house? I don't understand."

"He owns it because Francesca Fallon left it to him in her will."

"But why—if she disliked him so much?"

"Perhaps that's why. With her peculiar twist of mind, she might have thought she was insuring her own safety. The place had little value, but her leaving it to him has caused Tyler a lot of trouble and embarrassment. She made the will after that awful broadcast, and she told him what she was doing. In a way, I suppose she was saying, 'Leave me alone, or you'll be involved.' The worst of it was that Tyler came out here to see Francesca the day before she died. Luckily, he was elsewhere at the time of the murder. Ginnie Soong could vouch for that. He'd gone to the hospital in Monterey to take her to lunch and give her Ruth's invitation to visit their house. Ginnie was busy and couldn't accept just then, but she vouched for Tyler's being a long way from the Valley at the time of the murder."

"You said Francesca died from a blow to the head?"

Marisa pointed to a basket of firewood at one end of the hearth. "The police think a chunk of wood from that basket might have been used as a cudgel. Those are pretty sturdy sticks. Wood had been burned in the fireplace, which of course wasn't unusual. The piece of wood, if used, could have been destroyed as evidence. It seems to have killed her instantly."

Kelsey's knees had begun to feel shaky, and she sat down in a sheeted chair. "Why did you bring me here?"

Marisa sat opposite and closed her eyes, as if to concentrate.

A wind had risen outside, and branches made an eerie scratching against the porch roof.

"Perhaps it's because you have a gift," Marisa said.

"I don't know what you mean."

"I don't know exactly what I mean either. This place pulls me here—as though it held some answer. I've sat where you're sitting now, and spent an hour or more trying to get *something* to speak to me. But I can't make demands, and nothing has happened. Just the same, it's as though some part of me recognizes that mending for Tyler and Ruth and Jody—perhaps even for Denis—lies here at Flaming Tree."

Shivery words. Kelsey had the feeling that the brass mask was watching, listening. Unlike Marisa, she didn't want the house to speak to her. Every tense nerve in her body seemed to warn of danger in whatever it might tell, if ever the house began to reveal its secrets.

Marisa went on, her voice playing its musical scale eerily.

"Something came up on my tape of Francesca's interview that seemed to draw Tyler in. I'm not sure what it meant, but I never wanted to show that tape to the police. I don't think it would help, and it might lead to more questions. The radio station doesn't have a copy. If there was one, perhaps Francesca removed it herself. Kelsey, are you sure you don't have any—sensing—about this place?"

"You're wrong about me. I never have promptings of that kind. Nothing here speaks to me of anything but horror. There's a stain in the very air."

Marisa pounced on that. "Exactly! You do feel it. Perhaps the reason I've been doing a lot of reading on the subject of human evil, and even trying to set something down on paper, is because of what happened here."

Kelsey made an effort to quiet her inner trembling. "You said Francesca Fallon came down on your 'goodness' scale to a low two."

"I suppose I did say that, though it sounds presumptuous and judging. The trouble is, if there really are evil people, as some theologians believe, they fool themselves first of all. Rationalization becomes an art, so *they* are never wrong or guilty. It's always someone else's fault. They go through life sure of their own virtues and proper goals. And all the while they're sowing terrible damage along the way. They are the takers, never the givers."

"Was Francesca like that?"

"I thought so."

"Do you really believe that anyone is born that way? I mean that some people are beyond changing?"

"Jane Norman thinks it may even be partly chemical. There have been studies done with prisoners where a change in diet and the addition of vitamins made them less aggressive. Just the same, I feel there's more than that. More than can be put under headings like 'genetic' or 'environmental.' Perhaps the Bible had it right about good and evil, after all. But that's enough of my current soap box. Will you stay here while I go through the house? Or would you rather wait in the car?"

Kelsey stood up quickly. It felt better to go outside and escape the strange sense of panic that had begun to possess her in Francesca Fallon's house.

On the weed-grown walk, she turned to stare up at the gray frame, with it's oak-darkened windows, and then at the gaunt black skeleton of the tree standing guard.

The memory of Marisa's photograph of the tree was vivid in her mind. The way the branches had looked, flaming bright along every twig that flared against the sky—this had been caught forever in that marvelous, chilling picture. Now the tree's blackened, reaching arms revealed only its tragic ending, except for a tiny fluttering of green life in the upper branches. It seemed a symbol of the death that had taken place inside the walls of the house.

The only thing here that spoke to her was a sense of revulsion—for the deed and for whoever had committed it. Her one urge at the moment was to get away and never return to Flaming Tree Ranch.

Marisa locked the door behind her and joined Kelsey on the walk. "Don't look like that," she said at once. "Let what comes come when it will. Something always gets in the way for me. Perhaps I'm too closely involved with the people. You may see more clearly from the outside."

"You really feel there's a connection with—"

"There's a connection. Though who came here, and why, and what happened, I don't know. Maybe there's something in me that doesn't want to know and blocks the way."

Kelsey turned toward the car and Marisa came after her.

"Never mind. We must always come back to Jody's needs. Let the past alone."

"You didn't want me to let it alone," Kelsey said. "You brought me here."

Marisa didn't answer. As they drove away, Kelsey looked back, and the words *Flaming Tree* seemed to burn in her mind. Whatever wickedness Francesca Fallon had kindled could easily flare into another conflagration that might damage everyone—even Jody. If that was the message Marisa had wanted her to receive and guard against, it did no good. Premonition had never played any part in her life, and it wasn't going to now. Better to let "what comes, come," as Marisa had said.

Nevertheless, on the way back through the Valley Kelsey tried to put some sense of this into words. "The only feeling I have is that Francesca's house is a dangerous place. Is it possible that there may be evil in places, as well as people? Perhaps stamped there by human lives? I only know I never want to go back there. I don't *want* to know what happened."

Marisa drove in silence for several miles before she spoke again. When they were nearing Carmel Highlands she said quietly, "The choice not to know may not be yours to make, Kelsey."

XIII

KELSEY went directly to Jody's room when she returned, and stopped in surprise in the doorway. Tyler had set up a portable video tape recorder and was filming Jody as Ginnie sat talking to him. The boy, held upright in his chair, appeared to watch as though his eyes were really tracking. Kelsey noted the tiny lapel microphone clipped to his shirt.

When Tyler pressed the pause control and looked around at Kelsey, he seemed different—much more alive and interested than she'd seen him since Tor House.

"I've taken your suggestion," he said. "Do you suppose you can get Jody to say something?"

Kelsey sat down in the chair Ginnie vacated, feeling pleased that for once Tyler had listened. As she took Jody's hand, removing the soft cloth around which his fingers were always curled, she could feel his tension. Probably his father had been brusque again. Not because he meant to be, but due to his own uncertain state whenever he was near Jody. Grieving fathers could have more trouble being natural than mothers did.

Jody was looking at her now, and Kelsey spoke to him. "Who am I, Jody? What's my name?"

He made the sound that was like "Elly," and Kelsey stroked his arm to his fingertips, coaxing him to relax.

"That's good, Jody. Now I'm going to ask you something else. Would you like me to push you out of your chair?" She smiled, and Jody managed a grimace that was almost a smile in return. He said his best word softly, "No."

Often patients who were learning to talk again had so little confidence that they didn't want to speak loudly. With his father there, Jody was uncertain, and she needed to reassure him.

"You're doing fine, Jody, but I didn't quite hear that. Can you tell me again?"

This time his "No!" was louder.

She patted him in praise. "Of course you don't want to be pushed out of your chair. That was silly, wasn't it? Now I'm going to ask you another question, and this time I'd like you to think about the answer first. If it's 'yes,' don't say 'hai,' even if it's easier. You almost managed 'yes' once before, and I think you can. Here's the question. Would you like to taste a tiny bit of mashed banana? Ginnie can fix you some if you'll say you want it."

Jody's struggle was visible. The muscles of his throat tightened, his straightened arms turned inward, and his fists clenched. Then once more he made a hissing sound, blown between his teeth.

Kelsey hugged him. "That's almost it, Jody. We'll keep working on it so you won't have to say 'no' all the time. Ginnie?"

Ginnie had already stepped into the adjacent kitchen. "One taste of mashed banana coming up."

"You see how you can make things happen, Jody?" Kelsey said. She didn't look at the camera or at Tyler. What occurred now was between her and Jody and Ginnie, yet at the same time Jody must understand his father's purpose and sympathy.

"Every day you'll learn something new, and you'll remember all you used to be able to say. Your father will catch some of this on videotape, along with the sound—so you can watch how you're improving."

"Kelsey's right," Tyler agreed. "Ginnie's already making notes, but this is even better."

She'd never heard Tyler sound this relaxed with his son since she'd been here, and she smiled at him warmly. Perhaps a little too warmly, because her own emotions were too strongly involved. There was always this awareness of him that she didn't want to feel, and couldn't accept.

She spoke quickly again to Jody.

"You *are* going to talk properly. You know that, don't you, Jody?"

With a convulsive effort, Jody managed the hissing sound, and Kelsey gave him another hug. "We'll get that track from your brain to your tongue retrained. Sometimes it can even happen suddenly. Keep thinking the words, and someday they'll come."

She stepped aside to let Ginnie present her spoon with a bit of mashed banana on the tip. "Open up, Jody," Ginnie said. After a second of hesitation, he permitted the spoon tip to enter his mouth and took the tiny portion on his tongue. At once he made a face, but this time he didn't spit the food out. All tastes could seem strange and unpleasant to him now, and he must be persuaded to tolerate them, until his taste buds too were reeducated.

"Move it around in your mouth," Ginnie said. "Your tongue works. So get used to how it tastes and try to chew. Then you can swallow it." She stroked his throat gently until he swallowed.

Kelsey looked around at Tyler. "I hope you realize what an accomplishment this is?"

"I've got it on film with all the sounds," Tyler said. "How about more banana, Jody?"

Ginnie spooned more in without waiting for Jody's agreement. This time he opened his mouth more readily.

Tyler switched off the camera. "That's enough for now. Let him eat in peace, if he will. Where did you go with Marisa, Kelsey?"

"We had lunch in the Barnyard—at the Thunderbird Bookstore." She hesitated, and then decided that he might as well know the rest. "After that, Marisa drove us out to Flaming Tree Ranch. She had the key you gave her, and she wanted to check the house."

He stood quite still, about to take the camera off the tripod. "Do you know what happened there?"

"Yes. Marisa told me. I didn't like the place—there's an awful feeling about it. If houses are ever haunted, I think that one is."

"Swallow, Jody," Ginnie said. "It's all right—you aren't going to choke. Just let it go down easily."

Jody's face had turned red as he coughed and sputtered. Ginnie soothed him until the food went down and he quieted. But his eyes still looked wide and frightened from the near choking. He wasn't used to eating, and there would be episodes like this until he learned again.

Nevertheless, Kelsey thought, this had been more like a struggle to talk than a choking spell. And he couldn't manage talking and eating at the same time. Just the same, she felt encouraged. A good part of recovery was motivation. When Dr. Norman's nutritional treatment had time to take hold, everything might speed up. The very fact that Jody *wanted* so much to talk meant that he would keep trying.

"He'll be all right now," Kelsey told Tyler, remembering how he'd reacted at Tor House when Jody had had trouble.

Now, at least, Tyler said nothing as he removed his equipment from the room. When he'd placed the camera, videocassette recorder, and tripod in the hall, he spoke again to Kelsey.

"I'd like to talk with you for a minute, Kelsey."

Again she had stopped being "Mrs. Stewart," but with Tyler Hammond one never knew how long such progress would last. She followed him to his big airy office, where the view of pines and ocean seemed part of the room.

"Sit down, please," he said.

She took the chair across from his desk, bracing herself, but his words followed an unexpected course.

"Why did Marisa drive you to Flaming Tree?" he asked. "Whatever possessed her to take you there, of all places?"

"Why not? We were in that direction in the Valley, and Marisa said she looked through the house for you once in a while. So we might as well stop."

"What exactly did she tell you about the place?"

His tone of voice had hardened, and once more Kelsey felt an urge to provoke and challenge this arrogant man. She hated it that he could get under her skin so easily.

"Marisa said Francesca Fallon was murdered there. She told me the house had been hers, and now belonged to you."

"Francesca was an abominable woman! What else did Marisa say?"

"That Francesca left the Flaming Tree to you in her will. Perhaps as a—a sort of provocation. Marisa didn't understand why."

Suddenly Tyler looked so dejected that her need to challenge him evaporated. "I don't need to know any of this. My concern is with Jody."

He went on as though he thought aloud. "I suppose it was Francesca's way of threatening me—embarrassing me. You probably know from Marisa that I went to see her at the ranch the day before she died. After we'd talked, she told me she meant to write a will that afternoon and leave everything she owned to me. Not that she had much. She said if anything happened to her, it would look bad for me, so it was a precaution. I laughed at her. I suppose she thought, in her idiotic way, that she was protecting herself. From *me!* She saw too many television shows! There wasn't enough involved to make anyone think I was out for what she'd left me. And her blackmail notion was pretty foolish too, because I wouldn't stand for it. I'm not even sure what it was and I didn't want to know. Though it did upset Ruth that she singled me out in her will. How could I explain that? Of course that may have been what Francesca had in mind—to embarrass me in any way she could. If she'd lived, she would probably have publicized the will."

He sat looking out the window for a moment, and it seemed to Kelsey that the mask he usually wore had slipped, so that he became suddenly more vulnerable. That could be dangerously appealing in so strong a man.

"I'd still like to know why Marisa took you there," he said.

She spoke carefully, needing to hide her own uncertain emotions that could blow hot and cold in this ridiculous fashion.

"I'm not sure I can explain. It's so—nebulous. Marisa wanted the house to tell me something. At least that's what she said. Though I haven't any idea what it was supposed to tell me. She thinks I have some sort of sensitivity—which really doesn't exist. I've never had anything like that, and I think I'd fight it if I did."

Tyler picked up an onyx paperweight and studied it absently. "Marisa gets carried away. She sails off into some other world where there are different laws, different planes. Interesting, perhaps, but I don't like tampering with something that's so little understood."

"She did get some sort of message when Ruth and Jody fell, out at Point Lobos. If it hadn't been for Marisa, they might not have been found until it was too late."

"I don't understand what happened, or how she found

them. I wonder if she mixes reality up with her visions too much at times."

"I like Marisa very much," Kelsey said. "I'm willing to believe she knows more about these things than I do."

He tossed the piece of onyx from hand to hand. "When it comes to Marisa, I've learned not to entirely disbelieve—she's too often right. But I'd like to know what she's up to now. There's something I don't understand about this preoccupation with Francesca Fallon. Now she's drawn you into it, too. The woman's dead, so let it go. A nasty way to die, but maybe she asked for it."

Denis had said something of the same thing. What an unhappy life Francesca must have led—with no one liking her. A mean life.

Kelsey dared a direct question. "Why did you go there to see her? Especially after you'd had a public quarrel with her on the air?"

"That was why—unfinished business. I suppose Marisa told you about that?"

"She didn't say what happened on that broadcast, except that it was unpleasant."

"Francesca threw out something I couldn't ignore, so I went to see her. She invited me to come, right on the air. Her purpose was blackmail, but she didn't get anywhere with it."

"How could you stop her?"

"I told her if she went down that road I would fix it so that she'd do no more gossiping about anyone. I only meant to scare her. If she'd gone ahead, I don't know what action I could have taken. I still don't know exactly what she was getting at. She liked to play the mysterious adventuress—her best fake role. Maybe I'd have done what someone else did— picked up a piece of firewood and used it. *If* I were angry enough. As it happened, I didn't get the chance. Someone beat me to it."

"I suppose the police followed whatever leads they could about people she might have infuriated in her gossip columns, or her radio program?"

"That's why they came to me. They knew about the uproar on the air, of course. What with that and her stupid will, the police were pretty interested in me. The will must have been an afterthought. She always played her foolish hunches."

"Marisa told me you were with Ginnie Soong around the time when Francesca must have died."

He set the onyx down with an ominous thud. However, since so much was coming out, Kelsey went on doggedly.

"Marisa said that Francesca broke her Nairobi beads here in the library that day of the broadcast."

"What about the beads?" he asked, suddenly alert.

"She said Francesca was so upset with you that she jerked at the chain, and the beads flew all over the room."

"I remember. I'd have liked to wind them around her neck!"

"Are you always so violent about everything?"

He glared at her and she returned his look as steadily as she could manage. "Marisa told me that Jody found three of the beads after Francesca had left the house. What happened to them?"

"What difference does it make?"

"I asked because three beads turned up yesterday on Denis's desk at the inn. Denis seemed upset when he saw them, and he said you must have been in his office."

"He's crazy! Why should this interest you?"

"I suppose everything interests me. I keep telling everyone that I might be able to help Jody more if I understood what it is that frightens him so much. Do you realize how scared he is of you? Sometimes, when you merely stand in the doorway, he goes into that spastic stiffening. Perhaps he'd improve more quickly if you could help him not to be so frightened."

Tyler's expression darkened and his brows drew down. Kelsey was reminded again of the photograph she'd seen at Marisa's. This was a tortured man, and she wondered what had happened in his life to haunt him so. The long-ago childhood tragedy wasn't enough to account for his suffering now. Yet the photograph told her that his torment had been present before Francesca died and his wife and son were injured. She wished she could help *him* as well as Jody—and knew clearly the treacherous direction of her own feelings.

As she sat silent, waiting for an angry response, some of his tension seemed to lessen.

"Thanks, Kelsey. I'm glad you told me. I don't mean to go around scaring people. I know I'm to blame with Jody. I didn't dream he could understand, and I suppose I must have said a lot of things that upset him—words I'd never have spoken if I'd realized that he could hear me. I'll try to get past his fears, if I can, and if you'll help me. Maybe another outing?"

"That would be fine," Kelsey said, "if it doesn't end the way the last one did."

The thundercloud had lifted, and he managed one of his unexpected grins. "I'll try to behave. What Jody did scared *me*, and I suppose I took off. I'll tell you what happened to the beads. When the chain broke, Francesca had a fit. She said they were her good luck beads, and she had to retrieve every one of them. We all scrambled around looking for them. After she'd gone, Jody turned up three more. I took them from him, and when I came back to my study I put them here on my desk. Nasty looking little carvings—typical of Francesca's taste for the weird. Since I meant to pick up the invitation that she made on the air, I was going to take the beads with me and give them to her when I went to Flaming Tree the next day. But when I looked for them before I left, they'd disappeared. After what happened to Francesca, I didn't give them another thought until now. Does it really matter?"

"It seemed to matter to Denis. But it's only Jody who's important now."

He studied her with a new intensity, his look so direct that she felt disconcerted. It was as though he wanted to see inside her very brain.

"I like the way you care about him," he said. "The way you open yourself up to caring."

"Of course I care. I never want to reach the place where I seal off my own feelings."

"That must be rough at times. Isn't there a special danger of transference with Jody? I mean a risk because of your own loss. It might be hard to let go and give him up when the time comes."

He had reached inside her and stirred up the pain that always lay near the surface. She looked out the window at green pine tops and the distant ocean. She willed herself to walk on a beach with the fog coming in and a piper stepping slowly along the sand. If she could just recover that dreamlike moment, then perhaps she could put the pain away from her.

"I'm sorry," Tyler said gently. "Of course there's that danger, and I suppose you have to face it with each child from now on." He was silent for a moment, and when he spoke again, he surprised her. "What do you say, Kelsey—shall we find that dog for Jody?"

She blinked at his sudden change of course. "I'd like that, but what about Ruth?"

"Maybe we can just show her the dog, and then keep him out of her sight the rest of the time. She might even accept him for Jody's sake."

The trip to Monterey was strangely pleasant—almost as though Tyler had turned into a different man. She'd never seen him in a light mood before, and she knew he was making a special effort. She threw caution aside, and let herself relax and enjoy the trip. La Casa de la Sombra belonged to another world. For now, however recklessly, she accepted her pleasure in being with Tyler in his new mood. For this little while she would permit herself to like him.

He had brought with him an ad he'd torn from the *Pine Cone*, Carmel's local paper. A woman in Monterey was moving away and wanted someone to take her dog. No special breed, and not a puppy. A small dog. So they were going to see her.

Like San Francisco, Monterey was built on steep hills that plunged at several levels toward the water—with Cannery Row at the bottom. Only one active cannery remained, and the fame Steinbeck had brought to the street had turned it into a tourists' row, with shops, restaurants, and various attractions. They drove to a rooming house a block or two off the Row. Since Tyler had phoned ahead, the woman was waiting for them on the front porch, sitting in a rocker with a sandy little dog in her lap.

Her health forced her to give up her house, she explained a bit tearfully. She must move in with relatives, and she wanted a good home for her little friend. Sandy (naturally) had a muzzle that resembled that of a Scottish terrier, and a lively tail that was mostly mutt.

"He's very smart," the woman said. "And he loves everybody."

Sandy demonstrated this quickly, and seemed not to mind coming with them. He'd had shots and he owned a license on his collar, and a leash. Tyler carried him to the car, where he sat on Kelsey's knees, looking out the window with interest. He seemed to be the sort of dog who would adjust to change without too much brooding.

"We'll let Jody name him," Tyler said, optimistic for once.

It was strange and unreasonable, Kelsey thought, to feel happy and hopeful. Part of this emotional response was because of the dog, so warm and alive on her lap. But the greater part, as she recognized, was the presence of the man beside her. He too was warm and alive, and she was very close to wanting something she could never have. That was dangerous, since she mustn't open the way to still more pain.

Once, while they waited for a stoplight, Tyler looked at her with the same searching intensity she'd felt before, except that now there seemed an air of discovery—as if of himself as well as of her. He reached out to stroke the dog, and it was as if he had touched Kelsey. But this was no longer something she could be happy about, and she was afraid.

When they reached the house, and Tyler parked the car, he moved suddenly past her guard. Again, without touching her, without even looking at her, he gently destroyed the defense she'd needed to raise against him.

"Thank you, Kelsey. You've brought life into what was a hopeless situation before you came. Whether Jody and Ruth ever get well entirely, you've at least made *me* want to start living again. Can you take a responsibility like that?"

His last words teased her almost tenderly, and she put her cheek against Sandy's coat to hide any self-betrayal she might reveal. She couldn't endure kindness and gratitude from him. Not when so much more that was still unexpressed might lie behind the kindness. As long as no one spoke the words, she might still be safe.

She opened the car door hurriedly and got out, with Sandy in her arms. Tyler took her elbow on the way down the steps to steady her, and she knew very well that he recognized her confusion and distress. But she wouldn't give herself away any more than she already had.

When they were inside, Tyler carried the dog straight to Jody's room, where the boy sat in his chair. Kelsey followed, putting aside all except her eagerness to see what would happen now. Ginnie, looking delighted, watched as Tyler held the dog close to Jody's face, and then placed him on his knees.

After a moment of turning around uneasily, the animal stood on his hind legs with his front paws on Jody's chest, and looked him lovingly in the eye. When he started licking Jody's face enthusiastically, Ginnie pulled him off.

"Hey—Jody's been washed today. He doesn't need your help."

Jody's eyes followed the small dog as Ginnie held him.

"Let me have him for a moment," Kelsey said, and put the lively little body near Jody's hand. "Pet him, Jody. I think he'd like that."

The boy made a tremendous effort and moved a finger, touching the dog.

"That's good, Jody. We'll work on that." She took his hand and moved it to stroke the furry head. The dog wriggled his ecstasy.

"You can name him, Jody," Tyler said. "Can you think of a good name to give him?"

Jody allowed his hand to be stroked along the dog's back, and again he made a visible effort. Finally he blew out a new sound: "Woof."

"You want to name him Woof?" Tyler asked.

"No!" Jody was emphatic. "Woof!"

Kelsey tried an interpretation. "I think he means Wolf."

"Sss," Jody said, agreeing.

Tyler bent to give his son a hug. "Good—Wolf it is."

The un-wolflike little dog seemed pleased with all this attention, but after a few moments he settled down on Jody's lap and went to sleep—perhaps wearied by so much human emotion.

"It's going to work," Kelsey said softly. "Wolf is going to help a lot. Jody, we'll need to work hard to get you to stand and take some steps. Wolf needs you to walk him around. For now, I can do that for you some of the time. Remember, your new dog has just left someone he loved, and he'll need a lot of loving from you to make up for that."

Jody was staring at his father, and for once all the fear had gone out of him. He was behaving as he had at the beginning of the visit to Tor House.

"Ank," he said clearly.

Tyler understood. "You're welcome, kid," he said, and his voice broke a little.

"Does Ruth know you were going to do this?" Ginnie asked.

"We're going to tell her. I'll carry you upstairs, Jody, and we'll show your mother your new friend. We know she doesn't like dogs, but maybe she'll feel better when she sees this one."

Kelsey lifted the dog off Jody's knees and snapped on the leash, while Tyler picked his son up in arms that were very gentle. He carried him out of the room, and Ginnie rolled her eyes at Kelsey, clearly worried about Ruth's reaction.

Kelsey followed with Wolf trotting beside her, pulling away now and then to investigate a strange and interesting house.

Dora met them at the door, immediately uncertain at the sight of both Jody and a dog. "I'd better talk to Ruth before you come in," she said.

Tyler shook his head. "If you warn her, she'll object. Let's try surprise, so she can see how harmless this little dog is, and how much he means to Jody."

Ruth sat in her wheelchair, once more staring out a window. Tyler carried Jody to her and placed him deliberately in her arms. Kelsey held back with the dog, praying Jody wouldn't stiffen and make everything hard. For once he seemed relaxed, and when Ruth held him with his head on her shoulder, he stayed quiet, almost as though this was what he'd needed all along.

"We want you to meet a new member of the family," Tyler told her, and Kelsey pulled Wolf forward. "Jody has named him himself, and we're all going along with Wolf."

Ruth's eyes widened, but with Jody in her arms she managed to speak quietly. "You know how I feel about dogs."

"It will be all right, Ruth," Tyler said. "He's a small, harmless little fellow, as you can see. We'll keep him out of your room, and it isn't as though you'll be moving around the house where you could run into him."

It was the wrong thing to say, and Ruth's expression changed. "Take Jody, please. And take that dog away. Don't ask any more of me now. It's too much—the way Jody is . . ."

As Tyler lifted Jody from his mother's lap the boy stiffened, and his eyes rolled back.

Kelsey spoke to him quickly. "It's all right, Jody. Your mother doesn't understand how well you're doing. Mrs. Hammond, Jody is learning new words every day. He's trying hard to move and to talk. One of these days he'll show you."

Ruth moved a hand weakly and looked away from her son. At once Dora rushed forward, angry with Tyler.

"Just take that dog away, and leave—both of you! This is enough damage for one day. Everyone behaves as though Jody were the only one who needs help. No one thinks of Ruth but me."

Jody began to gasp for breath, and Tyler carried him from the room. Kelsey pulled at Wolf's leash and hurried after them. For the first time she wondered if Dora were really good for her daughter. That Dora already disliked and resented Tyler was very clear, and so was her obsessive determination to protect Ruth. From what? What could so frighten Ruth and her mother?

Back in Jody's room, the boy was put to bed and Ginnie ministered to him capably. While Tyler stood watching, Jody gradually relaxed. Wolf, no longer the center of attention, stood on his hind legs and pawed at Kelsey's knee.

"Jody will be all right now," Ginnie assured them. "Just let him rest for a while. Come back later, Kelsey."

Kelsey handed Wolf's leash to Tyler. "He's yours for now," she said, and fled from the room, not daring to wait for what he might say this time.

Outside, she hurried to her aunt's car and sat for a moment at the wheel, trying to collect herself. What had started out hopefully, if perhaps not wisely on Tyler's part, had turned into a disaster, and for the moment she wanted only to get away. Every time Jody seemed to make progress, either Tyler or Ruth turned emotional and threw him back into his helpless state.

She felt angry with both of them, yet she knew her anger was strong because she was also remembering her own weakness—something she couldn't accept. There was always Ruth and Jody to be considered, and she couldn't for a moment be selfishly free.

For now she would go back to the inn and escape them all, even though she couldn't escape herself. She started the car and drove down the hill to Carmel.

When she'd pulled into the space beside the cottage, Denis came out to talk to her. He saw her state of mind and opened the door on her side, drawing her out of the car.

"You look as though you need a change," he said.

Denis was a relief after all those angry, strong-willed people at the Hammond house. At least he could be quiet and understanding and sensitive to the needs of others. They sat on the bench outside the cottage and he put a companionable hand through the crook of her arm.

"Do you want to talk about it? Tell me what happened?"

She remembered the time on the beach when he'd told her he could be a good listener, and she found him that now. It was a relief to pour out an account of her visit with Marisa to Flaming Tree. She told him about her trip with Tyler to pick up the dog—but not everything about that trip. When she described Wolf, Denis looked doubtful.

"I'm afraid that was wrong. Ruth really is deathly afraid of dogs. And now that she's helpless and can't run away, it makes it all the worse."

So not even Denis knew that his sister could walk. Soon she must have another visit with Ruth and try to persuade her that what she was doing could help no one. Including herself. But this was something she couldn't discuss with Denis, though she did tell him of Ruth's reaction.

He heard her out sadly. "There's got to be an end," he said. "She needs to face living again. But I don't know what will happen when Jody begins to talk—maybe about that time at Point Lobos?"

"I know he wants desperately to talk. That's natural enough, but I don't know if it's about anything specific."

Denis took something from his jacket pocket and Kelsey saw that he held the three small black beads from Nairobi. He stared at them as though the evil little faces hypnotized him.

"Did you ever find out who left those on your desk?" Kelsey asked.

Denis started, as though he hadn't realized that he held the beads in his hand. He put them away at once. "No, I've asked questions, but I still don't know who came into my office and left them there."

"Hello!" From across the way Elaine called to them. "You're just the one I want to see, Kelsey. How are things going?"

"Up and down," Kelsey said. "Down right now. So I've run away."

"I've had a phone call from Marisa Marsh and she left a message for you. She'd like you to come to her house whenever you can make the drive."

"But I saw her at lunch today," Kelsey said.

"I know. She told me she took you out to Flaming Tree. She seems to have made up her mind about something she wasn't sure of then. So she's anxious to talk with you again." Elaine hesitated, and then went on doubtfully, "She seems to have a feeling that you need some sort of help, and that maybe she can give it."

"If that's one of her hunches, she's right," Kelsey said. "But I'm not sure I'm up to anything more today."

"You'd better go," Denis said. "I'll drive you out there, if you like. Then perhaps you'll have dinner with me afterwards? I'm off duty until this evening."

"A good idea," Elaine said. "Do go along, Kelsey. "I think you can trust Marisa." For an instant Elaine held Kelsey's eyes, and there was a perception in her own that Kelsey hadn't expected.

Denis pulled her up from the bench. "Seeing Marisa will do us both good. Thanks, Elaine."

In a few moments they were on their way around the Monterey Peninsula. Perhaps Marisa was the one she could talk to and trust. All the others—even Denis—existed too closely under the shadow of La Casa de la Sombra.

There could be no real relaxing, no leaning on others, while her own anxiety remained high. She couldn't rest until the kaleidoscope of shifting colors and emotions that swirled around her began to settle and make sense. In the meantime, it would do no good to run away.

What she might hope for from Marisa was some clue that would help the pattern to clear. Until it did, she could never be sure of her own role in events that seemed increasingly tragic.

XIV

Marisa was waiting for them—engulfed once more in flowing turquoise, with caftan sleeves that made her appear to float on wings. She seemed surprised and not altogether pleased to see that Kelsey had not come alone.

Denis apologized quickly. "I'm only the chauffeur, so pay no attention. Kelsey's had a bad day, and I thought I'd volunteer to drive her. I'll sit out on the terrace and commune with the view."

For an instant Marisa seemed undecided. Then she smiled at him. "I'm always glad to see you, Denis. And perhaps it's a good idea for you to hear this too."

She led them into the spacious living room with its redwood beams overhead, and hand-carved furniture, some of which had come from Tyler's workshop. The door to the adjacent studio stood open, and from where she sat Kelsey could glimpse the flying driftwood geese. She remembered that the first time she'd seen them they'd made her spirits soar. Now, when she thought of Tyler, she felt heavy with dread. It was no longer only Jody she wanted to help—his father was there, paramount in her thoughts.

Marisa had placed a tape recorder on a table, and as they sat down she slipped a cassette into place.

"Kelsey, I've decided that you should hear this tape of the interview Francesca Fallon did with Tyler. I don't know that it will tell you much, but perhaps there's something that should be done about it now. I'd like to know what you think."

Kelsey had heard enough about the broadcast to feel immediately uneasy, and she tensed against whatever might be coming.

Before she touched the play button, Marisa spoke to Denis. "Did you hear the interview when it went on the air that day?"

He shook his head. "I never liked Francesca, and I'm not especially eager to listen to Tyler. I hear him quoted too often as it is. I was in the library at the house when everything was being set up. But when they were ready to start, I went for a walk. I didn't come back until they were off the air, and by that time things had turned ugly. Savage, you might say. I was just as glad I missed the show."

"Then it's time for you to hear it now," Marisa told him.

Denis took the three small beads from his pocket again, and Kelsey was reminded of Bogart's Captain Queeg rolling steel balls in his fingers. Not a pleasant reminder, and she hoped it didn't fit Denis.

The tape purred and for the first time Kelsey heard Francesca Fallon's voice. It seemed eerie to listen, knowing that she had died only a few days later.

At the beginning, she seemed gracious enough. She introduced Tyler glowingly, and her voice possessed a pleasant timbre, though sometimes a little too silky, too smooth for the barbs that began to emerge slyly, inserted like glass splinters as the interview continued.

Tyler's voice recorded well, as Marisa had said, and the

sound of it brought his presence into the room so vitally that Kelsey could see him clearly in her mind as she listened.

Before long, Francesca's barbs turned into attacks that darted in and darted away, all with the pretense of lightness and amused laughter. Why on earth had Tyler been willing to do this interview at all, since he knew very well the sort of innuendo that she was likely to indulge in?

"Tell me," Francesca said at one point, "about the film you made on Salinas and the farm workers in the area."

A certain guardedness came into Tyler's voice. "What do you want to know about it?"

"I understand it didn't succeed as a documentary. The critics were pretty down on it, and you must have lost whatever you put into the project. Do you know what went wrong?"

Tyler answered carefully, still in control. "Nobody can tell for sure ahead of time what will succeed and what won't. Besides, I don't regard *Salinas* as a failure. I'm not trying for popular success."

"Of course not. Naturally, *you* don't have to worry about crass things like that the way the rest of us do. I've heard you called a genius by some—a few—who claim such films are worth making whether many people care or not."

Tyler held his temper and answered quietly. "A documentary ultimately has to make a statement about human beings if it's to matter, Mrs. Fallon. I think *Salinas* does that. It's a story of men and women who succeeded against all sorts of odds. From those Basque shepherds in the beginning to the beet growers and the artichoke fields of today, it's a story of struggle by individuals who interest me."

"You were both director and producer, I understand. Isn't there a risk in that?"

"I need to go my own way, and I'm willing to take the responsibility for my judgment. Though of course any film is the work of a number of people."

"With you in control, naturally. Who was your cameraman for that film?"

There was an instant of hesitation on Tyler's part. Then he said coldly, "Denis Langford."

"Oh, yes—your wife's brother. A good idea to keep it in the family. What would you say is the most necessary quality in a cameraman?"

"He needs to be free of emotional prejudgment—to have an objective lens that allows the shot to reveal itself. He certainly needs a sensitive eye that's quick enough to catch what can happen in fleeting seconds. Knowing where to turn the camera at the right moment can require a lot of expertise. Then there's always the problem of trying to be invisible. People who aren't actors can either freeze when there's a camera around, or else mug and show off. It's part of my job to get them to relax and forget the camera, but the man behind the lens plays a big role in that."

Kelsey stole a look at Denis, but his eyes were closed and he might have gone to sleep, except that his mouth twitched now and then.

"*Salinas* didn't seem a really dramatic story, in spite of the skill that went into making it," Francesca put in, the barb stabbing again.

Tyler said, "The individual struggle is always dramatic. I make films about subjects that seem important to me."

"It must be lovely to be independent so that you can do what the rest of us can't always manage. Your father was a bank president, I understand, and very successful and wealthy."

There was another instant of silence on the tape, and Kelsey could imagine Tyler's stiffening. But dead air was hardly Francesca's purpose, and she must have recognized ground too dangerous for even her insensitive foot. The tragedy of Tyler's childhood loomed large in that moment of quiet.

Francesca went on conversationally. "You know I love tidbits of gossip—everyone does—and an interesting one came my way that I've wondered about. Of course you've been to Nepenthe?"

"I've been there." Tyler was curt.

For a moment Kelsey lost the words on the tape because Denis dropped one of the carved beads, and bent to retrieve it from under a chair.

"I suppose you've met Olga?" Francesca was asking when Kelsey's attention returned.

"The fortune-teller at Nepenthe?"

"Oh, she's not reading her tarot cards actively anymore. But I ran into her a few months ago when she was up here, and we were reminiscing. Does the date of July 16, 1974, mean anything to you, Mr. Hammond?"

"Not that I can think of. Should it?"

"You might ask your mother-in-law about it sometime. Olga and I both happened to be at Nepenthe on that date when Dora Langford came there. Were you married to your wife then, Mr. Hammond?"

"What are you getting at?" Kelsey could hear anger rising in Tyler's voice, and she felt angry herself. He didn't deserve Francesca's viciousness and public probing.

Kelsey glanced at Denis, who looked sickened and disgusted, and he spoke over the voices to Marisa. "Must we listen to any more?"

"Just a bit more." Marisa had stopped the machine briefly when Denis spoke, but now she touched the button again, and the tape picked up after a slight break.

"Olga was very sympathetic about you and your family, Mr. Hammond. Whether you've troubled to remember that day or not. Some people think she has a talent for prophecy, and she seemed to be saying that still more trouble might be avoided if you took a proper course of action. Not that I believe in all that. When I saw Olga at Nepenthe all those years ago, she seemed to see trouble in *my* future, and I've really done all right."

"It can still happen," Tyler said testily. "Maybe you'd better tell me straight out whatever it is you're getting at."

Francesca turned coy. "Oh, not on the air. Sorry, dear listeners. Mr. Hammond, if you'll come out to my ranch at Flaming Tree very soon, perhaps I can help you to ward off fate. Or whatever. In private, of course."

Marisa stopped the tape abruptly. "No use listening to the rest. It gets even nastier after this. What a witch she was!" She wound the tape back to the beginning and took it out to hand to Kelsey.

"You'd better give this to Tyler," she said.

Kelsey didn't want to take the tape, and Denis reached for it. "Tyler won't want to hear any of this again, Marisa," he said. "Why not just destroy it?"

Marisa held the cassette back from his hand. "Because there may be something here that Tyler has forgotten. Something he ought to look into again. I'm convinced there are words, hints, on this tape that concern the present."

Meaning Francesca's death? Kelsey wondered. But Tyler had been cleared, and she'd believed what he himself had told her.

Marisa went on, puzzling aloud. "Why should Olga have brought that past date up with Francesca—or Francesca with her? What was Olga hinting at in her prophecy—if you want to call it that? It might be a good idea for Tyler to track Olga down and find out."

"Find out *what?*" Kelsey asked.

"Perhaps why Dora Langford went to Nepenthe on the date Francesca mentions on the tape."

"How can that possibly have anything to do with now?" Denis asked.

Marisa shrugged. "I don't know. The vibes seem all wrong, and I believe Tyler ought to see Olga. Give him the tape, Kelsey, and let him decide."

"Why me? Why don't you give it to him yourself?"

"Because, my dear"—Marisa's smile was unsettling—"you are the one who has an inside track with Tyler right now. Maybe you're the one he trusts. He's started to get very nervous about my—hunches. He thinks you are sensible, though fervent, and that you've placed Jody's health above anything else. So he might listen to you and go to Nepenthe."

"I doubt that. I'm not going to urge him, but I'll think about this." Kelsey took the tape reluctantly and put it in her purse. "What is Nepenthe?"

Marisa's face brightened. "It's one of my favorite spots in the area. It's down the Big Sur coast. A truly mystical place. I knew Olga rather well at one time. She used her first name alone because her last name was—for us—unpronounceable Russian. In her way, she became quite famous locally, and everyone used to go to her for readings. I suspect she was rather good—what they call a 'sensitive.'"

Denis disagreed. "She was good at picking up bits of information and feeding them back to the gullible. She never had what you have, Marisa."

"I'm not sure you're right," Marisa said. "Of course she's getting on in years now, and she doesn't work on a regular basis anymore. Big Sur is the name for that whole coast area, but I understand she has a house in the tiny post office location also known as Big Sur."

"Nepenthe is only a restaurant," Denis said to Kelsey, dismissing it.

Marisa shook her head. "It's more than that. Nepenthe is a Greek word that means 'no sorrow.' The phoenix is the symbol they've adopted—the bird that rises from the fire and renews itself eternally. Lolly and Bill Fassett built the place years ago.

They brought in a student of Frank Lloyd Wright to design the big redwood and adobe building so that it fits into that spectacular spot on the mountain. When the fog clears, there's a stunning view of mountains and ocean."

Marisa sounded almost dreamy, and Denis called her back by holding out the three carved beads from Francesca's necklace. "What do you know about these, Marisa?"

She took the beads from him, examined them with a shudder, and returned them as though she found their touch abhorrent.

"Francesca's bad luck?"

"Because of some sort of African curse." Denis sounded impatient. "She always bragged about getting those beads in Nairobi, and claimed they kept her safe from harm."

"Francesca bragged about a lot of things," Marisa said. "As a matter of fact, I don't think she was ever in Africa in her life. It was Olga who gave her those beads one time when she came to Nepenthe. Olga told her she needed protection unless she changed her ways, and the luck would hold as long as the necklace was intact. That's why Francesca went completely to pieces when she broke the chain during the interview with Tyler. She wanted to have the beads restrung immediately, but she knew how many there were, and that three were still missing. So she waited. That gave Olga's dark prophecy time to come true."

"God!" Denis threw the beads on a table beside the recorder and let them roll haphazardly. "Tyler, and most of all my sister, don't need to be upset with this kind of mumbo jumbo. Don't go spooky on us, Marisa."

She watched him sadly. "You're concerned because Dora was there that day, aren't you? I'm sorry if I've upset you. I only meant for Kelsey to hear the tape—not you."

"Well, she's heard it, and if she's as smart as I think she is, she'll erase it so no one else will ever listen to Francesca's nastiness again. Kelsey, if you're ready to leave, we can have dinner in Carmel. I need to be back at the inn by eight."

Marisa's turquoise wings had ceased to float her about the room. Indeed, she looked wilted as she came with them to the door. Denis said good-bye and went toward his car, but Marisa held Kelsey back for a moment.

"The ugly fact is that Francesca meant to blackmail Tyler with something she learned from Olga. If he knows what it was, then it no longer matters. If she didn't get around to telling him, then perhaps it does. Perhaps Francesca died because of her own vicious instincts."

"Can't we let it be forgotten?" Kelsey asked. "No matter what Dora might have been mixed up in years ago, shouldn't we leave it alone? There's enough trouble for all of them as it is."

"Not if you want Jody to get well," Marisa said. "I have such a strong feeling about this that it frightens me a little." She kissed Kelsey lightly on the cheek, gave her a slight push toward Denis's car, and then went inside, closing her redwood door firmly.

The sound seemed both warning and dismissal. Thoroughly upset, Kelsey went down the steps and got into the front seat beside Denis.

"What was that all about?" he asked.

"I'm not sure," Kelsey said. She couldn't repeat Marisa's words to Denis. It might be more useful to toss the tape into one of those restless seas as they made their way back to Carmel. Yet she couldn't bring herself to commit it to the water.

Since the hour was early, Kelsey and Denis found the small, charming restaurant in Carmel nearly empty. Denis asked for a table near a window, where they could watch the street and talk quietly. At first, however, he had little to say. He scanned the menu, ordered for them both without much interest, and lost himself in what were obviously gloomy thoughts.

Kelsey tried a question. "Listening to the tape has upset you, hasn't it? What does it mean, Denis?"

Over steaming onion soup he finally began to talk, but his words took an unexpected direction. Instead of discussing the interview, he told her more about Dora.

"I've seen pictures of my mother when she was young and she was very pretty. I think in his way even the General fell in love with her. Of course he wanted a suitable wife, children— a son. That would come first. She must have been quite a spirited girl in those days. It's strange about some men. They see what they want in a woman, but they don't want her to have the same attraction for *other* men so they stamp out the very qualities that drew them in the first place. Though the General never quite stamped them out of Dora. I'm afraid she learned to dissemble, to give him what he wanted, whether it was based on a lie or not—so long as she could keep something for herself and her children."

All this was part of the larger picture that Kelsey needed to understand, and she listened intently. Dora, the General, even Denis himself, were part of the past that had created Ruth, and now affected Tyler so strongly that he seemed at times a haunted man. Jody's recovery, as Marisa had pointed out, might hang in the precarious balance because of all that had gone before. The tape might offer a clue to this, yet somehow she was afraid of it.

After a moment of staring gloomily out at the street, Denis picked up his story again.

"By the time I was ten, I knew how strong Dora could be. If you can call it strength. Relentless is more like it. All that waffling she does is an act. I remember the times when she stood between me and the General, while not seeming to do so at all. I don't mean that she ever loved me as much as she did

Ruth. I knew when I was very young that it was always Ruth
who must come first. My sister came first with me too then, so I
could accept that. Though these days I sometimes don't even
like Ruth the way she is now. Dora has never changed toward
her at all. She's ready to fight Tyler for her, and I think she'd
even sacrifice Jody if it would spare Ruth. Of course 'Dora' is
the wrong name for her. It's a mousy, meek sort of name.
When I was around twelve, I used to play a game. I'd pick out
names I thought would suit her better."

He smiled at himself, remembering. His childhood couldn't
have been happy, Kelsey thought, yet, remarkably enough,
Denis seemed to have come through with an affection for his
mother, and without blaming her because she put his sister
first.

"What names did you give her?" she asked.

"Oh, I tried some pretty fancy stuff at first: Alexandra, Ber-
nadette, Yolanda—romantic names of heroines. But she wasn't
any of those, and I wound up calling her Judith. That seemed
to be a strong name that suited what she was like a lot better
than Dora."

"Did she know you called her that?"

"I told her once, and she laughed and said I'd better not tell
my father. He wanted a *Dora.* It's strange about names, isn't it?
Start thinking about her as Judith and you're likely to see a
different person."

"*Your* name seems right, Denis."

He shrugged. "I wouldn't know. What does it mean to you?"

"It's a name for a gentle man, a kind and considerate man."

"I'm not any of those things. I expect my father was right
about me a lot of the time. He thought I was weak because I
believe in people too easily. Or used to. And I'm too easily
influenced. Maybe I like to please the person I'm with—a sort
of chameleon. You're lucky, Kelsey. You have a name that's
unusual, so no one can hand you preconceived character traits.

You're a Kelsey—and that's it. A Kelsey, as far as I'm concerned, is someone who says what she thinks, who won't give up, and has enough imagination to pull her through all sorts of difficulties. Most of all, she's compassionate."

A waitress brought their broiled steaks, and Kelsey considered Denis's words in surprise, a little embarrassed. She hadn't realized that he'd been summing her up so carefully. But he wasn't altogether right, even if she'd like to accept some of what he'd said. He'd missed her foolish impulsiveness, her ability to dig unnecessary pits and then fall into them so that she had to fight to scramble out. And he'd missed her present confusion. Compassion wasn't enough, when she couldn't be sure what was wrong to begin with.

What had been said on the tape must still be worrying him, for he turned again to the subject of Dora. "Tell me what you think of my mother, Kelsey."

She tried to answer carefully. "I don't really know her. Sometimes she watches me. I mean literally—from windows. I think she's afraid I might actually hurt Ruth in some way."

"Maybe she's right."

"What do you mean? You know I've only tried to help."

Denis looked thoughtful, a little sad. "Will it help if you fall in love with Tyler? Ruth believes that's what's happening to you."

She hated the warmth in her cheeks, betraying her. "That's absurd! Tyler's only interest in me is because of what I might do for Jody."

"Ruth doesn't think he is interested in *you*, Kelsey. It's the other way around. I'm sorry—don't be upset if I say that. Just be on guard. He's a tremendously attractive man physically—sexually. And he's mentally stimulating and exciting to women. When he chooses to be. They've always responded to him, and Ruth knows that. She also knows that his fancies have been passing ones. It doesn't help much that she can see through him, now that it's too late."

Over her own impatience with herself, Kelsey had to rush into denial. "I don't even like Tyler's type of man! He's overbearing, inconsiderate, locked into his own ego, and—"

"I'm sorry you've fallen so hard for him, Kelsey."

She choked and closed her eyes against the wave of angry pain that enveloped her.

Denis took her hand across the table. "Don't look like that, Kelsey. I don't want to see you hurt. That's why I've had to speak frankly."

"Don't worry about me." She pulled her hand back. "I haven't any intention of getting hurt."

"That's fine, Kelsey. Hold on to that—if you can."

She wasn't at all sure she could and she stopped protesting.

"In the long run it's hard to hold on to anything," Denis said. "Maybe it doesn't matter whether it's love or hate—it all adds up to indifference in the end."

This, at least, she wouldn't accept. "Must I add the word 'cynical' to my list for you, Denis? Do you really believe that?"

He didn't answer directly. "Sometimes I wish that Ginnie and I had married years ago. Though I'm not sure it would have been right for either of us. I expect she'll be happier with her present plans. I've met Billy Yang, and I think he'll be good for her."

"Why didn't you two marry?" Kelsey said, glad of any side road.

"I'm not sure. Sometimes I think Tyler broke it up. At least that's what Ruth believed. Maybe he had a thing for Ginnie in those days himself, so that after a while Ginnie and I just moved apart. Of course when Ruth went after Tyler, he didn't stand a chance. My sister is a fascinating woman, and maybe he met his match. You've never seen her the way she used to be, Kelsey. Anyway, it was all a mess, with slightly splintered hearts all over the place. Ginnie went north, and I started a torrid affair with a minor movie actress. All silly and futile. And all past history. Next question?"

"I'm sorry. It's just that I care about what happened to all of you."

"It's okay." He grinned at her ruefully. "Anyway, I know the next question: 'Isn't there someone now?'"

"It's none of my business," she said, and knew she sounded stiff.

"Perhaps we've become your business—because of Jody, Kelsey. What did Marisa say to you a little while ago when you were leaving."

She could tell him now, since they'd seemed to arrive at a more open friendship—though perhaps a franker, more painful friendship than before.

"She said something strange. She said that if I wanted Jody to get well, I should give the interview tape to Tyler. Then he would probably go to Nepenthe and talk to that Russian fortune-teller. He would ask her why your mother went there on that date. I don't understand the connection with Jody, and it seems reaching pretty far."

Denis's expression had darkened. "What's the point of digging up something that happened so long ago? Jody wasn't even born then. I don't want to see my mother tormented anymore. She's had a harder life than any of us, and she's always given herself too much to others. If you follow through with the tape it will only bring back an unpleasant time in her life. Marisa's advice isn't always sensible."

Yet it was Denis who had called Marisa a "wise woman."

"I won't do it right away. I'm still going to think about it first." She couldn't promise more than that, being too uncertain herself.

Denis had lost his appetite, and Kelsey was no longer hungry either. While they waited for the check, she asked one more question.

"Denis, do *you* know why your mother went to Nepenthe that time?"

It was the wrong question. He looked at her despairingly and didn't answer. The more open friendship she thought they'd reached had its boundaries, of course. How little one ever really knew about other people. Summings-up were superficial, touching only upper levels, with so much more hidden underneath than one could penetrate.

At least, she thought, as they walked a block or two to where he'd left his car, Denis had made her aware of her own self-deception. There were emotions that she hadn't been willing to face or probe in herself, and she wasn't sure she could face them now. To let down her instinctive guard and admit that she was in love with Tyler Hammond—that could be devastating. Yet it might be the first step toward facing the problem of what she must do about it.

When they'd driven back to the Highlands, she put her hand on Denis's arm before she left the car.

"Thank you. I'm grateful for the things you said, and I really mean that."

His own guard was still up. "I enjoyed it," he said lightly. "I'll see you soon."

At the top of the steps she stood for a moment looking down upon red tiles and blue walls, hearing Denis as he drove away.

When she went inside she was sharply conscious of Marisa's tape in her purse. She wished she could destroy it without another thought—be rid of it. But she knew she must wait and avoid another of those treacherous pits into which she could so easily tumble. Too many mistakes lay behind her, beginning with her marriage. Strange—there were times when Carl's face seemed indistinct in her memory. The face of a stranger she'd known long ago. But every hair of Mark's head, every expression of his face, or movement of his sturdy little body was there to be vividly recalled, and there was no healing for her yet.

When she reached Jody's room, she found a night nurse with him, and she sat by his bed for an hour or so. He seemed to have recovered from his earlier upset, and she wondered how much he was able to remember of anything that happened to him. Or of anything that was said, no matter how much it disturbed him at the time. There were different layers of memory, and until he could talk it was impossible to gauge how much he'd forgotten of old happenings, or even of how long he might hold on to the new. Any talk of Point Lobos could upset him, so there must be something remembered there.

The days that followed were pleasantly uneventful, except for a slow but noticeable improvement in Jody. Dr. Norman came again to see how he was tolerating the treatment, and was pleased with his progress. No drugs were being used, but only the nutritional help she'd prescribed, and she felt that everything would move faster now as his own body worked toward healing.

For those who are ill good food is vital—something most hospitals still have to learn—but at this stage Jody needed so much more than food alone could provide. By this time he was beginning to take mouthfuls from a spoon, learning to chew again, and the vitamins had obviously increased his appetite, which was one of their functions.

Dr. Norman's positive and encouraging presence was in itself helpful, not only to Jody, who seemed to like her, but for those who worked with him as well. She had never needed to take "classes" in compassion. It was there in her eyes, in her warm smile, and always in her voice and reassuring words.

With each new step, Kelsey or Ginnie explained to Jody exactly what was about to happen. He seemed willing to accept what they wanted to do more readily now, no longer lost in a limbo where he couldn't reach out, and where those around him didn't realize they could reach in. Communication, though still elementary, had begun.

The woman acupuncturist visited every few days, and while Jody made faces, he was now willing to tolerate a little discomfort. The real pain he had suffered in the beginning had lessened a great deal, so he accepted needles that were placed at certain points to help relieve his spasticity. The treatment was still new for this purpose, but Dr. Norman welcomed everything that showed promise, providing it would do no harm. Massage treatments were introduced as well, and this seemed to help Jody's muscles to relax. Since there appeared to be real progress, everyone felt heartened.

Kelsey began several new exercises with him, both mental and physical. One of them was to help him learn to count out loud again. In a way, it was like teaching a small child from the beginning, though it was clear right away that his brain still knew how to count.

She sat close to him and made sure she had his attention. "Jody, I'd like you to think about the steps that go up outside the Hawk Tower at Tor House. You've climbed them lots of times, and I'll bet you know how many there are. So now you're going to tell me. Start up those steps in your mind, Jody. That's always the beginning of doing anything. First we imagine ourselves doing it, and then we can make it real. You're getting ready now for the time when you'll stand alone, and then take steps. You'll really climb the Tower again one of these days. Just take one step and then another in your mind, Jody, and count them for me. Let me hear you begin."

He understood and made an effort. He managed six steps up the tower, each a somewhat tortured effort, with sounds that might approximate the numbers. When he tired and stopped trying, Kelsey hugged him.

"That was very good, Jody. You don't have to climb the whole tower right away."

Now and then Tyler stopped in, and Kelsey felt an increasing awkwardness with him. Since having dinner with Denis, she'd tried to face her own feelings honestly. She cared too much about Tyler, and she knew that this must be hidden—not from herself, but from him and those around him. This wasn't easy to do because of her own awareness. Even the way his hair grew at the nape of his neck, the way his fingers touched Jody, smoothing his cheek, ruffling his hair—these were shivery to watch. Shivery in all the wrong ways. She'd been too long without a man in her life, and she had to be careful lest her own emotions lead her where she dare not go.

She still hadn't given him the tape. More and more she doubted Marisa's judgment on this, and held back. Once Tyler heard it, he might be reminded of something better forgotten, and he could very well choose a course that would lead to further trouble. So she waited, postponing, equivocating, marking time. She wasn't being dishonest now, but simply unwilling to decide about something so important. Perhaps she was even waiting for some sign that would help her to do what was right and wise.

These days, Ginnie hummed a lot as she worked around Jody, and he seemed to enjoy her cheerful presence. "I do think he's getting better," she said to Kelsey one morning. "He's stronger, more alert. Of course nothing can happen quickly, but I have a feeling now that he really will improve. He's so much further along than doctors ever thought he would come. One thing's for sure—he's no vegetable!"

Several times Tyler brought his video camera to Jody's room so that the record of small day-to-day changes could be caught, and even Tyler was less gloomy now.

His shoulders were straighter, as though the will to deal with whatever troubled him had returned, and his step seemed lighter. He even joked with Jody now and then. This didn't mean that the torment Kelsey had sensed in him had vanished completely. Always, underlying whatever he did, there seemed a deep anguish that he could submerge, but not entirely deal with.

For Kelsey this seemed both puzzling and a little frightening. Enough had happened recently in his life to weigh him down and cause any amount of anguish. Yet this seemed a deeper, older pain. The look of it had been clear in the photograph Marisa had hung in her studio. Perhaps since Kelsey's own acceptance of the way she felt about Tyler, her perceptions went deeper and she saw the troubling questions in him —the indecision he tried to hide. Disturbing in so decisive a man.

There was one vivid moment when Kelsey had stood on the balcony outside her room savoring a stormy day. The ocean rolled in and broke on the land, sending white froth high. Rain spattered her face, but she didn't mind. She was surprised to see Tyler climbing up through the trees, his head wet, the collar of his pea jacket turned up as he attacked the hill vigorously, not slowed by its steepness. He came to one place where wind tossed the brush about so that Kelsey caught a glimpse of white marble, and saw that he had stopped before the little statue that Ruth's mother had brought home from France. He seemed to study it for a long time, heedless of wind and rain as the storm beat about him. When he climbed again and neared the house, she caught a glimpse of the same look of despair she had seen in him before. Once more, his shoulders rounded under some burden he couldn't deal with, and she saw their heaviness as he disappeared into the house.

During all this time, Ruth remained shut away in her own sad, frightened world. Occasionally, she was brought down to see Jody, and at least she did nothing to upset him. In fact, when she was present he seemed to make more of an effort to talk—as though there were something he wanted terribly to tell her. The sounds were still unintelligible, except for a few words, and Kelsey suffered with him over his inability to say what he wanted to say. Sometimes the struggle would end in tears of frustration. Then there could be a setback, when he lost himself in an apathetic world where nothing seemed to reach him. Setbacks were to be expected, since progress was never entirely upward, but these times seemed especially upsetting. And Ruth responded with her own frustrated tears.

With tubes going into Jody's body, infection was always possible, and then antibiotics were needed. But those drugs brought their own undesirable aftermath, and then Dr. Norman increased the nutrients that would counteract such damage. She suggested a new type of catheter that seemed to help. She said that as his body grew stronger he would be better able to fight infections, and the treatment he was now under would increase this ability.

Ever since Kelsey had brought the tape home from Marisa's, she had felt increasingly uncomfortable about possessing it. She took to concealing it in a different place in her room whenever she left, though—except for that one unnerving phone call—she had no evidence that anyone held a grudge against her, or would be interested in the tape. Was she, after all, more sensitive to vibes than she realized?

One plus, without any reservations, was the uninhibited presence of the small dog, Wolf. By this time he knew how to jump up on Jody's knees, and he seemed to sense that this helpless young boy was his new family to whom he was ready to give loyal, loving allegiance. His uncritical attitude was good for Jody, since Wolf never asked for anything but love. In response, the boy began to blurt out a few syllables of a language that only he and Wolf understood. Everyone helped by taking Wolf for walks, and he cheered them all. The household fell into what was almost a comfortable routine. Almost—since

Kelsey still felt there were stormy seas ahead, and a rocky, threatening shore where sooner or later they had to land. More than once she asked herself what it was that Tyler seemed afraid to face.

Once she even questioned Denis about what might trouble Tyler so deeply. Denis had said, "Don't ask, Kelsey. You don't really want to know." She felt sure that whatever it was had to do with Ruth, and that Denis suffered some pain of his own for his sister.

One sunny afternoon Tyler arranged a special outing—their most enjoyable time with Jody before everything blew open and the strange, inevitable march toward Point Lobos began. Although it was not until much later that Kelsey could look back and see the inevitability.

On this occasion Tyler asked Ginnie to get Jody ready for a short trip. Kelsey was to come with them to help look after him. A new wheelchair that would fit Jody's specifications had been ordered, but in the meantime they still used Ruth's chair for outings.

This time they were going to Carmel Mission, where Jody could sit in the beautiful gardens and soak up the sun. It was a place he had enjoyed visiting, and it might give Tyler some good video shots.

The Mission of San Carlos Borromeo del Rio Carmelo, which Father Junipero Serra had founded in 1770, was the best restored mission in California. The first church on the site had been built of adobe bricks, and ten years later a sandstone structure had been erected, the stones quarried from the Santa Lucia Mountains in Carmel Valley. This building had fallen into neglect and ruin when all the California missions were secularized. It became a place haunted by bats, owls, and buzzards, to say nothing of vandals. Not until the thirties did real restoration begin.

Now the basilica raised its cross to the sky, and inside cool walls was the marble tomb of Father Serra. The tiny cell where he had lived and died had been restored, and the padre's library contained historic books and papers.

Jody, Tyler said, had shown some interest in the history of the Monterey area, so this place might stir a few pleasant memories.

As promised, the gardens glowed with color. There were fountains and cloistered walks, and small rooms that had once been the cells of monks. Over all rose two towers—one of them the bell tower, with the mud nests of swallows clinging high on the wall.

Jody managed to move his head to look around, and he didn't let it fall back to his chest. Tyler set up his video camera on its tripod and began to record Jody's reactions. He seemed more at ease with his son now, and Kelsey left them together while she wandered about a wide paved courtyard and into the quiet church. Not until she returned to sit on the stone edge of a fountain to watch Jody and his father did Tyler drop his bombshell.

He came to sit beside her, out of Jody's hearing. "I had a phone call from Marisa this morning," he said. "She wanted to know what I thought of the interview with Francesca that she'd taped. She said she gave it to you to give to me some time ago. So how about it, Kelsey? Why have you been holding it back?"

For a moment she tried to put him off. "After all, you did that interview, so you already know what's on the tape. Why is it important to hear it again?"

"Considering what happened, I don't remember a fraction of what was said. Marisa said I should hear it the way it went over the air—hear it objectively. I don't believe that's possible, and I dislike living through it again, but Marisa is insistent. She even thinks it might tell me something useful. Why didn't you give it to me, Kelsey?"

He seemed neither angry nor outraged, but merely puzzled —troubled in an unforeseen way.

"I'll get it for you as soon as we return to the house," she said. "I've been worrying about it long enough. I wasn't sure whether Marisa was right this time. I don't know why, but I'm afraid of that tape."

"I expect that's for me to decide. Have you any idea why Marisa wanted me to listen to it? She wouldn't explain."

"She said . . ." Kelsey hesitated, "she said it had something to do with Jody's getting well. There's some connection with Francesca Fallon, of course—perhaps something she said on the air. Though I don't understand how it can affect Jody now."

He stared at her for a moment, and then stood up. "Let's go home and you can give me the tape."

At least he was careful not to upset Jody with any suddenness about leaving. They'd seen all they needed for this time, he told his son, and they would come back again if Jody would like that. He'd take one more shot of Kelsey talking to Jody, and then they'd leave.

"I wonder if you can point at the swallows' nests, Jody?" Kelsey asked. "Can you lift your arm a little so your father can take a picture of you pointing at the nests?"

"Sure," Jody said quite clearly, and raised his arm at least three inches. Significantly, a forefinger pointed.

"Did you hear?" Kelsey cried to Tyler. "Did you see?"

Tyler had heard and seen, and he'd recorded the whole thing on tape. They both hugged Jody at the same time. Caught in their arms, he laughed between them. It was a lovely, close moment. Too close, because for those seconds Tyler's arms were around Kelsey as well as around his son, and for her it was a moment of trembling restraint. She kept very still, not wanting to lose the sense of their physical closeness. Tyler must have sensed it too, because he dropped his arms abruptly and began to get Jody ready for the trip home.

When they reached the house, Tyler had withdrawn again, and spoke to her curtly. "Get the tape now," he said. "I'll take Jody to his room and wait for you in my study."

The moment she stepped into her room, Kelsey knew that someone had been there. Not just Hana. Her cosmetic case had been opened and moved off center. Someone had looked into bureau drawers—not disturbing anything very much, but just enough so that Kelsey suspected there had been a rapid, cursory search.

This time she'd placed the tape inside a pillowcase when she'd made the bed that morning to save Hana extra work. When she thrust her hand inside the case, the small plastic box containing the tape was there. For a moment she held it in her hand, undecided. There was still time to destroy it, but if someone else was so interested then Tyler had better have it at once.

She went downstairs to his study and placed it on the desk before him. Then she hurried away, with no wish to hear the tape again, or to watch Tyler's face as he listened to it. More and more, she feared something that she didn't understand, but that Tyler would recognize at once.

The moment she reached the upstairs hall to her room, she knew someone was there waiting for her. She felt the sense of a breathing presence that never occurred in an empty place.

The upper hall seemed ominously dark, and she realized someone had turned out the lights.

XV

A WINDOW at the far end of the hall, though shaded by pines, let in a little green light. Otherwise the rooms with their closed doors made the hall seem all the more shadowy. She knew absolutely that someone was there, perhaps quietly watching her.

"Dora?" she said. There was no answer. Surely Ruth wouldn't risk moving about by day, but Kelsey spoke softly again. "Ruth?"

Still no answer, but a board not far away creaked under the weight of a foot. She realized that the door of her room stood ajar, though she'd closed it when she left. The sound had come from that opening. Suddenly she was frightened. The telephone was too far away, and the delay of trying to rouse someone might be too great a risk.

She moved a few cautious steps ahead until she was even with an elbow of hall that jutted toward the front of the house. Though she had no idea where the jog went or what blind alley she might step into, it seemed better to follow than to go blindly ahead toward her room—or try to escape toward distant stairs.

The new hall was short, its ceiling sloping with the eaves of the house, and it ended at another window that overlooked the front courtyard. This, she realized, was one of the windows from which she'd seen Dora watching her—a window that was well concealed. There seemed no place here to hide, however. Then as her eyes grew used to the darkness, another narrow, closed door emerged from the shadows on her left, its china knob gleaming palely. Since there was nowhere else to go, she opened the door and slipped into what seemed a dark closet, bumping her head on the low ceiling.

Inside, she stood very still, breathing quickly, wondering what to do now. In a moment, however, she realized that it wasn't a closet at all but a passage that led a few feet farther into the dark, where there appeared to be still another door.

Opening the second door, she heard voices below, and realized where she was. This was the small gallery built out over one end of the great living room. Denis had told her that musicians had played up here, and there had been poetry readings in the old days. Now, standing in this unlighted space, she could look down into the room below, where two people sat talking before the empty fireplace. The sofa on which they sat was set at right angles to the fireplace and to this gallery, so she could see them in profile. The two were Dora and Denis Langford.

She hadn't noticed Denis's car when Tyler drove in, and she wondered how he'd gotten here. The two were speaking softly, but the walls of the room formed a sounding board, and one word reached her clearly—her own name. Kelsey knelt behind the open balusters of the balcony.

"Kelsey's all right," Denis was saying. "She only cares about Jody. She won't hurt anyone. And she's helped Jody a lot."

"That's what we all want," Dora said. "You know that. But the moment he is able to talk—*if* he can remember—he will tell what he saw. Then you know what will happen. You know how violent Tyler can be."

Denis put his face in his hands, looking the picture of misery. "I want to help Ruth. But this is something no one can stop."

"She only told me a day or so ago about what happened," Dora said. "I've been thinking this out carefully. That's why I phoned you while Tyler and Kelsey are still away at the mission with Jody. Did anyone see you come in?"

"It doesn't matter. I left my car down the hill a little way, but I can certainly visit my mother if I like. What *did* Ruth tell you?"

"Never mind that now—there's no time. Marisa phoned me to say that she'd given the taped interview to Kelsey. But Kelsey hasn't given it to Tyler yet. She wanted me to ask Kelsey why she hasn't. What was on that tape, Denis? I need to know before I start meddling."

He seemed at a loss. "It concerns that time years ago when you went to Nepenthe. I still think that was an idiotic thing to do, Dora. It wasn't like you to be so impulsive."

"You know why I went. Denis, can you get that tape back from Kelsey before she shows it to Tyler?"

"It's already too late for that."

Dora stood up impatiently. "I can see that as usual you're no help. Stay away from Ruth, Denis. I don't want her to be any more upset than she already is."

She walked out of the room and Denis stayed dejectedly where he was for a moment. Then he rose and looked absently around, his gaze seeming to rise to where Kelsey knelt in shadow. He didn't see her, however, and after a moment he went out of the room.

Kelsey retraced her steps, stooping through the low doorway to follow the elbow toward the main hall. It hadn't been Dora up here, waiting for her in silence. So that left Ruth.

Ruth, taking a chance, and moving about by day, believing her husband was out of the house.

The long hall was very still, and now there was no sense of someone breathing, waiting. The door of her room had been closed, and that could mean that whoever had waited for her had gone away, or else that Ruth—it must be Ruth—had let herself into the room and was still there, waiting. Less frightened now, Kelsey opened the bedroom door and stepped inside, pulling it shut behind her.

At once her feet crunched over peanut shells strewn across the carpet, and she remembered the peanut-eating ghost Hana had mentioned. There was no one in the room, but Ruth stood outside on the balcony, and when she heard Kelsey she came in, smiling.

"A nice touch, don't you think—the shells? We always like to amuse our guests."

"Why didn't you answer a little while ago when I called you?" Kelsey asked.

Ruth shrugged and sat down in an armchair. She still wore a robe, but jeans showed under it. "Maybe I wanted to worry you a little."

"I don't understand why. Anyway, you scared me enough so that I explored and found a door that led to the gallery over the living room. An interesting side trip."

"Oh?"

"Your mother and your brother were there in the living room whispering to each other. That room magnifies sound, so I could hear what they said."

Ruth sat up, suddenly anxious. "I didn't know Denis was in the house. I don't want him to know that I can walk now. It's better if he doesn't. What did he want?"

"Your mother must have summoned him. She seems worried about the time when Jody may begin to talk. And she wanted to know what was on the tape Marisa Marsh made of

Francesca's interview with your husband. Is the tape what you've been looking for here, Ruth—or was it Dora who went through my things?"

Ruth blinked and ignored that. "What could Dora possibly expect Denis to do?"

"Maybe she thought he'd try to get the tape away from me. When he told her it was too late for that, she walked out. So this is a good time for you to explain to me what this is all about."

"That's why I came to your room, Kelsey. The last time I saw Jody he was struggling to speak, and I think it's all going to be blurted out before long. You're with him a lot, and he may talk to you. If that happens, you can save everyone a lot of grief and pointless trouble. Just listen and tell me what he says. Try to keep him from talking to anyone else until we know what he remembers."

Kelsey plumped up a pillow on the bed and sat against it, stretching out. "I'm ready to listen, Ruth."

Ruth's fingers plucked at the cloth of her robe. "I'm sure I behaved foolishly at the time, but I was too frightened to be sensible."

"Suppose you begin at the beginning."

"I hate to talk about it—it was so awful. But I know I must, because of Jody. Tyler wasn't the only one who was angry with Francesca after that radio interview. I wasn't there, but I heard it on the air, and I could see what she was up to. If she was going to blackmail anyone, it was better if it was me than Tyler. So I drove out to Flaming Tree to see if I could talk to her. There was no one to leave Jody with that day, so I took him along. I thought he could play outside while I talked to Francesca. Only that wasn't the way it happened."

She broke off, closing her eyes as though she were seeing again the scene she described. When she went on, Kelsey could hear the tinge of horror in her voice.

"The front door was open, so Jody and I walked in—right in on that ghastly scene. Kelsey, she was already dead when we got there. It was awful for Jody to see—all that blood! He was terribly upset, and the only thing I could think of was to get out of there quickly and take him home."

"You didn't report what you found?"

Ruth shook her head miserably. "I know—I'm a coward. But I didn't want Tyler to know that I ever tried to see her. If I'd said anything, the blackmail scheme might have come out—and why Francesca was doing this. It would have been dreadful for all of us."

"Why should it be, if you were innocent? Since Jody was with you, you could prove your innocence."

"I didn't want him questioned. Besides, who would take the word of a small boy? On the way home I pulled off the road and we talked awhile. I tried to be very calm and reasonable. I made him understand that it was better to say nothing. She was dead and there wasn't a thing we could do for her. I explained that it might mean serious trouble for Tyler and me if he talked about this. So he promised me he'd keep still. But it must have been boiling up inside him, and he kept edging toward blurting it out. Tyler knew something was troubling him, and we almost had a fight because he was asking Jody too many questions that day before we went out to Point Lobos. Jody was so upset that I took him away for a picnic and a chance to talk to him alone. And then—" Her voice broke. "Please believe me, Kelsey. I didn't have anything to do with what happened to Francesca. I wouldn't have had the strength to hit her that hard."

Kelsey sat up on the side of the bed. "So the lies have kept on piling up to smother the truth about what happened. And Francesca's murderer goes uncaught. You might have had something useful to tell the police. And you'd have spared

Jody." She knew she was condemning Ruth because of Jody, who was still harboring this terrible secret.

"Oh God, Kelsey—I'm not a monster. I know I haven't behaved well. In my life I've done a lot of crazy, spoiled things. But I didn't kill Francesca, and I didn't go out to Point Lobos and throw myself and Jody off the rocks. I've never been the suicidal type, and I'd never harm my son. You must believe me, Kelsey."

"I think I do believe you. Only I'm not sure what I'm supposed to do with what you've told me. This must be horrible for Jody, if he can remember."

"You have a choice. You can go to Tyler and open it all up. Maybe that's the best way, late as it is. I'm tired of all the subterfuge—and it's all going to come out through Jody anyway."

"Why should you be afraid to have Tyler know? Won't he believe you?"

"I can't be sure. Sometimes I think he hates me."

Kelsey knew what the other choice was. "If I keep still, what will happen then? Anyway, I'm not sure I can promise that. Jody needs to be comforted, reassured."

"I won't ask for your promise. The most I can hope for is that you'll be there when Jody begins to talk. Help him, Kelsey. Maybe that way you can help all of us. He may be confused about what happened, and you can keep things straight."

"Does your mother know?"

"I didn't dare tell her until a few days ago. Now *she's* crazy with worry too."

Before Kelsey could ask about Dora's reaction, the telephone rang in the hall.

"I'll get it," she said, no longer nervous about the phone—not with all that had come into the open. She went to answer it, and the voice was Tyler's.

"Come down to my study," he said. "Right away, Kelsey.

We're going out again. Not with Jody. I'll explain when I see you. We'll have lunch while we're away."

Watching the door of her room, Kelsey saw Ruth slip out and go quietly off down the hall. "All right," she told Tyler. "I'll be there in a minute."

When she'd hung up, she returned to her room and stood for a moment on the balcony, looking out at a white cruiser going by on the bay. Confusion was difficult to deal with, and sound decision impossible. When she thought of the horror Jody had experienced, she could hardly bear it. It wasn't Point Lobos he was trying so hard to talk about. Yet if she told Tyler, what would he do to Ruth?

Sooner or later, Tyler would recognize how she felt about him, and if that happened there would be no way to retreat, no pretense she could manage, and she would hate her resulting loss of pride.

She went inside and joined him in his study. He told her very little. In fact, when they were on their way he began to speak as lightly as though this were a sight-seeing trip.

"You'll be interested in Nepenthe," he told her. Yet the way he spoke belied his tone, and she felt chilled. His purpose wouldn't be peaceful, and she felt increasingly anxious about what lay ahead.

"I know we're going because of Marisa's tape," she said, "but I wish you'd explain a little. Why must I come along?"

He shrugged off her question. "Relax. Whatever will happen, will happen." Someone was always saying that.

"Because you'll *make* it happen. What sort of serpents are you stirring up?"

"Anything else is postponement. And that has already gone on for too long. I'm glad Marisa sent me the tape. I'd forgotten some of what Francesca said that day."

He was beginning to sound almost cheerful, as though taking any sort of action was a relief to him.

"I've phoned ahead," he added. "Olga still lives in Big Sur, though she's retired now—as a fortune-teller. Nepenthe is three miles south of the Big Sur post office, and Olga's agreed to meet us there for lunch. Try to enjoy the trip, Kelsey. Look out the window. This is one of the most famous roads in America, and one of the most beautiful. Highway One—the Big Sur coastline."

She couldn't relax, or think of much else but the awful scene at Flaming Tree that Ruth had painted in her mind. The horror that Jody had been allowed to see, but never talk about, must still burn terribly in his brain, when and if he remembered. And she suspected that Ruth was right—that he did. He must long to talk to his mother, to receive her assurance that everything was all right—and to understand. But no one had ever taught Ruth to face reality and deal with it. Her father had been grimly realistic about everyone but his own daughter. Now, unprotected by the General, she could only run.

"It's a thirty-mile trip from Carmel," Tyler went on, "though the road goes clear down to San Simeon and on."

It was hard to understand his lighter mood. It seemed almost frivolous, but then he didn't know what Jody had seen.

The day was a rare one, free of fog from the ocean or mists on the mountains. The strip of highway—the coast road—seldom ran straight. All along the rocky edge of the continent the ocean had cut into granite in sharp indentations, where water foamed white and the seas tossed restlessly. Their road followed the ragged edges of the land, the curves winding high above rocks that crouched with their feet in the water. On the left, mountain ridges crowded in, sometimes bare, sometimes green, the slopes often covered with plumy pampas grass waving gracefully in the wind.

Since there was little traffic, Tyler slowed as they crossed the Bixby Bridge that spanned a deep gorge between two mountains.

"Until the coast road and this bridge were built, people had to follow the old road inland," Tyler said. "A long way around."

As she listened, Kelsey tried to suppress her troubling thoughts about what would happen when Tyler learned where Ruth had taken Jody, and even worse, about the merciless silence she had thrust upon him.

Tyler's voice ran on. "When all this was a wilderness—as some of it still is back in the mountains—the Spaniards called it El Pais Grande del Sur. The big country to the south. So Big Sur has stuck."

Sometimes, looking far ahead, Kelsey could see where the highway wound above indentations made by the ocean, curving between mountains and water. The road, like the bridge, must have been a spectacular job of engineering—work that must continue, since there'd been times recently when parts of the highway had dropped into the water, buried by landslides from cliffs that had been weakened by too much rain. Now and then they passed ominous warning signs about falling rock. The Santa Lucia Mountains flowed along above the road, their ridges sometimes double, sometimes triple, as they followed the coast.

Once Tyler stopped at a turnoff, and they left the car on the pretext of looking at the view. But now he had made up his mind, and he began to talk.

"We're going to Nepenthe because Olga knows what happened on the date Francesca mentioned in the interview. I've tried to put what she said out of my mind, but I can't anymore. I have to know the whole thing."

"You needn't explain," Kelsey said, though she'd wanted him to only moments before.

"Yes, I do. You have a right to understand, Kelsey. You're the one who fought me for Jody's life. You believed when I couldn't, and I owe you a great deal."

She didn't want him to feel that sort of obligation, but there was no stopping him now that he'd begun to talk. His words took a suddenly personal turn that had nothing to do with Jody.

"No matter what happens, I want you to know the truth. I've tried for a long time to fool myself about my marriage. Because I loved Ruth a great deal in the beginning—because loving her became a habit, even after I knew the woman I thought I loved didn't really exist—I kept trying to close my eyes so I needn't believe what should have been evident. I absorbed myself in my work and my son, and pretended that the marriage was still working. I want no more of that. So we're going to Nepenthe to learn the truth—and I want you to be there and hear for yourself."

"I'll be there if you want me," she said.

"I've counted on that." He spoke gently. "We'll go on now, though there's a lot more to tell. You'll know it all soon."

On their way again, he let the personal go and told her about Nepenthe itself. "In a way, it's Marisa's sort of place. Lolly and Bill Fassett bought the property in 1947, and lived there for a time in a log cabin they built. Then they decided that they wanted to share that beautiful spot with whoever cared to visit it. So a building was constructed where the view is splendid, and a restaurant opened. It's not as elegant as the Ventana Inn that comes just before, lower on the mountain, but it's a place for families to enjoy, and it has a special fantasy quality of its own."

"Marisa says there's something mystical about Nepenthe."

"She's right. Lolly has always understood the magic. They hold what they call zodiac dances once a month on the great terrace, and people come in costume to celebrate one astrological sign. I've heard that these affairs can be exciting and colorful. Maybe it really is a place to rid oneself of sorrow!" His tone had turned mocking.

Kelsey was all too aware of his nearness and of the sound of his voice—a presence that stirred everything she wanted to forget, and could not. She picked up his last words.

"Is that what you mean to do today? Rid yourself of sorrow?"

"That will depend on Olga and what she has to tell me. If I can get her to talk."

"Tell me about her."

"There are often fortune-tellers-in-residence at Nepenthe. Olga worked with tarot cards. She made no charge, but received what anyone wanted to donate. In her way, she became well known for what she could read and foretell. She's getting old now, and she lives quietly in a cabin in the valley behind Big Sur. There are probably less than two thousand people living around there, and they all had a taste of the even more primitive a few years ago when the coast road went out on both sides of the town. They were isolated for quite a while."

The end of the trip was near, and they drove past the few stores and post office of Big Sur. In a few miles, a narrower road turned up the mountain. They drove to a parking space and left the car to climb to the restaurant on foot.

The Phoenix Gift Shop occupied a lower level, its low roof crowned by an arresting statue carved of wood. Kelsey stopped to look up at the tall figure that might be part angel, part devil. Its wings hung folded at its sides, and a metal halo with strands of fine wire raying out from it crowned the strange head. The eyes dominated a crudely carved face, seeming to stare down at Kelsey. She wasn't sure whether the eyes were kind or malevolent. As she and Tyler started up the mountainside, following a railed path, Kelsey looked back, and saw that the statue's eyes still searched her own eerily. She had a feeling that the creature—whatever it was—promised no good for them here at Nepenthe.

At the top they came out upon a broad terrace of terra cotta stone, and the view took Kelsey's breath away. The ocean seemed just off the edge of the terrace wall, though the water was more than eight hundred feet down. The California coastline went on into the distance, and mountains crowded in, so that this gem of a spot sat like a jewel mounted in a green setting.

Plantings of sturdy aloe vera were surrounded by a wooden bench that made a great circle on the terrace. From the midst of greenery rose a huge bird carved in redwood.

"That's the Nepenthe Phoenix," Tyler said. "Do you see that stump it stands on? That's all that's left of a big oak tree that grew there once. Lolly couldn't bear to accept the death of the oak tree, so in the Chinese Year of the Dragon the redwood Phoenix came to perch there, rising out of death to promise new life. That's what Nepenthe stands for—renewal."

The bird's legs were of bronze, anchored into the oak stump, and the carving itself gave an effect of flashing, jeweled color as light poured over it.

Plank tables stood about the terrace, some in the shade of bright umbrellas, with colorful canvas-backed chairs pulled up to them. Though the sun stood at high noon, a cool breeze blew over the mountain, so that few people were eating outdoors.

The main building looked like a rustic lodge built of redwood, its slanting roof seeming to follow the downward pitch of the mountain. As Tyler and Kelsey moved toward the doors, a woman who had been sitting on the bench near the Phoenix rose and approached them.

"Mr. Hammond?" She held out a thin brown hand.

The woman who called herslf "Olga" was very tall, all of six feet, and thin to the point of being gaunt. She wore beige slacks and a pullover sweater with zodiac figures woven into the wool. Her hair, cut in a surprisingly oriental style, hung short and straight to the line of her jaw, with bangs across the forehead. Its color was a somewhat unlikely black that shone like satin in the sun—probably a wig. The woman's features seemed sharply carved in her bony face, the eyes large and dominating, like the eyes of the angel-devil on the lower level of Nepenthe. There seemed nothing malevolent about her gaze, however, as her eyes rested on Kelsey with sudden interest. She looked at Tyler briefly, and then fixed her attention disconcertingly on Kelsey.

"Olga, this is Mrs. Stewart," Tyler said. "She's taking care of my son at present."

"I was sorry to hear about your wife and son," Olga said, still staring at Kelsey as though she saw something that fascinated her. "My friend, Marisa Marsh, told me about you, Mrs. Stewart," she added.

Kelsey wondered what Marisa could have said to cause this intense scrutiny. Kelsey was relieved when Tyler gestured them toward the dining room.

"Let's go inside where we can talk," he suggested.

They found a table on the far side of the room, near a great, metal-hooded fireplace that stood out in the center, its flames radiating a welcome warmth. Kelsey and Olga sat on a bench along the wall, with bright cushions piled behind them, while Tyler took the chair opposite. The beamed ceiling of the room slanted toward the outer edge to meet huge panes of glass that made the room an observatory.

Kelsey ordered an omelet, and Olga, a vegetarian, asked for a large salad. Tyler settled for hot soup and a sandwich. The moment she sat down, Kelsey could sense tension in the air, though she wasn't sure where the source of it lay. In Tyler, probably, since his lighter mood had vanished. Or perhaps merely in herself. Olga seemed serene enough outwardly, and whatever she'd read in Kelsey no longer held her fixed attention.

"Do you still read tarot cards?" Tyler asked.

Olga's smile revealed slightly crooked teeth that gave her

face a piquant character. Her age was uncertain—seventy? Eighty? She shook her head at Tyler in gentle reproach.

"I'm really not a fortune-teller, Mr. Hammond. Though I know I have that reputation. I am interested in parapsychology, and I use the cards to help me concentrate my energies. However, I don't think you're here for a reading."

Her speech held a slight accent—perhaps from long ago Russia—and the words had a formal ring as though she spoke each one with care.

"You're right," Tyler said. "I want to ask you to remember something."

The black points of hair moved against thin cheeks as she nodded. "Yes, I know."

"Marisa warned you?"

"She asked me to tell you whatever I knew. But I don't understand why you should want to learn about something that happened here nearly eleven years ago. What does it matter now?"

"It matters." He sounded grim. "Did you know Francesca Fallon?"

"She came to me a number of times—until I sent her away. I didn't want to face what kept showing up in her future." Olga stared at Kelsey again. "Stay away from high, rocky places, Mrs. Stewart. I don't believe in the inevitable. We can always make choices. Mrs. Fallon made the wrong choice."

"Francesca came here on the day Marisa mentioned?" Tyler asked.

"Yes. I'm not likely to forget. She phoned and asked me to have lunch with her, and I knew right away something was up. I can be almost as curious as she was, though I never used what I learned in the ways she did. We were sitting out there on the terrace bench when a man and woman arrived. Mrs. Fallon kept out of sight, but they wouldn't have noticed her anyway, because they were so absorbed in each other."

"The woman was my wife?" Tyler asked.

"Yes, though I didn't know that then. And I never learned who the man was. When they'd gone into the restaurant and were seated at a table, we went in too, and Mrs. Fallon chose a place not far away. There was an avidity in her interest that I didn't like, and I felt sorry for those two since I knew she meant trouble. I can still remember that there was a sort of enchantment about them, Mr. Hammond, though I'm sorry to tell you this. They were entranced with each other, completely absorbed. They couldn't have been more in love. This is what you had to know, isn't it?"

Olga paused, and Tyler spoke roughly. "Go on."

"Perhaps this was before your marriage, Mr. Hammond. Perhaps it really doesn't matter anymore."

"Just tell me the rest," he said.

"The only coincidence in what happened is the fact that those two had taken a cabin next to mine. Mrs. Fallon knew that—she always knew everything—and she was using me. All through that meal I knew she watched and waited for something to happen. When the two left the building, still involved only with each other, we went outside. They had disappeared, and we waited again. When an older woman arrived and came straight over to her I knew the next phase was about to begin. Mrs. Fallon didn't introduce her, but I heard her call the woman Dora once or twice. Later I learned that she was your wife's mother. Francesca Fallon had brought her there by a phone call she'd made the day before. Dora seemed a strange little woman—nervous and unsettled, yet furiously determined all at the same time."

Again Olga paused, remembering, and Tyler barely concealed his impatience for her to continue. Kelsey began to wish herself anywhere else. She didn't want to witness Tyler's pain and anger, and recognized how strongly he was still involved with Ruth, no matter what he'd said. It wasn't over yet, and Kelsey could only listen unhappily.

Olga went on again. "We went to my cabin, and Mrs. Fallon told Dora that those two were in the next cottage. My windows looked out through a few trees, and we could see any coming and going clearly. But they didn't come out, and Dora suddenly tired of waiting. She stopped Mrs. Fallon in the middle of a sentence, ran from my cabin and over to the next one. Mrs. Fallon went out on the porch to watch, and I came with her. Nobody bothers much to lock doors around here, and the man and woman must have felt perfectly safe. They weren't. Dora pulled open the door. From my porch we had a glimpse of them entwined on a bed before Dora went inside and slammed the door shut. Mrs. Fallon seemed disgustingly pleased with what she'd arranged, and her pleasure was ugly. I knew that her livelihood was nasty gossip, and the only thing that surprised me was that she never used what she learned that day."

"She waited for an opportune moment when she thought she could make the most of it," Tyler said.

Olga had no more to tell him, and after a meal they'd hardly eaten, they wandered toward the spot where the Phoenix stood, and Tyler motioned them toward the circular bench. "Let's sit down for a moment before you go," he said to Olga.

The woman looked up at the great carved bird as though it held some mystical quality for her. Sitting very straight, she closed her eyes as though she listened to something far away. Whether this was an act or not, Kelsey couldn't be sure, but when she spoke again Olga's voice had the ring of an oracle, the words even more formal and stiff.

"In their own eyes the evil are never guilty," she pronounced. "There is a fatal flaw that makes them always innocent of their own actions. Nor is the instrument guilty. It is never the will of the knife that kills in the hand of the murderer."

Wind hummed through carved feathers of the Phoenix, and Olga's strange words seemed to hang ominously on the air. When she opened her eyes she looked as though she wasn't quite sure what she had said.

"There's one more thing." Tyler took a small, wallet-size picture from his pocket and held it out to Olga. "Was this the man you saw with my wife that day?"

Olga accepted the picture and studied it for a moment before she gave it back. "As I've said, this was so long ago—I can't be sure. But I think it is the same man."

Tyler nodded grimly and something in him seemed close to the breaking point. Kelsey saw his hand shake as he put the photo away. Tyler needed to hold his grief private for now, as she must conceal her own awareness of how wholly he was still tied to Ruth. To offer a bridge over a dangerous moment, she spoke quickly to Olga, her tone light.

"Mrs. Marsh told me that you gave Francesca Fallon a string of carved beads from Africa. Do you recall that?"

"Of course. Those beads have changed hands many times since they left Kenya. There is a stipulation that accompanies the gift each time. They are to be worn until one meets someone whose danger is great. Then they must be given again. I was wearing the strand that day here at Nepenthe. So I gave them to Mrs. Fallon, who needed protection. It wasn't for me to judge her, no matter how much I disliked what she had done. It seemed necessary to give her a chance to save herself. Perhaps even to change. The beads must have failed, however, or else she had given them away before her death."

"She didn't give them away," Kelsey said. "She broke the string two days before she died."

"So who knows?" Olga's shrug was eloquent.

Kelsey didn't dare to look at Tyler, silent beside her, lost in his own painful thoughts and paying little attention.

"I've seen those beads," she told Olga. "They're exquisitely carved, but very ugly—wicked-looking."

"Of course. Among primitive peoples one frightens off evil with masks and images that are malevolent and threatening. It was unfortunate—for her—that Mrs. Fallon broke the strand."

Tyler seemed to come back in time to hear Olga's words, and he made a sound of dismissal for this nonsense about beads. At once Olga stood up, told them good-bye quickly, and went off to visit Lolly in her rooms behind the restaurant. She had known the right moment to leave, before Tyler's control broke.

He barely waited until she had gone before he took the small photo from his pocket. "There's been enough concealment and deceit, Kelsey. It's time for you to see this."

Troubled, Kelsey took the picture of the man Ruth had been with. She looked at the glossy print of a rather gentle, smiling face and eyes that seemed unbearably sad. The photo was of Denis Langford.

"Oh no!" It was hard to say anything because she felt almost ill with shock. She gave the print back to Tyler, and he let it drop from his fingers unnoticed, and it blew away across the terrace. When he bent forward to put his face in his hands, Kelsey knew how scalding and bitter such long-held tears would be. After a moment, she touched his shoulder gently. That was all the comfort she dared to offer, but it seemed as though her love must pour out to him through the pressure of her fingers. She wanted desperately to put her arms around him, but his grief was apart from her and must not be invaded.

Tears, however angry and despairing, brought some relief, for in a few moments he sat up and moved away from her, letting wind from the ocean dry the wetness on his face. Now there were words he needed to speak—and could speak at last.

"I'm not sure how to get out of the trap we're all caught in, Kelsey, but now I have to try. In some ways I'm sorrier for Denis than I can ever be for Ruth. This must have begun in their growing-up years, and her brother could never have stood up to her, or resisted her. She always used her sexuality to get what she wanted—and she wanted *him*. More than any other man. I know that now, though I could never accept it. For years I hid from the truth, shutting myself into my work. I loved her enough so that what couldn't be faced was destroying me."

For the first time she could fully understand the photograph that hung in Marisa's studio.

"It's part of my own shame," he went on, "that I allowed this to continue covertly while I pretended nothing was wrong. She married me because the General had taught her that respectability was necessary. Perhaps she even wanted me in the beginning. But she wanted the forbidden more, and she must have enjoyed manipulating her brother."

The story was tragic for so many. It would have affected Jody too, even though he couldn't understand the currents that swirled around him.

"Dora must have known all along," Kelsey said. "She tried to break it up here at Nepenthe."

"Dora's own weakness was loving her daughter too much, and trying always to protect her. Of course in the long run that did no good. After we were married, the relationship with her brother simply went on. Probably destroying Denis too, since he wasn't strong enough to escape."

Kelsey thought of the marble statue in the woods below La Casa de la Sombra—the small boy with his arm protectively around the girl who clung to him, and she felt like crying—for Tyler, for Denis, for herself. And most of all for Jody. At least she had been freed of any loyalty to Ruth, and no longer owed her silence.

"Your wife can walk," she said abruptly.

Tyler stared at her.

"I found out that night in the library before you came in. She's been able to get around almost from the beginning. I believed everything she told me, and I'm ashamed now that I listened, that I kept still about it."

It took him a moment to absorb what she'd said, and then his relief was enormous. "Thank God! Don't feel ashamed, Kelsey. Ruth is an expert at deception. What matters is that she *can* walk, and that opens one side of the trap. If I hadn't believed that she was helpless and dependent on me, she knew I'd have walked out and taken Jody with me before this. I can do that now. Thanks to Olga, and to what you've told me."

So much had surfaced, but so much that was still submerged lay ahead. Denis had been caught desperately by his own terrible enthrallment to his sister. Now Kelsey could better understand the sadness she saw in his eyes. There was one more thing she must tell Tyler. He must know about the time when Ruth had taken Jody to Flaming Tree. He must know about the burden she had placed on a small boy by forcing him to keep silent. Yet she held back for the moment. This was not the time to add to Tyler's burgeoning anger. She had always feared the violence in him. And Ruth might be in real danger if he learned this now. His rage must cool a little before she told him the rest. As it was, the look in his eyes made her shiver.

He noticed at once and misread the reason. "The weather is changing, and the wind's sharp out here. We'd better go back."

"I still don't fully understand why you brought me here," she said. "It might have been better if you'd come alone, and let me stay with Jody."

"No! I wanted you to hear this plainly from someone else. I wanted you to believe—in *me.*"

A strange new hope she hadn't felt in years had begun to rise in her. She had every reason to be afraid of a great many things about this situation, and especially afraid of what action Tyler might take. Yet this unreasonable hope swelled and turned into something like happiness. He had brought her here, he had turned to *her* in his pain, and this was a beginning.

There seemed a new tenderness in him, something apart from his anger. Without touching her, it was as though he held her warmly, lovingly. Hope was a promise—and still very fragile.

Unwarranted happiness continued to brim in Kelsey as they drove toward Carmel. Drifts of fog were blowing in from the water, wreathing the mountains, and the sound of the ocean had risen.

Her new sense of happiness lasted only until they reached the front door of La Casa de la Sombra. There Ruth met them, running frantically outside, making no effort to hide the fact that she could walk.

"Jody's gone!" she cried. "Ginnie says he was trying to talk— disjointed words. My mother was with him and she got upset. Ginnie says that Dora was going to take him to Elaine's, but I don't know if I believe that. She just got in her car and drove away without even telling me. You've got to go after them, Tyler!"

"I'll phone Elaine right away," Tyler said and rushed into the house.

Ruth ran toward Kelsey. "He never listens! I don't think Dora's gone to Elaine with Jody. I know where she'd take him, and I'm going after them myself. If you want to come with me, you can."

Without waiting to see if Kelsey would follow, Ruth ran up the outside steps toward her car. Kelsey hesitated, and was suddenly aware of another person in the doorway. Denis

Langford stood watching, his smiling mask gone—perhaps forever—a haunting look of despair in its place.

But she had no time now to pity Denis. "Tell Tyler I've gone with Ruth," she called to him, and ran up the steps, reaching Ruth's car just as it began to move. Ruth braked, and Kelsey jumped in.

XVI

RUTH seemed both fearful and excited as she turned the car away from the Highlands on the road north.

"Dora thinks she's protecting me!" she cried when they were on their way. "Kelsey, I love my son, and we've got to stop her!"

Always there was this mixture of truth and lies in whatever Ruth said, and it was impossible to tell which was which. That Dora was governed by her own obsession and might do anything was true. It was better to go with Ruth and find out. Denis would tell Tyler, and if he was in time to follow them, he would.

Clouds had darkened the sky by the time they reached Ruth's destination. Kelsey saw in dismay that this was the entrance to the Point Lobos State Reserve. Ruth switched off the engine and got out of the car, again paying no attention to whether Kelsey came with her or not.

Kelsey ran after her and caught her by the arm. "Wait, Ruth. Surely Dora would never hurt her grandson. There's a storm coming up—I don't think you should go out there."

Ruth shook off her hand. "Do you want to take the chance of not finding Jody? There's no time to argue, and I don't care whether you come with me or not. If Jody's out there, I've got to reach him. This is just what Dora might do—so there can be *another* accident." She began to run again.

Kelsey went after her into a grove of cypress trees. The cypresses closed around them, dark and sepulchral, and wind rattled through the branches, fighting their progress. On ahead the sea roared in full voice. In a few moments they came into the open, and Kelsey could see the rocks of Point Lobos, black and wet and craggy. The ocean crashed against the resisting land, and spray leapt high in the air like a shower of white fire, falling back with a clatter, only to leap again. Borne by the wind, drops stung their faces.

Ruth rushed straight toward the rocks.

Once more Kelsey caught up with her. "Don't go out there —it's too dangerous. We can see there's no one there. Ruth, let's go back."

"That's the way it was when Jody and I fell—no one could see us. If it hadn't been for Marisa Marsh we wouldn't be alive now. I *know* Jody's on the other side of those rocks. I can feel it. You stay here where it's safe, Kelsey. I'm going to find him."

There was such desperation in her voice that Kelsey ran after her to where the outcropping of rock began.

"Listen!" Ruth cried as they reached the foot of the pile. "Did you hear that?"

Kelsey could hear nothing but the wind and the sea. "It must be Dora," Ruth shouted above the clamor. "Jody can't call to us."

"He might if he had to." Kelsey began to clamber over the rocks but Ruth passed her quickly, alive and exhilarated in her own wild element. She wasn't the least afraid for herself, and she didn't look at Kelsey.

Moving more cautiously, Kelsey clung to the ridges of stone, pulling herself along. When she reached the ridge, it was terrifying to look down into wild deep water, surging through gashes in wet black granite, retreating and then hurling itself in again in endless repetition—mindless motion. The wind force thrust against the tiny strength of the two women.

"It's only a little way farther!" Ruth cried, and now there was a new sound in her voice—wild and triumphant.

Already she stood between Kelsey and the less precipitous pitch of rock they'd just climbed. Kelsey could see now that no one clung to the rocks below. If anyone had been there, they'd have been swept into the sea. Perhaps Ruth really had expected to find Jody and Dora here, but that purpose was gone now, and Jody's rescue was no longer first in Ruth's mind.

She perched on the ridge of rock like some seabird, at home in these stormy elements, and Kelsey began to crawl away from her on hands and knees, fighting for a hold, no longer daring to stand upright against the buffeting wind. She could see in Ruth's face what she intended.

There was still no rain, but in the flying spray Kelsey was soaked through and half blinded. Ruth must be too, and that was a small advantage. Somehow, she must climb down and run for the cypress grove. Once on level ground there was nothing Ruth could do. But the rock was too steep here, and when her foot slipped she scrambled back to the ridge and clung there, drenched in spray.

They were only a few feet apart now. "Why, Ruth?" Kelsey shouted above the wind. "Why must you do this?"

Ruth screamed at her. "Do you think you could take my husband? Take my son? Oh no, Kelsey! You're afraid now, aren't you? Afraid of *me!*"

Any struggle here might send them both into the surging seas below, and this time Ruth might not even care whether she lived or died—if only she took Kelsey with her.

The *watcher* hesitated in the shelter of a straggling cypress, torn by momentary indecision. Ruth stood visible against the sky while Kelsey clung precariously to the rock. No one could stop what was about to happen. Months before, the watcher had walked away, sure that the two who had fallen were dead, and nothing could be done except to leave and pretend ignorance of what had happened. On that other time, the watcher had followed Ruth and Jody here, fearful that harm might come to the boy. If some unconscious part of Ruth's mind had intended her son's death that other time, the conscious part would have gone on playing its games, believing in her innocence. It was Jody himself who had thrown the two off balance and pitched them from the cliff.

This time, the watcher knew, it was different. Ruth would push Kelsey over, and perhaps she would manage somehow not to fall herself. The man began to run toward the mound of wet, slippery rock.

As he climbed, he shouted above the noise of wind and sea. Ruth heard him and paused in her progress along the ridge. When she turned and saw him she laughed again, triumphant. The high pitch of her voice carried to the man above the tumult.

"You couldn't stay away! You had to come back—I knew you would. You never guessed that I saw you that other time, Denis. You looked down at us and then you went away. So I hated you. The only one I ever told was Marisa, and she kept still about it. But you've been punished enough, and you'll make up for everything by helping me now. You know what must be done, Denis. You know, just as you knew that day when I put a stick of wood in your hands at Flaming Tree and told you what must be done about Francesca. You've always understood. You've always done what I needed, Denis. You can't help yourself!"

She was right—he had never been able to help himself,

though he always knew the blame was hers. He held out his arms and ran along the ridge, reaching out toward her. It was easier to balance when he ran, and in a moment he had wrapped his arms lovingly about his sister. The hard impact of his body gave her no chance to resist as he deliberately flung them both outward into space together, their arms still clasped about each other. Only the wind and ocean screamed, and there was no sound of their fall to be heard above the sea's uproar.

Denis, at last, had taken responsibility for his own actions.

Kelsey clung to the ridge, trying to peer down through flying spray to where water churned in the cauldron below, and nothing living—or dead—could surface in roiling black water. They might already have been swept out to sea. She was trembling too hard to stand, and she could only crouch on the spine of the ridge, trying to gain an inner equilibrium so she could move again.

The wind paused to hold its breath and in the comparative hush she heard someone shouting her name. Her attention had been riveted on Denis and Ruth, and she hadn't seen the other man until now. Tyler had climbed the rock until he was just below her.

"Come down to me, Kelsey," he directed. "You're all right now. Take my hand and I'll help you the rest of the way."

The strong clasp of his fingers about hers steadied her, and she could move again. Together they inched their way back, and when solid ground met their feet, Tyler held her, kissing her wet face over and over, stilling her trembling.

After a moment of clinging blindly to each other, they started back through the trees. Tyler's arm was about her, but her shivering started again when they reached his car.

"Don't shake so, Kelsey. It's over now. The whole nightmare's over, darling."

But it wasn't over. There was still Jody, and the awful thing Ruth had shouted out there on the rocks.

"What about Jody?" she asked when they were in the car and on their way.

"He's fine. I reached Elaine on the phone, and she said Dora had brought Jody to the inn. He started to talk, Kelsey—he was really saying a lot of words. Whatever he said frightened Dora. I guess she didn't want anyone to hear him, so she took him to Elaine—her one friend around here. I asked your aunt to get Dora calmed down and then send them back to the house."

"How did you know where we'd be?"

"Denis came to get me before I finished phoning and he sounded desperate. He told me that you'd gone with Ruth, and there was just one place she'd take you. So we couldn't have been far behind you. Kelsey, Denis did what he had to do."

She knew that was true. In the end he'd had tremendous courage.

When they reached the house Dora met them in the living room, anxious and questioning. She told them at once that Jody was with Ginnie, and he was all right.

Tyler went off to make his grim phone calls to the park rangers and the Coast Guard, and then rejoined them in the living room.

Since Kelsey wouldn't go to her room to change, he brought a coat to put around her. Then he sat beside Dora and told her as gently as he could what had happened. Once more she seemed to summon an inner strength, and she listened, sitting stiffly upright, her hands clasped tightly in her lap. Dora didn't speak until Tyler was through.

"I protected them for too long. Though I didn't know until a little while ago what really happened out at Flaming Tree. Perhaps I didn't want to know." Her voice was steady and her eyes tearless. When Dora cried, it would be later, alone, and she would let no one see her suffering. The General would have taught her this stoicism. "Of course I am guilty too. I loved my daughter too much. We've all paid for that—most of all my son."

"Can you tell us what happened at Flaming Tree when Francesca died?" Tyler asked.

For an instant Dora's voice broke, then she steadied herself and went on. "Francesca knew about that time when Ruth persuaded Denis to go with her to Nepenthe. She'd seen us all there, but she did nothing until after the interview with you, Tyler. She saw a chance to be paid for her silence, and she roused your curiosity enough to agree to the interview. Afterwards Ruth went out to the ranch to see her, not knowing that you had been there the day before. Francesca understood by that time that she'd get nothing from you, Tyler, so she put pressure on Ruth—and really frightened her. Denis went there with his sister that day, and I think Ruth terrified him into the action he took."

Dora's voice had steadied until it was as if she spoke mechanically, suppressing all the emotion she would not display.

"All they intended in the beginning was to scare Francesca into keeping still. Ruth sent Jody outside to pick up kindling while the grown-ups talked. But everything got out of hand. Francesca must have been at her nastiest, and Ruth took the sort of action her father might have chosen. Francesca had to be stopped—for good. My daughter never accepted the fact that she was guilty of murder. Even though she put the weapon into Denis's hand, and gave him her will to act. She believed herself innocent of wrongdoing because others were always to blame. Denis knew that he was used, so he felt innocent too—helpless in Ruth's hands."

The knife was innocent, Kelsey thought, remembering Olga.

"How much of this did Jody see?" Tyler asked bleakly.

For the first time, Dora found it hard to continue. "That was the awful part. He saw it all. He came in the door with a basketful of twigs and branches, and he saw his uncle being urged on by his mother. He saw Francesca killed. Both frightened him into saying nothing. She told him that she and Denis would be hurt if he talked. So he kept still and suffered terrible nightmares during that time—until the whole thing was ready to burst out of him."

"Oh, God!" Tyler's anguish grew acute. "Did she take him out to Point Lobos that day to—to—"

"She took him on a *picnic,*" Dora said grimly. "That was all she could accept in her conscious mind. In her way, she loved Jody, and she never faced the part of her that didn't love him. That day, Denis was afraid of what she might do, and he went after them. He watched from a safe distance where Ruth wouldn't see him. He told me this only a day or so ago. When Ruth and Jody fell together because of Jody's larking, he went to the edge and looked down. He saw them on the ledge below, and really believed they were dead. So he came away, feeling safe for the first time since Francesca died. But he didn't dare tell anyone until he finally told me. Then I knew that the story Ruth had told me about arriving at the ranch after Francesca was dead was all a lie."

The same lie she had been told, Kelsey thought.

"Afterwards," Dora finished, "Ruth wouldn't see Denis or talk to him, and he didn't know what to do. Of course I had no idea then of what was really wrong."

For a few moments no one was able to say anything. Then Dora spoke directly to Kelsey.

"I have no excuses left for myself. I was just as weak as Denis. Ruth asked me to make the telephone call that day on the hall phone, hoping to catch you. She wanted to frighten you into leaving. When you first came, she thought she could have you report to her and keep you under her control, since

Tyler told her so little. But you weren't cooperative and she was afraid of the time when Jody might begin to talk. Ruth took those beads from Tyler's desk and told me to leave them in Denis's office as a warning. Denis was getting a little out of hand, perhaps even interested in you, Kelsey, so she wanted to remind him that *he* had killed Francesca. Once Denis might have escaped her if he'd married Ginnie, but Ruth broke that up too—and made him think it was Tyler's fault."

Another lie at Ruth's door, Kelsey thought.

"What about Jody talking?" Tyler asked.

"I didn't know he could manage this until I heard him today. He was trying so hard—words that sounded like 'flaming' and 'tree.' And he said, 'Ma' and 'Denis' and 'blood' quite clearly. I had to stop him somehow, so I took him out in my car before anyone could overhear him, and I went to Elaine. She's always sensible and she'd been my friend for a long time. But he'd stopped trying to talk by the time we got there. And then you phoned, Tyler, and told me to bring him home. Somehow I knew that everything was over. I suppose in a terrible way I was relieved, and I'm glad they escaped—Ruth and Denis. There wasn't any other way. That's all I have to tell you."

Dora rose with a quiet dignity that became her, and went out of the room.

Neither Tyler nor Kelsey moved for a moment. Then Kelsey said, "The truly evil one in all this was the General. I suppose evil can breed evil unless it's turned around."

Tyler stood up. "Come with me to see Jody. It's time I behaved like a father."

When they reached Jody's room, Ginnie seemed to understand, and slipped away. Perhaps she'd heard enough from Jody to know that they must see him alone.

He sat in his chair, straps in place, and his eyes were round with terror as his father came in. Tyler went to him at once, and sat down close, taking Jody's hands in his.

"It's all right," he said. "You needn't be scared and worried anymore. We know everything you wanted to tell us. We know what happened at Flaming Tree, and it's all right for you to talk about it anytime you want to. Do you understand me, Jody?"

" 'Stand," Jody said, and began to cry quietly.

"That's good—crying," Tyler went on. "I've been crying some too. We're going to talk a lot now, and you can say anything you please. I'll listen, and so will Kelsey, and we'll all help each other. Ginnie will help too, when she's been told. Jody, you remember what happened to my parents when I was your age and they died? We've talked about it before. So now you're going to learn how to live with that, just as I had to. Sometimes it will be pretty hard, Jody, but it will get better—I promise you. There's something I have to tell you. Something bad. Today . . ." Tyler stopped and took Jody from his chair to hold him in his arms.

Kelsey too went quietly out of the room and joined Ginnie down the hall. These were words to be spoken only between father and son. Full healing would take a long time for Jody, both emotionally and physically, but now in his father's hands, it would begin. She had been right about Tyler Hammond the very first time when she'd seen those soaring geese at Marisa's and had thought he must be a sensitive man. All along he had been fighting demons too awful for him to handle.

She talked to Ginnie for a little while, though not about all that had happened. Then she left her and went toward the stairs. As she started up, Tyler caught up with her and covered her hand on the rail with his own. She looked down with tears in her eyes.

"Thank you for my life today," she said. "In so many ways."

"Thank you for mine. In just as many. And most of all, Kelsey, thank you for Jody's. Maybe now there's hope for something better ahead. If we give it a little time."

She leaned over the rail and kissed him gently. Then she ran up the stairs to her room. She didn't want him to see her own private joy that couldn't be expressed right now.

In her room she began to get out of wet clothing. Sounds came in from the balcony—sounds of wind and ocean still roaring wildly. She closed the door with a firm click. She didn't want to think about water and wet black rocks.

There was so much to do, and as soon as she was dry again she would go to Jody and his father. And begin.

Note to My Readers

Why did I write about Jody and the particular treatment he was given? This grew from personal experience because of a tragic happening in my own family.

Nearly four years ago my grandson, who was only nineteen, tried to commit suicide with carbon monoxide. He was taken to a California hospital, and my daughter flew out from Long Island, not knowing whether he would be alive by the time she reached him.

Michael was in a deep coma, and doctors told her that he would never be anything more than a "vegetable." Because many so-called "vegetables" have made a recovery, we did not accept this verdict and give up. We decided instead to make every effort to save him, and brought him home to private care.

We knew that Carlton Fredericks, long a pioneer in the field of nutrition, had worked as a consultant on brain-damaged patients. He was able to help us in conjunction with a medical nutritionist, and the treatment was begun.

Improvement was gradual, barely discernible at first, until something dramatic happened. After about six weeks of talking to Michael, reading to him, playing music tapes and television, but getting no response we could be certain of, he suddenly laughed at a funny story told by a nurse. Now we knew he was *there*.

Today Michael speaks clearly, using difficult words, and he understands complex ideas. One of my favorite incidents occurred when he overheard a meaningless conversation nearby. After the talk stopped, he said, "That was uneventful." His mother asked what he meant and he said, "Nothing happened." This was not the thinking of a "vegetable." Physically, he still has a long way to go, but since he has never stopped improving, we will continue to hope and try.

The treatment given Jody in my novel is much the same as that which helped Michael—though Jody was less seriously injured. Now, at this writing four years later, my grandson is in an institution that employs trained therapists and has a fine reputation for helping brain-damaged young people. Nevertheless, we feel that more could be done. It is sad that so many medical authorities who lean heavily on drugs have closed their minds when it comes to the nutritional approach.

If there is a "message" I have tried to convey in this novel, it is that we must never stop seeking for alternative and supplemental help, no matter how grave the problem. New answers are always coming in.

Phyllis A. Whitney